ACCOMPLICE LIABILITY

David Brunelle Legal Thriller #7

STEPHEN PENNER

ISBN-13: 978-0692773147

ISBN-10: 0692773142

Accomplice Liability

Joy A. Lorton and Lynette Melcher, Editors.

Cover by Nathan Wampler Book Covers.

Testimony of an accomplice, given on behalf of the State, should be subjected to careful examination in light of the other evidence in the case, and should be acted upon with great caution. You should not find the defendant guilty upon such testimony alone unless, after carefully considering the testimony, you are satisfied beyond a reasonable doubt of its truth.

State of Washington
Pattern Criminal Jury Instruction 6.05
"Testimony of an Accomplice"

CHAPTER 1

"Snitches are bitches who end up in ditches."

King County homicide D.A. Dave Brunelle lifted his gaze from the dead body behind the gas station to look at his friend, Seattle Police Detective Larry Chen. The cold, night rain cut at Brunelle's cheeks. "Nice eulogy," he said.

Chen shrugged and a dark smile tugged at the corner of his mouth. He didn't look up from the corpse lying in the drainage ditch just a few feet below them. "It works as an epitaph too. A lot of people put poems on their gravestones."

"Nobody puts anything on their own gravestones," Brunelle disagreed. "They're dead. It's their loved ones who add the poems."

Chen finally looked up from the ditch. "I'll be sure to tell the widow," he offered. Then he turned and walked back toward the makeshift command center in the gas station parking lot—basically where the first two patrol officers parked their cars next to each other. The vehicles' emergency lights were still flashing, backlighting Chen's large frame in red and blue as Brunelle watched him walk back to check in with his officers.

After a moment, Brunelle looked down again at the murder

victim. It seemed doubtful the man had a widow. He was lying face up, one arm under his body, the other raised over his head, and his legs splayed unceremoniously in the wet grass. He was in his early twenties, with long hair, a stubbly face, and a gaunt frame becoming increasingly apparent as the rain soaked his dirty clothes against his body. He didn't look the part of family man. He was clearly a drug addict. Two years earlier, Brunelle might have guessed methamphetamine, but heroin was back, and with a vengeance. They were scraping O.D.'ed bodies off First Avenue every morning. And Broadway. And Denny.

But Ditch Boy hadn't overdosed. Three dark blood stains on his gray hoodie attested to the gunshots that had torn through his chest. The autopsy would say for sure, but Brunelle could guess that at least one of them had perforated a lung. Tough way to go. The lung collapses, then blood fills the chest cavity, crushing the other lung as well.

Brunelle scanned the crime scene. Or more accurately, the secondary crime scene. The man had been shot elsewhere. Brunelle wasn't a detective but he'd reviewed enough investigations for charging, defended enough investigations to defense attorneys, and explained enough investigations to juries, that he knew what to look for. They were standing in the heart of Seattle's Lake City neighborhood, which sounded fancy but was anything but. It wasn't even on any of the lakes Seattle abutted or surrounded. Instead, it was the lower income neighborhood northeast of the University of Washington, filled with high-density housing, medium-quality bars, and low-profile strip clubs. The gas station was next to an all-night convenience store and directly in front of a hundred-unit apartment complex.

It was a terrible place to shoot somebody. Some neighborhoods were deserted at night, suburban families getting their beauty rest before another day of school and work. But a gas station next to a convenience store in front of an apartment complex? It was hard to think of any place more likely to be active at night. Shooting a man in the middle of all that would almost certainly be seen by multiple witnesses, even the ask-no-questions types who lived in that particular part of the city. But backing up to the edge of the gas station and quickly rolling the body out of the trunk was exactly the kind of thing the drug addicts and criminals awake that time of night would be happy not to notice.

And it was more than just the unlikelihood of the location for a murder. The body had obviously not simply fallen where it was shot. His tangled arms and legs attested to that much. Also, there were no footprints anywhere in the wet grass. Instead, there was a wide matted path of wet grass leading from the asphalt under Brunelle's feet to the ditch under the dead man. Brunelle was certain the man had been murdered somewhere else and rolled down the hillside into the ditch, D.O.A.

The rain picked up as Brunelle ruminated over the remains of yet another stranger. The drops stung his face and his scalp started to get wet as his short hair became saturated. He was warm enough in his lined raincoat—a necessity in Seattle—but he had refused to get one of those fedora-like rain hats. It wasn't 1950 any more. And as he pushed through his mid-40s toward his late-40s, he wasn't looking for anything that made him feel, or look, even older than he was. Besides, it was just a little rain. Cold rain. In the middle of the night. He pulled his coat tighter, then slicked his hand over his head, squeegee-style. He was drenched.

So too was the dead heroin addict. Brunelle wondered whether the rain might not impact the investigation. Was there some piece of vital forensic evidence that was being washed away, forever lost into the mud beneath the body? But he supposed that was unlikely. Any bullets that had lodged in the body weren't going anywhere. They would be extracted at autopsy. And a little rain wasn't going to wash away the blood stained into his clothes. Besides, it was pretty obvious whose blood it was. If there had been a struggle, there might be assailant DNA under his fingernails, but the whole point of shooting someone was to avoid a struggle. The only thing likely under the victim's fingernails was dirt. It wasn't a forensics case. They were going to need witnesses.

Somebody shot the man. Gunshots are loud. Somebody heard them.

People don't usually shoot people for no reason. There was likely an argument. Somebody heard that too.

Drug addicts usually hung out in packs. Somebody knew the victim. Somebody knew his enemies.

Dead bodies were heavy. Even an emaciated heroin addict would still be well over a hundred pounds. Somebody helped the killer dispose of the body.

And there was blood wherever he was shot and in whatever vehicle was used to transport the body. Somebody saw the blood. Somebody cleaned it up.

Chen walked back up to Brunelle. "The patrol guys interviewed everybody," the detective announced. "They talked to the clerk who found the body when he was taking the trash to the dumpster. A couple customers who were inside the store when he came running back in. Even the crazy homeless lady on the corner. But nobody saw anything."

Brunelle frowned, and not just because of the trickle of cold water that ran down the back of his neck. "No. Somebody saw something. We need to find those somebodies."

CHAPTER 2

The door to the King County Medical Examiner's Office was just a little bit too heavy. It took Brunelle some effort to pull the door through the loud metallic clank of its latching mechanism. It was as if the door were asking, 'Are you really sure you want to be here?' Brunelle wasn't sure, in fact, but Chen had called him from the autopsy and told him to come down right away.

Brunelle hadn't questioned the request. He trusted Chen. But on his way over, he wondered what was so special about this autopsy that the D.A. needed to attend. Three shots to the torso. What was left to wonder about it? Brunelle had guessed it was a perforated lung, but a nick to the heart would be just as possible and just as deadly. And it wouldn't impact the case at all.

There was a small squawk-box in the lobby, next to the elevator to the upper floors that held the offices and examining rooms. Brunelle was familiar with the place. Intimately familiar. Which was another reason he wasn't thrilled at the prospect of visiting the M.E.'s office. But he was a professional. They both were. And there was work to do.

But he still hoped the assistant M.E. doing the autopsy was

anyone but Kat Anderson, his ex-G.F.

There was no receptionist, just the squawk-box. He pressed the button and spoke. "Hello. This is Dave Brunelle, from the prosecutor's office. I'm supposed to meet Detective Larry Chen here."

After a few moments, there was a staticky, unintelligible response, and the elevator door dinged open. Brunelle knew the drill. He stepped into the elevator and pressed '2.' The examining rooms. The elevator lurched and shuddered and then opened again to reveal the sturdy frame of Det. Chen, and the wiry figure of Dr. Jeremy Albrecht, another of the assistant M.E.s who worked for the office.

Brunelle was glad to extend his hand in greeting as he stepped off the elevator. "Dr. Albrecht. Good to see you again."

But Albrecht raised his own hands to display the blue latex gloves still covering them. "I don't think you want to shake my hand right now, Dave. We just finished the autopsy. "

"Damn," Brunelle replied. "I missed all the fun."

In truth, he didn't mind missing yet another dissection, but he was a little irritated at rushing down there for no reason apparently.

"No, you missed the incisions," Chen answered. "But the fun stuff was on the outside anyway."

Brunelle frowned, confused, but Chen grabbed him by the arm and started toward the examining rooms. "Come on. I wanted you to see this for yourself. "

Brunelle allowed himself to be led down the hallway, but instinctively looked at Chen's hand to see if it too was gloved. He'd just had that suit dry-cleaned. But, mercifully, there was no blue glove.

The body was still on the examining table, naked and purply

pale. An M.E. technician—like a nurse, but for dead people—was already sewing up the stomach. Brunelle knew they had piled all of the organs inside the stomach cavity, even the brain, before sewing it up. He didn't need to know it; he just did. Like a lot of messed-up things he knew after working twenty years in the criminal justice system.

"Guy's name was Derrick Shanborn," Chen informed Brunelle. "Pretty easy I.D. He still had his wallet on him. Suspended driver's license, Subway punch card, and a fortune cookie fortune that said, 'Better days are just around the corner.'"

Brunelle ignored the irony of the fortune. "So it wasn't a robbery," he remarked, almost absently.

"Yeah, this guy doesn't look like he had anything to rob him of anyway," Chen replied.

Brunelle just shrugged. He'd figured as much while Mr. Derrick Shanborn was still in the ditch. "So what was so interesting," Brunelle asked, "that it pulled me away from all the paper I was planning on pushing this morning? Did he die of something other than the bullets through his chest?"

"Oh, no," Dr. Albrecht replied quickly. "He definitely died from those gunshot wounds. Perforated a lung, nicked the heart, and shredded the aorta. Completely unsurvivable."

"Good," Brunelle said. Then, realizing how that sounded, even among professionals, he clarified, "I mean, I'm glad there are no surprises there."

"Nope, no surprises there," Dr. Albrecht confirmed. "The surprises are elsewhere."

The doctor pointed to the leathery skin of the corpse's thighs, then gestured to the scab-covered forearms, and finally he used a gloved hand to pull apart the dead man's toes. The technician didn't even seem to notice as she continued sewing the stomach shut with twine.

Brunelle squinted between the splayed toes, then glanced at the arms and legs. "Injection tracks," Brunelle recognized. "I'm not seeing the surprise."

"That's why I wanted you to see them in person," Chen said. "Their condition probably won't show up in the photographs."

"Condition?" Brunelle leaned down to squint even harder at the lines of red and black dots on the dead man's arms. "What condition?"

"Healed," Dr. Albrecht answered. "The injection sites are old. The veins in his arms collapsed long ago. The thighs were leathery from all the times he'd shot up there. And the injection sites between the toes really show how bad of addict he was. But he'd kicked it. I can't find a single injection site that isn't fully healed. He hadn't injected a needle into his skin for at least two weeks before he died, probably longer. I'll send fluid samples to the toxicology lab, but I'll be stunned if it doesn't come back one hundred percent clean. Maybe marijuana or alcohol—something you don't inject— but there won't be any opiates."

Brunelle looked to Chen. "You think he switched to meth or crack? Something you smoke?"

But Chen shook his head. "It's possible. But not typical. I mean, he might have been doing that other stuff too, in addition to the heroin, but heroin addicts don't just stop taking heroin. Heroin withdrawal is some pretty serious shit."

Brunelle nodded at that. "But Dr. Albrecht says he did stop."

"Correct," the medical examiner confirmed. "Something got him to stop."

"More like *someone*," Chen said.

Brunelle supposed that might be more accurate. Maybe a girl, he thought. Probably a girl. "Any clue who it was?"

Chen smiled slightly. "Actually, yes."

He nodded to Dr. Albrecht who then reached over to the instrument tray next to the examining table. He picked up a ragged business card for Brunelle to see.

Brunelle instinctively reached for it, but Chen grabbed his wrist. "You don't want to touch that, Dave."

Brunelle pulled his arm back. "Right. Because it's evidence."

"Because it was in his underwear," Chen corrected.

"And it was damp," Dr. Albrecht added.

Brunelle frowned. "Because of the rain?" he hoped.

"Sure," Chen offered. "Let's say it was because of the rain."

Brunelle's middle-aged eyes couldn't quite make out the lettering on the card. "So what does it say? Is it a rehab clinic or something? "

"Nope," Chen answered without even looking at the card. "It says, 'Detective Tim Jackson, Seattle P.D.'"

"Jackson?" Brunelle replied. "I know him. Is he doing homicides now?"

Chen shook his head. "Drugs."

Brunelle grimaced. "So why does a dead drug addict have a narcotics detective's business card in his underwear?" he asked. But it was rhetorical. They both already knew the answer.

"Because," Chen said, "this bitch in a ditch really was a snitch."

CHAPTER 3

"Dead?!"

Tim Jackson slammed his fists onto his desk and lurched to his feet. "Derrick Shanborn is dead? God damn it! He was almost done. Just one more and he was done. He was going to go to Montana. He had an uncle in Montana." Jackson dropped his head into his hands. "God damn it."

Jackson's office was small and cramped. A bookshelf full of binders practically blocked off the only pathway behind the file-covered desk. There were two guest chairs but Brunelle and Chen both had to stand because one chair held two stacked file boxes and the other had an open file box with loose papers stacked on top of the files already jammed in to capacity. Brunelle wondered whether all three boxes belonged to the same investigation or if it was a one chair, one case system.

Jackson himself mirrored the compact feeling of the space. He was on the short side, but with a thick chest and arms, and a full mustache that matched his salt-and-pepper crew cut. His gun holster hung from a hook by the door, but he wore his badge on his hip and, apparently, his heart on his sleeve.

"Damn it," Jackson repeated. He pushed past the bookshelf and slumped back onto the front of his desk. "I really thought he was gonna make it out." He looked up to Chen. "What happened?"

"He was shot," Chen explained. "Three times to the chest. His body got dumped behind the gas station at a Hundred-and-Twenty-Third and Lake City Way."

Jackson looked down again. "Damn it. He was a good kid. He deserved better than that. "

"So you were working him?" Brunelle confirmed. "He was your informant?"

Jackson stood up again and put his hands in his pockets. "Oh yeah, I was working him. Had been for a few months. I popped him with a half-kilo of black tar heroin. He had syringes, baggies, the whole bit. I thought he was dealing but he insisted it was all for him. After a few minutes I could see how strung out he was and I believed him. Then I recognized him."

"You'd arrested him before?" Brunelle supposed.

But Jackson shook his head and chuckled a little. "No. He played little league with my son. They're the same age. I think he even slept over at our house once when Neil had a birthday party sleepover."

"Oh," Brunelle said.

"Yeah, 'oh' is right," Jackson agreed. "I didn't recognize him at first. For one thing, he wasn't that good of a friend. They just played little league together, hung out sometimes. You know, stuff like that. By the time they were in high school, I don't think they were really friends any more. But the other thing was, he looked like total shit. You know how these heroin addicts get. Filthy walking skeletons. I was gonna book him for possession of a controlled substance with intent to deliver, but when I ID'd him, I recognized the name. I was like, 'Derrick, is that you? You used to play right field for my kid's little league team.'"

Jackson took a moment to gather himself, then continued. "He looked at me with those huge skeleton eyes, and then he just started bawling. Sobbing. He couldn't stop."

"So you turned him into an informant," Chen surmised.

Jackson nodded. "Maybe I just shoulda booked him. Let him and his public defender figure it out. But the only way I could justify not booking him was to turn him. He was begging me to just let him go. I couldn't do that of course. Not unless he agreed to work for me. Then I have to let him go. I'd need him out on the street so all the other druggies would think he was still on their side. And I needed to establish his credibility first. I had plans for him, but first I had him do a couple of controlled buys. Small time stuff. Just to prove he was reliable so I could use him to go after my real target."

Jackson shook his head. "We had a whole plan. He was gonna kick the heroin and go stay with his uncle in Bozeman. I hooked him up with a methadone clinic down in the Rainier Valley so no one in Lake City would see him."

"You can't inform on druggies if they know you're clean," Brunelle knew.

"Exactly," Jackson confirmed. "He did a couple of small buys. Went great. No problems. The methadone was working. Uncle Larry had a bedroom and a job waiting for him. He just had one last job and then he was all set to take his life back."

"Instead," Brunelle observed, "he lost it."

"What was the last job?" Chen asked. "Who was the target?"

"The same bastard who shot him," Jackson answered. "I'm sure of that. Derrick's cover must have been blown. He dumped his body so everyone would know what happens to snitches."

"Who?" Brunelle asked. "Who shot Derrick? Who dumped

his body so everyone would know?"

"The biggest heroin dealer in North Seattle," Jackson answered. "Elmer Hernandez."

CHAPTER 4

Brunelle liked hanging out with cops, but he knew they were the real heroes of law enforcement, not him. He helped. He took their hard work and carried it across the finish line. But they were the ones out there, knocking on doors, talking to witnesses, even literally risking their lives sometimes. The other part of being a prosecutor and not a cop was that he didn't get involved until the cops finished their job, or at least the initial part of it. Dead body in a ditch? That's a job for a detective. But the lawyers don't get involved until the killer is identified, arrested, and charged.

Usually.

Brunelle was gazing out his office window when his phone rang. It wasn't as nice a view as his boss had, but then again, it probably shouldn't be. Matt Duncan was the elected District Attorney for King County; Brunelle was one of his Assistant D.A.s. An experienced, talented, successful assistant but an assistant nonetheless. Still, it was hard to have a bad view from two dozen stories above downtown Seattle. Everywhere you turned there was water, mountains, and/or glass skyscrapers. Beautiful. Which is why it took a few rings before Brunelle managed to tear himself away from the view and answer the phone.

"King County Prosecutor's Office, Dave Brunelle speaking." He'd considered copying Chen's gruff, 'Chen, Homicides,' intro, but again, he was a lawyer not a cop.

Good thing, too. Chen would have teased him about it. "Dave, it's Larry. We have a ... situation."

That didn't sound good. Brunelle said as much.

"I know," Chen answered. "Can you come down to the station right now?"

"Right now?" Brunelle questioned, although he considered that he'd just been staring out his window. "Why?"

Chen sighed into the phone. "Jackson went a little rogue. He had Hernandez picked up on some old probation warrants. I guess he thought he could scare him into confessing to the Shanborn murder."

Brunelle rolled his eyes. "Let me guess. The biggest heroin dealer in the north half of the city wasn't intimidated by some old misdemeanor warrants and an angry detective?"

"Not even close," Chen confirmed.

"So why do you need me?" Brunelle wondered.

"Hernandez isn't scared," Chen repeated, "but he isn't stupid either. He said he wants to talk to the D.A. That's you."

"Why does he want to talk to me? He should get his own attorney and talk to them."

"Maybe because there are no charges yet," Chen guessed. "I don't know. But you better get down here while the iron's still hot. We can book him on the warrants but he'll be out again tomorrow. And we don't have enough to arrest him for murder."

"Of course you don't," Brunelle agreed. "What did Jackson think? He'd just confess or something?"

"Between you and me," Chen offered, "he wasn't thinking.

He was feeling. A dangerous thing to do when you're a cop. But now we have Hernandez here and he wants to talk to you. So get your ass down here and maybe we'll get that confession after all."

Brunelle reluctantly agreed then hung up the phone. He looked out the window. The sun was shining and there were few places more beautiful than Seattle when the sun was shining. Everything looks perfect from twenty-four stories up. Then he shrugged and headed for the door. It was time to trade the sunshine of perfect Seattle for the drug dealers and murdered of real Seattle.

* * *

Brunelle observed Hernandez through the two-way mirror into the interrogation room. He was a large man, as thick as Jackson but much taller, with a full black beard and a bald head. His clothes were fashionable but not gaudy. Undoubtedly, he was doing well selling heroin, but he was smart enough not to flash it around. Cops would notice, and so would potential rivals. Brunelle already admired the man's style. On the other hand he sold poison to little league friends and dumped bullet-ridden bodies behind gas stations.

"What does he want again?" Brunelle asked before going into the room.

"He just said he wanted to talk to the D.A.," Chen answered.

"And you're sure he said D.A., not attorney?" Brunelle confirmed. "There was a prosecutor who did that once, pretended to be a public defender so they could get a confession from a murderer. The confession got suppressed and the prosecutor got disbarred. I'm not signing up for that."

"No, no," Chen assured. "He was very specific. He said D.A. We even clarified. Asked him if he meant defense attorney. He said, 'I know how to call my own attorney. I want to talk to the D.A.' Not sure why. Seems like he should be talking to his own lawyer. I don't know what you can offer that the defense attorney couldn't."

Brunelle frowned. "I do."

"What?" Chen asked.

"Immunity," Brunelle answered. "He wants immunity in exchange for information."

Chen nodded. "That makes sense."

"For him, maybe," Brunelle said. "Which usually means it doesn't make sense for us." He bumped Chen on the arm. "Come on, I'm not going in there alone. Let's you and I get this over with."

They exited the observation room and joined their subject in the interrogation room. Although one look at Hernandez's sharp eyes and Brunelle wondered who was really whose subject.

"Mr. Hernandez," Brunelle began. He always made a point of addressing criminals with the respect anyone else deserved. A little respect could go a long way. "I'm David Brunelle. I'm an Assistant District Attorney with the King County D.A.'s Office. Detective Chen said you wanted to talk to a prosecutor."

Brunelle was no detective. He'd watched plenty of interrogations, hundreds if not thousands, both live and on tape. But his questioning expertise was in a courtroom. Pulling information from a civilian witness, a reluctant victim, a testifying defendant. In a bright courtroom, with a book of evidence rules and a judge to settle disputes about whether any given question was phrased properly to admit only relevant evidence and not confuse a jury. But Brunelle found himself in a windowless room in the basement of a Seattle P.D. precinct, with no judges, jurors, or defense attorneys, and just one cop in case the drug dealing murderer on the other side of the table decided to get violent.

"Good morning, Mr. Brunelle," Hernandez replied in a smooth, almost soothing voice. "Thank you for agreeing to speak with me."

Brunelle tightened his poker face. He'd been expecting something gruffer, more street-hardened. He supposed Hernandez was plenty hardened. But he was polished too. Brunelle immediately considered that he'd play well in front of a jury—if they ever got that far. "I didn't do it for you. I did it for Detective Chen. When he asks for a favor, I'm usually agreeable."

"Of course, of course," Hernandez replied. "Then I am indebted to Detective Chen. I sensed that Detective Jackson is less amenable to accommodating my requests."

"He gets that way when his friends get murdered," Brunelle quipped.

"Ah, then Derrick was a friend of his," Hernandez said. "Or more than just another doper on the street anyway. Good to get confirmation of that."

Brunelle cursed himself. He never should have offered information to Hernandez. He didn't know what Jackson had or hadn't already told him. Although apparently Jackson hadn't revealed the informant relationship. No, that was left for Brunelle to stumble across.

"What do you want?" Brunelle snapped.

Hernandez raised a thick black eyebrow at Brunelle's changed tone, but then shrugged it off. "It's not what I want, Mr. Brunelle, it's what you want."

Brunelle wasn't in the mood for games. He'd given up a nice view and a fresh cup of coffee for this. "And what is it that I want?"

Hernandez grinned. He had nice teeth too. "You want, Mr. Brunelle, to know who killed Derrick Shanborn."

Brunelle offered a grin of his own. "I think I already know that, Mr. Hernandez."

Hernandez smiled more broadly. "Let's be careful with our word choice, Mr. Brunelle. You may suspect who killed Derrick, but you don't know. If you knew, then I would have been picked up for murder, not for failing to report to probation on a two-year-old misdemeanor case."

"So you're admitting to the murder?" Brunelle parried.

"Not at all," Hernandez dodged. "I'm pointing out that you and these fine detectives think I did it, but you don't have any evidence or else you would have already arrested me."

"So, if you're smart enough to figure that out," Brunelle asked, "why bother talking with me? Why not just wait to get released tomorrow and go back to selling heroin to hopeless drug addicts?"

Hernandez's smile lost some of its warmth. "We can discuss the ethics of the criminalization of drugs another time perhaps. No, the problem I face is that so long as Detective Jackson and the rest of the Seattle Police Department believe I'm responsible for a murder, they will be watching my every move and making themselves quite apparent to everyone I know, both friends and business contacts."

"And that would be bad for business," Brunelle remarked.

"Terrible for business," Hernandez replied. "I have as much interest as anyone in bringing this investigation to a speedy conclusion."

"But first you want immunity, right?" Brunelle asked. "That's why you wanted to talk to me. Detectives can't give you immunity. Defense attorneys can't give you immunity. Only the D.A."

"Correct," Hernandez confirmed. "I knew you'd understand."

"I understand," Brunelle replied. "But I haven't heard anything yet that would make me want to give you immunity."

"Right, well, that's really the problem," Hernandez said. "You won't hear anything until I get immunity."

Brunelle shook his head and surrendered a dark chuckle.

"But if I give you immunity first, and you confess to the murder, I can't prosecute you."

Hernandez smiled. "I suppose that's just a risk you're going to have to take, if you want to solve this case."

Brunelle frowned and crossed his arms. He regarded the man across the table from him. He was smart, well-spoken, and ruthless—he'd have to be to have become a major player in Seattle's heroin trade. A jury would likely believe him, whether it was testifying for the state that someone else had killed Derrick Shanborn, or testifying for himself after getting charged with that murder himself.

"I'm sorry, Mr. Hernandez," Brunelle said. "I'm a prosecutor. I don't take risks. I lock the case down and give it to the jury so they hold killers responsible. If you want to tell us who killed Derrick Shanborn, great. No one's stopping you. But there's no way I'm giving you blanket immunity before I know what you're going to say."

"And there's no way," Hernandez replied, "that I'm going to tell you what I know without that immunity."

"Then I guess we're at an impasse." Brunelle stood up.

"You won't solve it without my help," Hernandez insisted. "If I don't talk, no one else will."

Brunelle smiled. "That's why we need to hurry up and tell people you did talk before you get out again."

For the first time since Brunelle walked in, Hernandez was rattled. "What? You can't just—"

Brunelle turned to Chen. "Go ahead and book him on the warrants. Then round up every known associate and bring them here. We've got a long day ahead of us."

CHAPTER 5

"Any luck?" Brunelle asked a few hours later, after the police had swarmed into Lake City to round up any known associates of Elmer Hernandez they could find. The good news was, Hernandez had a lot of known associates. The bad news was, people like that were good at not being found.

"The patrol guys are still looking for more people to grab up," Chen answered, "but they've got two for us to start with. The easiest two to find."

"Who's that?" Brunelle asked.

"Hernandez's girlfriend, Samantha Keller," Chen answered. "And his right-hand man, Nate Wilkins. Keller was at their house, and Wilkins was on Lake City Way, making sure business was running smoothly while his boss was temporarily out of commission."

"So, the two people closest to him," Brunelle observed.

"And probably the most loyal," Chen finished Brunelle's thought. "Imagine how surprised they'll be when we tell them Hernandez snitched them out."

* * *

This time, Brunelle waited in the observation room and Jackson accompanied Chen for the interview. They started with the girlfriend. They figured it didn't hurt to let the junior drug dealer sweat a little, wondering who was saying what. They also figured, with no known involvement in Hernandez's drug activities, and the best info they had putting her relationship with Hernandez at just under six months, Samantha Keller might hear the word 'murder' and crack wide open.

They figured wrong.

"Fuck you, pigs. I ain't saying shit."

Nice language, Brunelle thought as he watched through the glass. *You kiss your murderous, drug-dealing boyfriend with that mouth? Oh right, of course you do.*

Samantha Keller was one feisty little ball of nerves. She was small, barely five feet tall and thin as a rail. She had long black hair that fell onto her shoulders in a tangled heap, and her eyes were oversized and deep brown. Dark red lipstick decorated that aforementioned mouth of hers.

"Samantha," Chen soothed, "nobody's saying you knew anything about this. We just need to know what happened. You're a witness, not a suspect."

Chen was playing good cop. Brunelle wondered if Jackson really had a bad cop in him. It might just be good cop, good cop. But then again, that might be just as effective with such a lovely young lady.

"Eat shit, mother fucker. I don't know shit. I ain't saying shit. Fuck both of you, you fucking cock-gobblers."

Brunelle understood what Hernandez saw in her. What she lacked in class, she more than made up for in hatred of the cops. A good quality for the girlfriend of a drug lord.

"Come on, Sammy," Jackson intervened. "There's no need to

get so nasty. Somebody's dead, and we're just trying to figure out why."

Keller narrowed her eyes. "If you don't know why, then you don't know shit." She crossed her arms, which mostly succeeded in stilling the uncontrollable shaking she'd exhibited since she'd set foot in the room. She was as high as a kite. Probably another desirable trait in a drug lord's girlfriend, Brunelle guessed. At least she supported her man's work.

"We know a lot more than you think," Chen replied.

"Oh yeah?" Keller challenged. "What do you know? How do you know it?"

"We know Derrick Shanborn was murdered for being a snitch," Jackson said.

"And we know it because Elmer told us himself," Chen added.

Keller's eyebrows knitted together. "Elmer? Fuck, man, ain't no one calls him Elmer. You call him Elmer, you gonna get a round in your ass. Maybe that's what happened to Derrick fucking Shanborn. And I ain't surprised to hear he was a snitch. He was a short little, rat-faced fucker. He deserved to get shot."

There was a lot there to work with, Brunelle knew. Chen put a hand on Jackson's arm to quiet him, then started in. "We know his street name is Burner. And we know how he got it. We also know that Derrick was killed for giving information to the police, not for calling your boyfriend by his real name."

Keller shrugged and looked away. One of her legs was bouncing uncontrollably. "Whatever, man."

"We also know that we never told you Derrick was shot," Chen continued calmly. "I was careful to say murdered. You're the one who knew he was shot to death. So why don't you just go ahead and tell us what else you know?"

Keller looked back at the detectives, but her arms stayed crossed and her leg kept bouncing. After a moment she said, "I don't know nothing about nothing, asshole, but I know if someone snitched on me, I'd shoot his bitch ass."

"That's exactly what Elmer—er, Burner—said," Chen replied. "He said he shot him because he was a snitch and dumped his body where it'd be found so everyone would know."

Keller took a few beats to size up her opponents. Finally, she asked, "Burner said that?"

Chen nodded. Jackson too. "Yep. Although he said it better than that," Jackson said. "He's better with words than we are."

"Yeah, and he's better with reality than you two shit eaters. Now I know you're lying to me. No way he said that. No way he said anything. Fuck you. We're done. Let me go or get me a fucking lawyer, but I'm done talking with you two ballsacks. Fuck you."

The detectives tried one more time to get Keller to engage, but the request for an attorney pretty much brought the questioning to an end. They didn't have to get her an attorney—they just couldn't talk to her any more. They left her in the interrogation room, and checked in with Brunelle.

"What do you think?" Chen asked.

"I think she's a lovely girl," Brunelle answered. "Real 'bring home to mom' material."

"Well, now that you're single again, I could introduce you to her. I feel like I have a real rapport with her now."

"Oh, yeah, absolutely," Brunelle replied. "You cock-gobbling ballsack. Maybe I'll just try my luck online."

"Bad idea," Jackson interjected. "That's how I met my ex-girlfriend."

Brunelle looked at Jackson. He had to admit, he was interested, but they had limited time. "So anyway. That didn't go terribly well."

Chen shrugged. "Well, I mean she didn't confess to seeing the murder and helping dump the body, no. But it wasn't a complete waste of time either."

Brunelle nodded. "She was almost buying it until you told her Elmer said he shot him."

"Right." Chen returned the nod. "So maybe that part isn't true and she knows it."

"Which means," Jackson added, "Hernandez isn't the one who shot him, but she knows who did."

The three men stood in thought for a moment. Then Chen stepped into the hallway and grabbed one of the patrol officers who was standing guard. "Let her go. Just right out front. She can find her own way home. Then bring Wilkins into the interrogation room and leave him there to sweat a little more."

* * *

"He doesn't look very nervous," Brunelle remarked as he and the two detectives observed Nate Wilkins through the two-way mirror. "He just looks kind of tired."

Chen grunted. "Well, you probably don't get to be number two in a major drug-running operation if you scare easily."

"Yeah, he's known on the street for being a pretty cool cucumber," Jackson added. "Basically unflappable. A good quality for someone you need to rely on."

"Great," Brunelle replied. "I'll keep him in mind if we ever have any openings."

"Don't worry, Dave." Chen rested a hand on his shoulder. "This whole interrogation thing is a little like judo. We'll use his strength against him. Unflappable people are good at running operations, but they rarely get angry enough to kill someone. If he was involved, he's freaking out inside, no matter how calm he seems on the outside."

"And what if he wasn't involved?" Brunelle asked.

"Then we better hope the boys have found some more associates for us to talk to, because so far, as sweet little Samantha Keller would say, we ain't got shit."

Chen and Jackson departed the observation room and Brunelle settled in for the next interview. He wished he had a cup of coffee.

"Mr. Wilkins," Chen practically shouted as he threw open the door to the interrogation room. "I'm Detective Larry Chen, Homicide Division. I believe you already know Detective Jackson of our Narcotics Division."

The thing about unflappable people is that they have the same flapping triggers as anyone else. They just have an extra filter that clamps down the reaction to the flapping. They're cool under pressure, but that doesn't mean they don't feel the pressure. And a constant barrage on those flap-filters can wear them down, just like anything else. Brunelle knew that. Chen did too. Hence, the loud entrance.

Yeah, it was going to be a good show. Brunelle needed popcorn to go with that coffee.

But the filters were still doing just fine, thank you. Wilkins nodded toward Jackson. "I know him. He's always trying to get all up in our business. Not very good at it, though."

Brunelle smiled slightly at that. They all knew that was a dig about Derrick Shanborn. Jackson had tried to catch Hernandez using Shanborn and Shanborn had ended up dead. So Wilkins scored a cheap shot. But it confirmed Wilkins knew Shanborn was an informant.

"We're better at it than you think," Chen replied. "Shanborn got us enough info to put you away for a long time."

But Wilkins just laughed. "Not without a witness. It's gonna be hard for Derrick to testify from the cemetery."

"You think we build our cases on just one informant?" Jackson challenged. "Derrick got us some initial info. But then we follow up with more witnesses, more informants, cell phone records, bank records, surveillance video from every business on the street. Oh no, Nate. We know what we're doing. And we know what you've been doing."

Wilkins didn't have a ready comeback. He shifted uneasily in his seat, a cheap and intentionally uncomfortable plastic chair.

Chen pressed their advantage. "And that's just the drug activity. We also know about what happened to Derrick. There's no honor among thieves. There sure as hell ain't no honor among drug addicts."

Wilkins looked down and frowned. After a moment he looked up. "You're bluffing."

"My officers are picking up more of your friends right now, Nate," Chen answered. "Do you trust them to keep their mouths shut? This isn't some little drug delivery. Shit, this isn't even a big drug delivery. Somebody's dead, Nate. Somebody's murdered. This shit is real now. The others, the other people we're picking up, they get it. They're gonna talk, Nate. They're already talking."

Wilkins didn't say anything.

"They're already talking, Nate," Chen repeated. "Samantha Keller, Nate. We just talked to Samantha. And the reason we picked you and Samantha up is because we talked to Burner this morning."

That got Wilkins' attention. His head shot up. "No way Burner talked. No way."

"So how did we know to scoop up you and Sammy, huh?" Jackson asked.

Before Wilkins could figure out a response, Chen threw

him—and Brunelle—a curve ball. "Nate, there's somebody I'd like you to meet." He tapped on the mirror. "Dave, come on in here."

"Fuck," Brunelle hissed under his breath. *What the hell are you doing, Larry?*

Brunelle ran a hand over his head. It was one thing for him to look on while the cops lied to a potential defendant. It was completely different if he was the one lying. He had Rules of Professional Conduct he had to worry about. One of those rules was candor to opposing parties. He wondered, as he let out another hushed, "Fuck," and headed toward the door, if he had to be honest and candid with a suspect before he became an actual opposing party. It wasn't a distinction he wanted to have to explain to a bar investigator in three months' time in order to save his law license.

As soon as Brunelle opened the door to the interrogation room, Chen started in with the introductions. "Nate, this is Dave Brunelle. He's a homicide prosecutor with the King County Prosecutor's Office. Do you know why he's here?"

Wilkins lowered his eyebrows in thought, but then admitted, "No."

"He's here, Nate," Chen said, "because Burner talked and I can't cut deals. Only the prosecutor can cut deals. Burner is getting booked into the King County Jail right now, and unless you want to follow him in on first degree murder charges, I'd advise you to start talking too."

Wilkins hesitated. His eyes darted back and forth under those lowered eyebrows. He looked up at Brunelle. "What kind of deal you offering?"

Brunelle shrugged. "Depends on what you say. And if I think you're telling the truth."

That much was true, Brunelle supposed. That was always how he approached snitches—or as his office liked to call them, 'cooperating codefendants.'

Wilkins crossed his arms. "First tell me what Burner said."

But Chen swatted that idea down. "Sorry, Nate. That's not how it works. We're not gonna let you just parrot back whatever Burner said. You just tell us the truth. Then it doesn't matter what anybody else said."

Wilkins sat there for several long moments. He was clearly conflicted, weighing the pros and cons of snitching out a major drug dealer. Brunelle knew what the rational decision was. Unfortunately, so did Nate Wilkins.

"Nope," he finally decided. "I ain't a snitch. If Burner talked, then he had his reasons, but I ain't talking."

Chen sighed. Jackson tapped the table with his fist. But Brunelle was actually a little bit relieved; the bar was going to care a lot less about him being involved in a police ruse if the ruse failed.

Chen stepped past Brunelle and opened the door again to the hallway. "We're done," he informed the patrol officer standing guard outside. "Take him to the jail and book him in on three counts of delivery of a controlled substance."

"Not murder?" Wilkins asked as he stood up.

"Not yet," Brunelle growled. He couldn't help himself.

Once Wilkins was gone, the three of them let down their guards.

"Damn it," Chen complained. "This is going nowhere."

"Everybody's too scared of him," Jackson said. "Or too loyal."

"Both, most likely," Brunelle suggested.

The detectives both nodded.

"What we need," Chen started, but the rest of his thought was cut off by screaming in the front lobby and a call for assistance over the P.A. The detectives ran toward the lobby; Brunelle hurried behind. When he got there, it was quite the sight: five patrol officers were trying to hold back two scraggly drug addicts, a man and a woman. The man was fully compliant with the two large officers holding him. In fact, he appeared to be barely conscious and definitely able—unlike everyone else in the vicinity—to ignore the ratty-haired woman struggling against three even larger police officers and screaming at him, "You better not talk, you mother fucker! You talk and you're dead, man! You fucking talk and you're fucking dead!"

CHAPTER 6

Chen looked back at Brunelle.

"Start with the guy," Brunelle suggested. "So she has time to calm down, and he doesn't have time to sober up."

Chen smiled and nodded. "Agreed."

A moment later, he'd barked out the appropriate orders to his officers. The belligerent woman was dragged out of earshot and the compliant man was dragged into the interview room.

"Battle stations, everyone," Chen said.

Brunelle went back into the observation room as the detectives got their subject's name, rank, and serial number from the patrol officers, then headed into the interrogation room for the introductions.

"Mr. Rittenberger?" Chen began. "I'm Detective Chen and this is Detective Jackson. We'd like to ask you a few questions about a man named Derrick Shanborn."

Rittenberger's head was flopped to one side, his eyes open, but fixed on the table top. He didn't respond to Chen at all.

"Mr. Rittenberger?" Chen repeated. "Josh?"

The use of his first name seemed to stir something inside

Rittenberger. He managed to raise his head and his eyes slowly upward until they focused on Chen, still standing over him. "I'm Josh," he said.

Chen smiled slightly. "Hi, Josh. I'm Larry." He sat down and gestured to Jackson. "This is Tim. We want to talk to you about Derrick. Do you know Derrick?"

Rittenberger took several moments to process what had been said to him. His face was blank as the neurons tried to fire amidst all the heroin or God-knew-what his brain was pickled in. Then his already bloodshot eyes suddenly teared up. "Derrick. Oh God, Derrick. He's dead."

This was the first confirmation that any of the people they'd questioned even knew Derrick was dead. And Josh Rittenberger looked like he was ready to spill a lot of information. Without standing up, Chen reached around to the small table behind him and pulled a form off the stack of papers there. Now that they were going to actually get some information, it was time for the formalities.

"Okay, Josh. I want to hear all about Derrick, but first, I have to read you something, okay?"

Rittenberger didn't respond. But he didn't protest either. Chen proceeded. "Okay. You have the right to remain silent..."

Chen went through each right, one by one, and then asked Rittenberger to sign the form if he was still willing to talk to them. Rittenberger signed the form.

Brunelle wasn't thrilled about the interrogation of an obviously intoxicated suspect. Even though the case law was on his side—getting yourself drunk or high was your own fault—it still felt a little dirty. On the other hand, they didn't even know if they had a case yet, let alone against whom. Even if a judge would suppress this particular question-and-answer session, Josh

Rittenberger might still lead the investigation to other, more admissible evidence. Brunelle deferred to his cops and made a mental note to research "intoxication + confession + admissibility" when he got back the office. If Rittenberger actually gave them anything worthwhile.

"Burner shot Derrick, man!"

Yep, worthwhile, thought Brunelle.

Chen had reengaged with a simple, open-ended, "What happened to Derrick?" Rittenberger jumped right to the conclusion. Chen would need to back him up a bit. Still they knew how the movie ended, and it was a good ending.

"Okay, let's back up," Chen said. In part because the homicide was his investigation, but another part was that Jackson looked like he was ready to explode. "What happened, Josh? Why did Burner shoot Derrick?"

Rittenberger's eyes were as wide as saucers. They almost looked like dinner plates in his gaunt, yellowy face. "He just shot him, man. Right there in front of everybody. Just," Rittenberger mimicked pulling a gun out from under his jacket, "blam, blam, blam! Dead. Fucking dead, man."

So, good information, but not exactly responsive to the question. Not really surprising. Chen pressed ahead. "Okay. And why, Josh? What happened before Burner shot him?"

But Rittenberger just shook his head and answered a different question. "He made us clean up, man. Said we'd be next. We had to wrap the body up in the rug, man. We had to clean the floor too, man. With bleach. I got it on my coat, man. I ruined my coat, man. I don't have another coat, man."

Rittenberger looked down at his dirty, ragged jacket. So did the detectives, and Brunelle. There were definitely bleach stains, areas where the yellow-beige of the coat had been turned nearly white. But far more importantly, there were darker stains. Brown stains. Blood stains.

"I think we're going to need your coat, Josh," Chen said. Brunelle would have preferred a warrant to seize someone's personal property, but there wasn't a judge handy right then, so Chen went for one of the exceptions to the warrant requirement: consent. And maybe a bribe. "Can we keep your coat, Josh? We can give you a brand new one from our lost and found. It'll be a lot cleaner and warmer."

Rittenberger glanced down at his coat again. Then he shrugged. "Sure. I guess." He started pulling himself out of it.

Jackson stood up and took the article of clothing. He took a moment to hand it to the patrol officer outside the interrogation room, directing him to book it into property and return with a new, warm jacket for Rittenberger. "Thanks, Josh," he said as he sat down again. "Your new coat is on its way."

Rittenberger nodded and hugged his jacketless self against the chill of the concrete-walled room. "What, uh, what were we talking about?"

"Derrick Shanborn," Chen answered. "You said you got your coat stained cleaning up after he was shot."

"Oh, right, right," Rittenberger said. "Yeah, there was blood everywhere, man. Just everywhere."

"Where, Josh?" Chen asked. If they knew where the murder had actually taken place, they could find that judge and get that warrant. There would be trace amounts of Derrick's blood there still. It was next to impossible to completely clean up a murder scene. That would require a lot of planning beforehand, and an amazing attention to detail afterward. There was no way a couple of drug addicts like Josh Rittenberger could have pulled that off.

"We were at Burner's place, man. He lets us crash there

sometimes when we're tripping."

"Who would crash there?"

"Everybody, man. Me. Lindsey. Derrick. Whoever."

'Lindsey' was likely the woman who was screaming at him in the lobby, Brunelle figured. Hopefully, Rittenberger was too high to remember what she'd been screaming, but his face had that same gears-turning expression as earlier. Chen didn't have much time left.

"Why, Josh?" he pressed. "Why did Burner shoot Derrick?"

Rittenberger's face clenched up in concentration. Those dinner-plate eyes narrowed to fat slits. Then they flew wide again. "Derrick was a snitch, man! Holy shit. Derrick was a snitch. He was working with the cops." Then clarity really set in for Josh Rittenberger. "Oh, shit. I just talked to the cops too. Oh, fuck, I just snitched out Burner. Oh, shit. Shit, shit, shit!"

Rittenberger lurched to his feet. Chen and Jackson sprang to theirs. "Calm down, Josh," Chen said, placing a hand on Rittenberger's shoulder. "It's going to be all right."

But Rittenberger shook himself away from the detective's grasp. "No, man, it's not. Oh, shit. Burner's gonna kill me. Just like Derrick." Then he grabbed his hair, and those eyes darted all around. "Oh, shit! I just did it again. I just snitched again. Oh, shit. Fuck. Shit."

"Josh," Jackson tried, but Rittenberger would have none of it.

"No way, man! I ain't saying shit more, man. We're done. We're done, man. I want a lawyer, or whatever. I don't wanna answer any more questions. I'm done, man. I'm done."

He stopped bouncing around the room and dropped his head into his hands. "Oh, shit," he murmured. "I'm so fucking done."

Brunelle could hardly disagree. Hernandez wasn't going to

be happy once he found out Rittenberger had implicated him. It seemed unlikely that Hernandez would give him a pass because of the whole high-as-shit thing. But that was Rittenberger's problem. Mostly. They finally had confirmation Burner was guilty of the murder. But they were going to need to keep Rittenberger alive until the trial.

"Book him for rendering criminal assistance first degree," Chen told the patrol officer who had just returned with Rittenberger's new, not blood stained coat. "You can put the coat in his personal property, for whenever he gets out again."

The officer nodded and took Rittenberger out by the arm. Rittenberger didn't resist. He was too relieved the interview was over.

Brunelle exited the observation room and joined Chen in the hallway. Jackson was a few steps away, talking with another patrol guy. "That was helpful," Brunelle remarked.

Chen shrugged. "It was a good start. We know who, where, and why. When isn't hard to figure out either. But he's scared to death of Hernandez, like all of them."

"Rational, I suppose," Brunelle said. "They saw him kill Shanborn for being a snitch."

Chen frowned but nodded. "Well, maybe the girl will talk now that she's had time to calm down."

But Jackson nixed that idea. "That's a no go. She tried to kill herself in the bathroom. Smashed her head against the toilet bowl."

Brunelle shook his head. "That's never going to work."

Jackson shrugged. "No one said she was smart. But she was injured. They took her to the jail infirmary."

"Fuck," Chen sighed. "I don't think we can even book her. Rittenberger said there was a Lindsey present, but he didn't say she helped." He frowned and looked to Brunelle. "What do you think,

Dave? We got enough to prosecute anyone?"

Brunelle frowned as well and considered. "We have the intoxicated ramblings of a drug addict who will likely refuse to testify against anyone." He shook his head. "No. We don't have enough. We have enough to know Hernandez did it, but not enough to hold him responsible."

CHAPTER 7

The next morning, Chen came to Brunelle's office, to discuss successes, failures, and strategy.

"Did you pick anybody else up after I left?" Brunelle asked. He was pretty sure he already knew the answer. If they'd had success there, they would have called him. Silence equals failure.

"No," Chen confirmed with a shake of his head. "We shook down some more dopers, but nobody had any info. Nothing of value anyway. Word spreads fast. They knew we had Hernandez, and of course everyone knew what happened to Shanborn."

"Of course," Brunelle agreed. "That was the point."

"So now what?" Chen asked. "Are you going to charge Hernandez based just on Rittenberger's statement?"

Brunelle offered a lopsided frown. "I'm inclined not to. Hernandez got booked yesterday. That means he's going in front of a judge at one-thirty today. I've got three choices: charge him based on Rittenberger's drug-addled allegations, don't charge him and he walks out of custody, or ask the judge to hold him for forty-eight more hours to give us a chance to get more evidence. I don't think we win a trial based on Josh Rittenberger alone, but it would probably be enough, barely, to establish probable cause for murder so the judge would hold him. "

"So why not just do that?" Chen asked. "That'd give us more time to try to find another witness."

But Brunelle didn't like the idea. "I'm not supposed to ask a judge to hold someone short of actual charges unless I really think there's additional evidence coming in, and right away. Like some forensic testing that takes an extra day or two before we get the results. Not just more time for a fishing expedition, hoping we find someone who knows something."

"I could make another run at Lindsey Fuller," Chen suggested. "She was too doped up on painkillers last night to talk to. She's probably got a hell of a headache this morning but I bet she's conscious. That's not a fishing expedition. Rittenberger said she was there."

Brunelle wasn't so sure. "That's still pretty fishing-y," he started. Then his phone rang and he took a moment to read the caller ID. If it was Duncan, he'd interrupt the meeting to take the call. He'd always interrupt a meeting for his boss. He probably would've answered if it were Jackson as well, since a call from him would probably mean more info on the case. But it wasn't a number he recognized. He let it go to voicemail.

"She was pretty clear," Brunelle returned his attention to Chen, "that she doesn't support cooperating with the authorities. I'm not sure I can represent to the judge that I expect that to lead anywhere."

"We're getting that search warrant today," Chen tried again. "What if we find something at Hernandez's house that ties him to the murder?"

"That's not bad," Brunelle admitted. "Murder victim blood in your house is pretty good evidence you were involved. But I won't have it by one-thirty."

The phone rang again. Brunelle checked the caller ID. It was the same number as before. He let it go to voicemail again.

"I hate just letting Hernandez walk," Brunelle said, "but there's another consideration. As soon as I charge him, he has a right to read all the police reports, everything we have against him. If this investigation is going to take a while, which it looks like it is, giving him copies of everything done to date could compromise the investigation. If I don't charge him, well, then he doesn't have any right to see the reports. He's just a suspect, not a charged criminal defendant with constitutional trial rights. And Rittenberger is safer if Hernandez doesn't get his hands on that interview until Hernandez is charged, arraigned, and held on a million dollars bail."

"He might be able to post a million," Chen warned.

"Fine. Two million," Brunelle replied. "Anyway, the point is, there are reasons to hold off charging, and I really don't have enough evidence right now to justify charging him. Maybe you'll turn up something in that search that we can use against Hernandez."

"Yeah," Chen agreed, "but they won't be done processing that scene until late tonight. I told them to check for blood in every crack and crevice."

"Yeah, tonight is too late," Brunelle confirmed. "I need something that can be done in the next three hours."

The phone rang a third time. It was the same number. Brunelle rolled his eyes and sighed. "Hold on, Larry. Whoever this is, they keep calling. Let me just make sure it's not some kind of emergency. "

He grabbed the receiver impatiently. "Brunelle."

"Mr. Brunelle, hello," came a smooth male voice on the other end of the line. "It's nice to speak with you again. This is William Harrison Welles. I'm a local criminal defense attorney. I'm sure you don't remember me, but we had a case against each other some time ago—"

"Oh, I remember," Brunelle interrupted. "I couldn't forget that case. Or you, Mr. Welles." Brunelle made a thumbs-down gesture to Chen, who nodded in agreement. "What can I do for you?" Brunelle asked his caller.

"Actually," Welles replied, "I think it's more a matter of what I can do for you."

Brunelle rolled his eyes. He didn't have time for games. If he was going to charge Hernandez, he'd need to get busy on the paperwork. If not, he and Chen needed to come up with a game plan. "I don't really have time for riddles, Mr. Welles. I'm kind of busy right now."

"I'm sure you are, Mr. Brunelle," Welles answered. "No doubt you're examining your evidence and trying to decide whether you have sufficient probable cause to charge Elmer Hernandez with murder."

Brunelle was stunned, but just for a moment. Then irritated. "What do you know about the Hernandez case?"

"It's not what I know, Mr. Brunelle," Welles oozed over the phone. "It's what my client knows. And she knows a great deal. A great deal, Mr. Brunelle. Interested?"

Brunelle put his hand over the receiver. "He claims he has a client who has info on the murder," he whispered.

"Is it Lindsey Fuller?" Chen whispered back.

"Is it Lindsey Fuller?" Brunelle asked Welles.

"Oh, no," Welles chuckled. "It is definitely not Lindsey Fuller. Although my client knows her as well, and her role in all this. But no, Ms. Fuller is well known in the relevant community as being mentally unstable. My client, on the other hand, is intelligent and articulate, with a spotless record. I believe she could be of significant value to your prosecution."

There was that saying about not looking a gift horse in the mouth. On the other hand, the Trojans got tricked by a gift horse. "Why would your client want to help my prosecution of her friends?"

"Careful, Mr. Brunelle. Don't try to trick me. I'm not one of your public defenders there. I never said the people responsible for this were her friends."

Yeah, there was no way Brunelle could forget this pompous ass. "The question stands. Why would she help me?"

"Simple self-interest," Welles answered. "She is not without potential criminal liability in all this. She'd like to tell her version first, before someone else tells a less accurate version that implicates her unfairly."

Brunelle nodded. "And let me guess, she wants full immunity, right?"

"Please, Mr. Brunelle. I'm no fool. And as I recall, neither are you. I don't expect you to give her full immunity right out of the gate. You need to hear what she has to say. I can assure you that she has valuable information and she is willing to testify for the state when the matter goes to trial. But I know you can't take my word for it. You need to hear it from her directly. Simply give her transactional immunity for the statement. Nothing in it can be used against her, so you can't listen to her and then charge her. If I let that happen, I'm quite sure the bar association would, and should, revoke my license. If you find what she has to say valuable—and I believe you will—then we can discuss a mutually agreeable resolution for my client. If you don't like it, you can walk away and my client doesn't have to worry about being charged with a crime in exchange for her effort to do the right thing."

Brunelle couldn't help but laugh at that last bit. "The right thing? We're talking about drug addicts and murderers, Mr. Welles. Throw in a couple of lawyers and a cop and we won't get anywhere close to the right thing."

Welles didn't return the laugh. "Well, then, the right thing for my client. Are you interested in speaking with her?"

Brunelle looked for a cue from Chen. He'd heard enough of the conversation to get the general idea. He shrugged and nodded.

"Be at the Seattle P.D. main precinct in one hour," Brunelle instructed. "Ask for Detective Larry Chen."

"Ah, Detective Chen," Welles replied. "This is turning into a regular reunion."

"One hour," Brunelle repeated. "See you then."

He hung up the phone and sighed.

"We got another snitch?" Chen asked.

"Yes," Brunelle answered. "But one smart enough to hire a lawyer before snitching."

"Well, let's hope she fares better than Derrick Shanborn."

"Agreed," Brunelle sneered. "If anyone else ends up bleeding in a ditch, let's hope it's William Harrison Welles."

CHAPTER 8

"Welles is here," Chen announced as he hung up the phone in the conference room where he and Brunelle had been waiting. It was considerably nicer than the interrogation room they'd used for the other interviews. There were still no windows, but there also wasn't a two-way mirror or table full of *Miranda* rights advisement forms. That was for cops and criminals. Lawyers and clients needed a conference room. They could at least pretend to be civil. "I'll go get him."

Brunelle nodded in assent and waited while Chen fetched their guests. The clock on the wall said 10:30. He guessed the interview would take about an hour. Everything seemed to take about an hour. That would give him two hours to get the paperwork ready to charge Hernandez with the first degree murder of Derrick Shanborn. Assuming Welles's client was as good as Welles had promised.

But Brunelle knew what happened when you assume...

Chen entered first, followed by Welles, then Welles's client. Welles was the same well-suited, gray-pony-tailed attorney Brunelle remembered from when they'd last tangled. That is, typical

Seattle attorney, nothing remarkable. His client's appearance, however, was striking, and Brunelle couldn't decide if it was in a good way.

She was tiny—maybe five feet tall, if she stood on her toes— and thin as a rail, with a black pixie haircut. She wore a red tank top and jeans, both hanging loosely from her bird-like frame. She looked like an eighth grader. A small, skinny eighth grader. The only thing that made her look old enough to be involved with a pack of murderous druggies were the tattoos completely covering her arms, chest and neck. Then again, Brunelle supposed that might be all the rage in middle school any more. The universe seemed to have no limit to its ways to make a man in his mid-40s feel old.

"Mr. Brunelle," Welles presented his client. "This is Amanda Ashford."

Brunelle extended a hand. "Nice to meet you."

Ashford stuck her hand in Brunelle's. If it were possible for one hand to swallow another one, that's what it would have felt like. Ashford avoided eye contact and pulled her tiny hand back quickly.

"Let's get started then, shall we?" Welles said as he selected seats at the conference table for himself and his client. He opened his briefcase and took out a file. "I've prepared a written immunity agreement—"

"Whoa, whoa," Brunelle interrupted. "Slow down there. First of all, we'll use my agreement. This isn't the first time I've done this. My agreement is fair. I don't know what yours says and I don't have time to read it looking for the ways you're going to screw me over later."

Welles grinned. "I've put all of those in section six," he quipped. "But seriously, I'm familiar with your office's standard agreement. I believe mine is superior in its draftsmanship and cogence, but I believe we can deign to sign yours."

Brunelle pinched the bridge of his nose. He didn't have time to get sucked into a verbal joust with Welles. "Great. It's the standard deal. Transactional immunity for this statement and this statement only. Anything she says can't be used against her unless she testifies differently at trial. Sign at the bottom and let's get started."

Welles made another remark but Brunelle ignored him as he and Chen took their spots around the conference table. Chen placed a digital recorder in the middle of them all and the interview began.

"This is Detective Larry Chen of the Seattle Police Department. I'm present with Assistant D.A. David Brunelle of the King County Prosecutor's Office, Amanda Ashford, and Ms. Ashford's attorney, William Harrison Welles. Ms. Ashford, why don't you just tell us what you know about the death of Derrick Shanborn? Then we can go back over any details we have questions about."

Ashford looked to Welles. He nodded. "Go ahead, Amanda."

She turned back and lowered her eyes. She took a deep breath. "Okay, I didn't actually see him get shot, but—"

"Wait. What?" Brunelle interrupted. "You didn't see the murder?" He turned to Welles. "Why are you wasting our time?"

But Welles raised a calm hand. "Patience, Mr. Brunelle. We are not wasting anyone's time. Least of all our own. I too have other cases and clients to attend to. I wouldn't have contacted you if I wasn't both aware of your time constraints and certain of the value of the information Ms. Ashford can provide you."

Brunelle narrowed his eyes at Welles. But then he looked to Chen, who nodded. Brunelle turned back to Ashford. "Okay, Ms. Ashford, go ahead. I won't interrupt again."

Ashford hesitated, her eyes wide in her frail face, then

sighed. "Okay, like I said, I didn't see Derrick get shot. But I know Burner did it 'cause he told me before that he was gonna do it, and he told me after that he did it.

"See, me and Burner, well, I was one of his girlfriends. I mean, Sammy is his old lady. They're, like, a couple. But a man like Burner, he's too much for just one woman. Sammy lets him get some on the side, so long as it ain't serious. Just sex for drugs, or a place to crash or whatever. So, when I showed up, Burner was all like, 'You and me are gonna be good friends.' He made sure I had enough dope and a place to sleep. And in exchange, I gave him whatever he wanted whenever he wanted it." She shrugged. "I'm not proud of it, but I ain't gonna be ashamed either."

Brunelle had promised not to interrupt, so instead of saying, 'I don't need to know your sexual habits. I need to know who killed Derrick Shanborn,' he just nodded encouragingly.

Ashford continued. "So, like I said, Burner told me he was gonna kill Derrick. Derrick had been hanging out with us for a while, but he kinda stopped using. He always had some excuse, but they were lame. Like one time he said he had the stomach flu, and every time somebody offered him a needle, he was like, 'Oh man, I gotta take a shit.' At first, it was like, whatever, man. But after a while it got really suspicious. So Burner had somebody follow him and he saw Derrick meeting with some cop."

She looked over at Chen. "Not you," she said. "A white dude. Burner knew him. Said he worked drugs, so Burner knew Derrick had turned snitch. Man, you don't cross Burner. Derrick was dead as soon as Burner found out. It was just a matter of time. Whenever Burner wanted to kill him, that's how much longer Derrick was gonna live.

"Burner told me what was going down and what he was gonna do. He told me the whole plan. They were gonna lure

Derrick over to his place and confront him. Make him tell them what he'd told the cops, then they were gonna kill him."

Brunelle didn't interrupt, but Chen did. "Why would he tell you all that?"

Ashford shrugged. "It wasn't like he was really telling me. It was more like he was just talking to himself. We had just boned, and he was talking afterward. You know, just lying there and talking after you fuck."

Brunelle wanted to make a comment about all the times he'd laid there after sex, talking about who he was gonna murder. Instead, he just said, "Go on."

Ashford did. "Well, Derrick was kinda sweet on me. I mean, he knew I was fucking Burner, so he wasn't gonna try anything, but I saw the way he looked at me. So my job was to call him and tell him to come over to Burner's place. They figured if Burner called him, he might get suspicious, ya know. He might be paranoid and think Burner knew and not come over. So I called him and told him I was alone over at Burner's house. I told him I came over with Burner but then Burner and Nate left and so I was all alone. I didn't say I was gonna fuck him or anything, but I knew he'd come over just in case maybe I woulda."

Brunelle nodded. *Yeah, that's how guys think.* At least Ashford was credible. So far, anyway.

"After I made the call, Burner gave me a shitload of dope and told me to go shoot up in the back bedroom. Well, I wasn't gonna say no to that. I went back there and shot up. It was good shit too. I was fucking tripping. I passed out, I think. When I woke up, Burner was pulling me out of bed and telling me I had to clean up.

"When I came out front, Josh and Lindsey and Nate were all there, and Derrick was wrapped up in a rug. There was blood all over the walls and the floor. Burner gave me a bucket and a sponge and told me to start cleaning up the blood. And it was hard, 'cause Derrick was still there, ya know, on the floor. So I just worked on the walls. But Burner said they had to leave his body there until it was dark. Then they were gonna take it down to Nate's truck and dump it someplace where people would find it. He wanted everyone to know, you don't snitch out Burner Hernandez."

Brunelle finally interrupted with a question. The obvious one. "So why are you snitching him out?"

"I'll handle this one," Welles interjected, much to Brunelle's irritation. He'd rather hear the answer directly from the witness. Plus, he just really hated listening to Welles talk. "Ms. Ashford came to me because she was aware that the authorities might misconstrue her actions as those of an accomplice to murder."

"Calling the victim to come over so the murderer can kill him is pretty much the definition of accomplice," Brunelle replied.

"Yes, well," Welles smiled. "There's a bit more to it than just that, I assure you. I believe my client may be overstating how much Mr. Hernandez actually told her before the murder—a vital point for any theory of accomplice liability. But I don't believe you have time for that right now. Suffice it to say, I listened to Ms. Ashford's story, then made some inquiries into the status of your investigation."

Brunelle raised an eyebrow and looked to Chen. Chen lowered his own eyebrows and shook his head. "My officers better not be giving information out to defense attorneys."

"My sources are strictly confidential," Welles responded. "The point is, I knew you needed additional information and I knew you needed it now. The iron was as hot as it was going to get for my client and so I struck."

Brunelle frowned and began chewing the inside of his cheek. Welles was right: what Ashford had just admitted to was sufficient to charge her as an accomplice to the murder. But she only said it after Brunelle agreed not to use any of her statements against her. Still, if the others threw her under the bus and were willing to testify against her, she could still be facing a murder conviction and the next two to three decades in prison.

"What do you want?" Brunelle asked.

"Rendering criminal assistance in the second degree," Welles was ready with his answer. "For aiding with the cleanup."

"Assisting after a murder is rendering criminal assistance in the first degree," Brunelle pointed out.

"And first degree is a felony," Welles returned. "Second degree is a misdemeanor. She pleads guilty to the misdemeanor and testifies against Hernandez and the rest of them at trial."

It wasn't a great deal. Brunelle hardly wanted to hand a misdemeanor to someone who was probably an accomplice under the law. On the other hand, she was his best chance of holding Hernandez responsible, and giving an accomplice a misdemeanor was a lot better than giving the murderer a free pass.

"She testifies first," Brunelle said, "and if she tells the truth, then she gets her misdemeanor."

Welles stood up and smiled broadly. "I believe we have a deal." He extended his hand to Brunelle.

Brunelle hesitated, then stood too. With no smile at all, he reached out and shook hands with the devil.

CHAPTER 9

Chen escorted Welles and Ashford to the lobby then returned to the conference room.

"So, you gonna charge Hernandez now?" He asked Brunelle.

But Brunelle had been asking himself that same question. "What happens when I file charges based on what Amanda Ashford just told us?"

"The judge will set bail at a million dollars and he sits in jail awaiting trial on first degree murder charges."

"Correct," Brunelle said. "But what about all the other people who were in on it? What happens with them?"

Chen thought for a moment. "Well, Wilkins is in on those drug charges. We bring him in and add charges of murder."

Brunelle nodded. "Okay, easy enough. What about Samantha? Fuller? Rittenberger? What do they do?"

"They scurry like cockroaches when you turn on the light."

"Exactly." Brunelle stood up. "I can ask the judge for those extra forty-eight hours now. You use that time to scoop up those three. Then, come Wednesday, I'll charge all five of them with the murder of Derrick Shanborn and we can have one big happy arraignment."

"Should be a hell of a show," Chen said.

"Yeah," Brunelle answered. "Bring popcorn and your tasers."

Chen surrendered a chuckle, but his expression remained grim. "That's gonna be a security nightmare. Maybe we should see if we can have each of them arraigned in front of a different judge."

But Brunelle shook his head, and he had no trouble smiling. "No," he said. "I want them to see each other."

CHAPTER 10

The judges were less enthused about a quintet of murder codefendants sharing a courtroom. There were only so many corrections officers available, and assigning ten of them to one courtroom was a bit more than the court wanted to allow. Instead, the compromise was to have them heard all by the same judge, but one after another, in the secure courtroom up on the eleventh floor of the King County Courthouse. One judge, three guards, and five holding cells on the other side of a secure door. Also, one prosecutor—Brunelle—and five defense attorneys, one for each defendant.

Each defendant needed to have his or her own attorney because every one of them might decide to sell out any other one of them. One attorney couldn't advise a client to snitch out another client of theirs; that was an insurmountable conflict of interest. No, each defendant got their own attorney, and they could each consider selling out some or all of the rest. A wonderful system.

The problem was, Brunelle needed at least one of them to agree to testify against the others. Amanda Ashford was a good start, but she couldn't give Brunelle the information he needed most: what exactly happened when Elmer Hernandez shot and killed Derrick Shanborn. So Brunelle decided to charge them all and wait for 'the race to the phone' that would ensue as each attorney explained to each client just how fucked they were.

"Good afternoon, Dave," greeted the first of the day's attorneys as she entered the secure courtroom and approached the bar where Brunelle stood, five different files in front of him, ready to start the show. It was Jessica Edwards, one of the senior attorneys at the King County Public Defender's Office. Whichever defendant drew her was lucky. She had defended at least as many murder cases as Brunelle had prosecuted, and all for a middling government salary. Top shelf representation at rock bottom prices.

"Afternoon, Jess," Brunelle returned the greeting. They were routinely adversaries, but that didn't mean they couldn't also be friends. "Who have you got?"

"Mr. Wilkins," Edwards answered simply. She was ready for battle, dressed in a black suit and a pale yellow blouse to match her shoulder-length blonde hair.

Brunelle nodded. "Yeah, I figured you'd get either Hernandez or Wilkins. They seem to be the biggest fish."

"Well, I don't know about that," Edwards replied. "But Mr. Hernandez hired private counsel. I took Mr. Wilkins. The rest we farmed out to local attorneys willing to handle a murder case for the paltry sum the county pays on conflict cases."

That conflict of interest rule extended to all attorneys in the same firm, and the public defender's office was essentially a law firm. So Edwards took the biggest fish who needed public counsel, and sent Keller, Fuller, and Rittenberger out to three private attorneys who were struggling enough to agree to represent a murder defendant for ten percent of whatever Hernandez's lawyer was charging.

Brunelle reached into the Wilkins file and pulled out Edwards' copies of the charging paperwork. "Here you go. We're going in reverse-guilty order. Hernandez will be last. Wilkins is right before him."

"Again, no comment," Edwards replied, but with a smile. "I'll just take a seat then. Mr. Wilkins and I are ready."

Brunelle spread out the files on the bar and looked at the clock. 1:24. The judge would be out in six minutes. Edwards, of course, was early, and prepared. Brunelle wondered which attorney would arrive next, and who they'd be representing. But court was about to start, so they didn't show up neatly, one at a time. Instead, they all walked in together at 1:29, talking amicably in the relaxed way the defense bar always seemed to have when they were hanging out together. Brunelle had to admit, his office was a lot more uptight. Probably had something to do with what kind of people were attracted to the job of forcing other people to follow the rules. Not a bad thing necessarily. Just different.

Brunelle recognized all three of the attorneys who walked in. One was Nick Lannigan, a local DUI and misdemeanor attorney who was trying to graduate to more serious felonies. Brunelle hoped he was representing Josh Rittenberger. In part, because Lannigan shouldn't be representing anyone more seriously involved than that, and in part, because Brunelle wanted to cut a deal with Rittenberger and Lannigan was going to be scared to death to go to trial.

Another was Barbara Rainaldi. She was a former prosecutor who left Brunelle's office about five years earlier to set up a private practice with her husband. By all accounts, she had been a competent prosecutor and was doing fine out on her own too.

But it was the last attorney that made Brunelle's heart jump, and not from the fear of a superior litigator. From the rush of seeing a former love—or at least, lover—and the confused combination of excitement and pain at interacting again with someone, his feelings for whom he hadn't ever taken the pain to really work through. He'd just ignored them and figured it would be a long time until Robyn Dunn was doing homicide cases.

Lannigan and Rainaldi took their seats next to Edwards. But Robyn strutted right up to Brunelle. "Hello, Mr. B. Long time, no..." She grinned. "Well, we probably shouldn't talk about that right here."

Brunelle could actually hear his heart pounding in his ears. She looked even more amazing than the last time he'd seen her. She had a slightly different hairstyle, shorter and sharper, the curving red hair framing her perfect face and bright blue eyes. That face with its dimple on one cheek, and a beauty-mark scar on the other. Perfect.

Brunelle had been a trial attorney for over twenty years. He was practiced at concealing his nervousness and presenting a calm facade to judges and juries. He could extend it to former lovers. Maybe.

"Oh, hey, Robyn. Are you here on this case? Aren't you still with the public defender? How can you and Jessica both be on the case?"

That was all way too fast, man, he thought. *Ugh.*

Robyn smiled, making that dimple pop. "I left three months ago, Dave. Set up my own practice. I was tired of waiting my turn to work on big cases." She lowered her voice a notch and looked up at him with lidded eyes. "You know how impatient I can be."

Brunelle did know. He also knew that she was playing him, trying to rattle him right before the arraignments, keep him from thinking straight. The worst part was, it was working. And they both knew it.

Luckily, the judge came out and the bailiff called the courtroom to order. Brunelle could turn his back on Robyn without it being rude. And just in time.

"Are you ready, Mr. Brunelle?" the judge asked as he took his seat above the participants.

It was Judge Michael Jankowski. He'd been around for a while, although most recently he'd been in the family court rotation, handling contested divorces and child dependency petitions. He'd grown a salt-and-pepper beard while he was away. Brunelle was glad to see him back doing criminal again.

"Yes, Your Honor," Brunelle responded. He grabbed the file on top of his stack and nodded to the corrections officer standing at the secure door to the holding cells. "The first matter that's ready is The State of Washington versus James Rittenberger."

The guard unlocked the door and shouted, "Rittenberger!" into the concrete holding area. Then, to Brunelle's slight disappointment, Barbara Rainaldi stood up and walked to the bar to wait for her client.

A few moments later, a disheveled, gaunt, and cowering Josh Rittenberger skittered into the courtroom. Rather than the standard jail outfit—like nurse's scrubs, but red—he was dressed in the padded gown they gave to the inmates on suicide watch. A determined inmate could hang himself with a standard shirt and pants; not so with two baseball catcher's chest pads connected at the shoulder and waist by Velcro. Apparently, Josh wasn't taking his current situation well.

Brunelle handed the charging documents to Rainaldi, who reduced the arraignment to its most efficient form with a professional, "We acknowledge receipt of the information, waive formal reading, and enter a plea of not guilty."

Brunelle   appreciated   the   professionalism.   Very

prosecutorial. Efficient, no drama.

They moved next to the bail argument. "The defendant is charged with murder in the first degree, Your Honor," Brunelle started. "He has prior convictions for simple drug possession and traffic matters. He has a history of failing to appear for court on most of his cases. The state would ask for bail in the amount of one million dollars."

Standard request for a murder case. Unfortunately, Rittenberger wasn't quite the standard murder defendant.

"Your Honor, Mr. Rittenberger is charged as an accomplice," Rainaldi responded, "not a principal. A million dollars may be appropriate for the person who pulled the trigger, but it is clearly excessive for someone who, even by the state's account, was a minor player. My client can likely make arrangements to post bail in the amount of ten thousand dollars, and I will work with him to ensure he makes all of his court dates."

Judge Jankowski only considered for a moment before declaring, "Bail will be set at five-hundred-thousand dollars. Other standard conditions apply, including no criminal law violations and no contact with witnesses or codefendants."

Brunelle nodded and began filling out the form for conditions of release. Rainaldi stepped away and the in-court corrections officers guided the still handcuffed and apparently confused Josh Rittenberger back to the other guard, who opened the door, pushed Rittenberger through and called out the next name Brunelle announced. "Fuller!"

Lannigan stood up. Which meant Robyn had Samantha Keller. Brunelle had mixed feelings about that. The case against Keller was probably the weakest, at least so far. That, combined with her probable loyalty to Hernandez, meant she was the least likely to cooperate and the most likely to tell Brunelle to fuck off and take the case to trial. Part of him wanted to work collaboratively with Robyn, but another part of him wanted to see her mouth form the word 'fuck.'

When Brunelle shook himself back to his senses, Lindsey Fuller was at the bar next to Lannigan. Brunelle handed Lannigan the paperwork and prepared for the bail argument. Lannigan tripped on his words but managed to mimic Rainaldi, acknowledging receipt, waving reading, and entering the 'not guilty' plea. Brunelle asked again for a million dollars bail. Lannigan could barely form a coherent sentence. And Judge Jankowski set bail at the same amount as Rittenberger: $500,000. Next!

Next was Samantha Keller. Robyn stood up and sauntered to the bar. Brunelle tried, but failed, to not look at her legs wrapped tightly in her suit skirt as she took her place next to him. The pounding returned to his ears.

Somehow he managed to call the case and Keller joined her lawyer in front of the judge. Same song and dance, same arguments, same result. "Bail is set at five-hundred-thousand dollars. Other standard conditions."

Not bad, Brunelle figured. Three-fifths done and Robyn was in his rearview mirror. The problem was, Edwards was in his front windshield, and he was vaguely aware, amid everything else competing for his attention, that no one claiming to be Hernandez's lawyer had arrived yet.

"Wilkins!" the door guard bellowed. A moment later, a confident looking Nate Wilkins strolled into the courtroom. He took his place next to Edwards, and the judge began. Arraign, rinse, repeat. Bail was set at $750,000, reflecting Wilkins' greater role in, if not the murder, then at least Hernandez's general business. The proceedings had become rote. Everyone relaxed. Mistake.

With four of the five arraignments finished, everyone knew who the last defendant was. The corrections officer at the door called out for "Hernandez!" before Wilkins was actually safely back in the holding area. When Hernandez stepped into the courtroom and saw a cocky, grinning Wilkins walking toward him, he only paused a moment before leaping on Wilkins and tackling him to the floor.

"I'm gonna fucking kill you!" Hernandez shouted as he punched Wilkins repeatedly in the face, a staccato of blood and bone. "Kill you! You hear me? You keep your fucking mouth shut! Shut! Or you're fucking dead!"

Even as the guards pulled Hernandez off the bloodied Wilkins, he continued shouting, "Dead! You hear me? Fucking dead!"

Hernandez was slammed into a chair and handcuffed behind his back. Wilkins was half-carried into the holding area, blood all down the front of his shirt. Brunelle suspected the arraignment would be delayed. But Hernandez's attorney had slipped in during the excitement and announced his readiness to proceed.

"Good afternoon, Your Honor," the attorney called out. "Ronald Jacobsen appearing on behalf of the accused, Elmer Hernandez."

Brunelle winced and turned to see Jacobsen grinning at the bar. He was a partner at Smith, Lundquist, Jacobsen and Brown, one of Seattle's many mid-sized corporate firms. Brunelle had dealt with him once when a white-collar criminal decided to hire a white-collar lawyer. When that case was over, Brunelle figured he'd never see Jacobsen again.

"Don't you have a polluter to defend or an orphanage to sue?" Brunelle asked under his breath.

"I'm sure I do, Mr. Brunelle," Jacobsen replied with that same money-eating grin. "But I got a taste for the criminal practice on our last case. Mr. Hernandez was referred to me by some other attorneys who have worked with him in the past."

"Laundering his drug money," Brunelle quipped, although it wasn't really a joke.

"I look forward to battling you again, Mr. Brunelle," Jacobsen said. Then he looked up again at Judge Jankowski. "The defense is ready to proceed with the arraignment, Your Honor, the earlier excitement notwithstanding."

The guards waited for the judge to authorize moving Hernandez from his secure chair to the usual defendant's spot next to Jacobsen. He didn't.

"That wasn't excitement, Mr. Jacobsen," Judge Jankowski declared. "That was assault, intimidating a witness, and contempt of court. You can acknowledge receipt of the information, waive formal reading, and enter a plea of not guilty, but you'll do it from where you're standing while your client remains where he's seated. If you want to be heard on bail, I can't stop that, but I wouldn't expect a good result. Are you sure you want to proceed today?"

"Quite sure," Jacobsen answered without hesitation. He was dressed a step above his government-employed colleagues, in a tailored suit and designer shoes. His silk tie alone probably cost more than Brunelle's entire outfit. And he wore it all very well, with an athletic frame and dark, thinning hair atop his 50-something head. "And I would like to be heard on bail as well."

Judge Jankowski scowled at Jacobsen for a few moments, then looked to Brunelle. "Proceed," he instructed.

Brunelle knew to do what a judge told him, especially a pissed off judge. He called the case, handed Jacobsen the paperwork, and asked for two million dollars bail, since Hernandez was the actual shooter.

Jacobsen acknowledged the paperwork, and said "Not guilty" on behalf of his client. Then he started his bail argument. "The defense asks you to release Mr. Hernandez on his own recognizance, Your Honor. He has gone to the trouble and expense of hiring private counsel. This shows his commitment to taking this matter seriously. He is presumed innocent of the charges against him and we look forward to holding the state to its burden of proving every element of the charge beyond a reasonable doubt. He was born and raised right here in Seattle, so he is not a flight risk and he does not pose a threat to the public. Therefore, under criminal rule three-point-two, which presumes a P.R. release, he should be released on his promise to appear."

"He assaulted a witness in open court," Judge Jankowski interjected. "*My* court."

Jacobsen raised a pointed index finger. "*Allegedly* assaulted, Your Honor."

Sometimes civil lawyers could be too clever for their own good. Civil practice was about deposition and bank records, trying to find some secret piece of information to trip up the other side with. Criminal practice was more real. Real victims, real blood, real consequences. And real assaults.

Jankowski turned back to Brunelle. "What bail did you ask for, Mr. Brunelle?"

"Two million, Your Honor."

"Bail will be set at *four* million dollars," Jankowski ruled. "This hearing is over. Return the defendant to the jail."

Jacobsen opened his mouth to argue, but the opportunity was lost. The guards were hardly silent about ordering Hernandez to his feet and laying hands on him to make sure he complied. Brunelle quickly stepped away from the bar. His work was done, and if Hernandez decided to fight the guards, it could easily spill in his direction.

As it turned out, Hernandez was perfectly compliant, and in just a few moments, the door to the holding area was closed and Jacobsen was left standing alone before the judge.

"We're done, Mr. Jacobsen," Jankowski said.

But Jacobsen regained his grin and replied, "For now, Your Honor."

CHAPTER 11

Five defendants, one uncharged informant, and six defense attorneys. That was too much for even Brunelle to handle by himself. It was standard practice to assign two prosecutors to murder cases anyway. The only question was, who was going to be Brunelle's second chair?

Matt Duncan, the elected District Attorney, called a meeting to answer just that question. Brunelle would have preferred to make his own choice of who to work with on a complex, challenging first degree murder case. But that wasn't how Duncan ran the office. And it was his office to run.

So a few days after the arraignments, Brunelle found himself at a mid-morning meeting in Duncan's office, coffee and pastries on the conference table, and a view of Elliot Bay out the window. It was actually a nice environment for a meeting. And almost everyone in attendance was as pleasant as the surroundings. Almost.

"So this one's a little too much for you, huh, Brunelle?" Joe Fletcher jabbed as he lumbered in and threw himself in a chair opposite Brunelle. Fletcher had been at the office just about as long as Brunelle. Somewhere along the way, they decided they didn't really like each other, although Brunelle couldn't recall why. Fletcher seemed committed to it, though, so Brunelle never bothered trying to bury whatever hatchet had appeared between them. Which was easy enough, because Fletcher was pretty much a loudmouth jerk.

Brunelle didn't reply to Fletcher's jab. He simply nodded in acknowledgement and decided that his paramount goal of the meeting would be to make sure he didn't get paired up with Fletcher. Anyone would be better than Fletcher.

Fletcher was the last one to arrive for the meeting, so Duncan closed the door to his office and took a seat at the head of the table. The attendees were Duncan, and a hand-selected few of his top homicide prosecutors: Brunelle, Fletcher, Linda Kirkpatrick, and Cameron McLain. Brunelle had hoped to see Michelle Yamata, his co-counsel on a couple of his prior cases, but no such luck. This was the old guard of the most experienced homicide prosecutors. It looked like Duncan was going to pair him up with someone old and experienced.

"I think," Duncan started, "we should pair Dave up with someone new and fresh."

Crap, Brunelle thought. But his spirits lifted when he realized 'new and fresh' excluded Fletcher. Still, he had his concerns.

"Well, not too new or too fresh," Brunelle said. "This isn't a slam-dunk case. There's no shooting on surveillance video or full confession on tape. We're going to have to piece it together witness by witness, and we're going to have to cut deals to do it. It's a bit more complex than your typical murder."

"Exactly what I was thinking," Duncan replied.

Brunelle wasn't sure what that meant. Was Duncan already

backpedaling on 'new and fresh'?

Fletcher interrupted his thoughts. "So you're gonna base your entire case on the word of the fellow murderers?"

Brunelle shrugged. "I don't have any choice. There aren't any other witnesses. Everyone who saw it helped out in some way. That means cutting deals."

"No one is going to believe a bunch of snitches who are getting deals to throw one guy under the bus," Fletcher scoffed. "Every defense lawyer in that courtroom is going to argue that every other defendant is lying. And they'll all be right."

"Well, luckily," Brunelle replied, "not all of the defense attorneys want to end up arguing anything in front of a jury. One of them contacted me before we even charged it so he could get a deal in place right away."

"Who was that?" Kirkpatrick asked. She was a straight shooter, no time for insults and jabs.

"William Harrison Welles," Brunelle practically groaned.

"That guy is such a windbag," McLain said. "But he's not afraid of trial." McLain was probably the quietest of the five of them. But a quiet lawyer still talks a lot. He'd been at the office a few years less than anyone else in the room, but had distinguished himself with a calm demeanor in even the most stressful situations, and a quiet command of the courtroom while in trial. Maybe that's who Duncan had in mind. Brunelle could live with that, he supposed.

"Oh, no doubt about that," Brunelle answered. "Welles loves a courtroom. It just so happens, the least culpable of the group was also the smartest. She got him on board before we even knew who she was."

"No, I was thinking more about Nick Lannigan," Brunelle continued. "He's got one of them. The last place he wants to be is in front of a jury."

"Who's Nick Lannigan?" Kirkpatrick asked.

"Exactly," Fletcher laughed. "He's a nobody. He's got no business being on a murder case."

"He's a nice enough guy," Brunelle defended him. "But yeah, he's in over his head on this one. He might bluster a little bit, but there's no way he doesn't talk his client into a deal, even a crappy deal."

"Which is exactly what it'll be," Fletcher said, "since we know he's scared of going to trial."

Brunelle supposed there was some truth to that. There probably shouldn't be, but there was.

"Who represents the main guy?" McLain asked. "The shooter."

"Ron Jacobsen," Brunelle answered. If the others didn't know a defense attorney—albeit small-time defense attorney—like Nick Lannigan, he doubted they'd know a corporate guy like Jacobsen. And he was right. Blank faces stared back at him.

"Is he new?" Kirkpatrick asked. "I don't recognize that name."

"Me neither," McLain added.

Fletcher just shrugged. He wasn't the type of person to admit when he didn't know something, even when that something was a someone nobody else knew either.

Well, almost nobody else.

"I know him," Duncan announced. All eyes turned to the boss. "He's a partner at Smith Lundquist. They mostly do civil litigation, a mix of insurance defense and plaintiff's personal injury. They've sued the county a few times. Somebody tripping on an uneven sidewalk at a public park, stuff like that."

The criminal division of the prosecutor's office was so large and dominant, the criminal guys like Brunelle—and Fletcher and Kirkpatrick and McLain—tended to forget the office had an entire civil division. But Matt Duncan was the lawyer for the entire county. The majority of his lawyers prosecuted crimes, but he also had lawyers who enforced zoning laws, negotiated labor contacts, and defended the county against lawsuits. The lawyers in the civil and criminal divisions didn't interact very much, and there wasn't usually a lot of transfer between the divisions, although every now and then a prosecutor would burn out on broken bones and recanting victims, or a civil attorney would get tired of motions for summary judgment and sanctions under civil rule 11. Yawn.

Brunelle and the other criminal prosecutors didn't need to know what was going on in that other part of the office. But Duncan did.

"He's a very zealous litigator," Duncan went on. "He's like a pitbull. Once he locks his jaw onto something, he doesn't let go. He just files motion after motion after motion."

Brunelle nodded. That had been his experience as well.

"Yeah, but criminal practice is different," Fletcher said. "This isn't a drug case where you can suppress evidence if the search was bad. It's a murder. Bad guy shot dead guy. Simple."

"He'll file the motions anyway," Brunelle interjected. "Especially because that's not how we do things on this side. He knows we don't like paperwork. We like jurors and evidence tags. The last thing we want to be doing is responding to yet another motion to compel production of the receipt for the pen the detective used to take notes at the crime scene, or whatever."

Fletcher huffed. "Sounds like somebody needs to teach him how we do things."

Kirkpatrick disagreed. "No, we need someone who understands how he does things."

"And can meet him, blow for blow," McLain added.

"We need a criminal trial attorney with experience as a civil litigator," Brunelle summarized.

Duncan nodded and smiled. "Yes. We need Gwen Carlisle."

The other attorneys in the room exchanged blank stares and shrugs.

"Who?" Brunelle asked for them all.

"Gwen?" Duncan was surprised. "You don't know Gwen Carlisle? She's been doing burglaries for two years now."

Brunelle shrugged again. "Sorry. I guess I haven't had a chance to get down there. It's a pretty big office."

"How does prosecuting burglary cases make her indispensable to a murder case?" Fletcher questioned.

Brunelle wondered the same thing himself.

"Because before that, she was the lead of our civil litigation team for five years," Duncan explained. "She's worked here for over ten years. Do you really not know her?"

"Again, big office," Brunelle defended. "If I don't know everyone doing burglaries, there's no way I know the civil guys."

"I think I saw her name on the phone list," Kirkpatrick offered. "Didn't she used to have a different last name? Flannigan or Flaherty or something?"

"No, it's always been Carlisle," Duncan said. "She got divorced a few years ago, but she never changed her name."

Everyone waited a moment for Fletcher to make some inappropriate remark about divorced women. When he didn't, Duncan finished his explanation of Carlisle's qualifications. "She defended the county against three different lawsuits filed by Jacobsen's firm. She won them all too. Then she turned forty and got a divorce. She wanted a change, so she asked to come over to the criminal side. Now she's kicking butt at that too. She's ready for something more than burglaries and car thefts. She's ready for a murder case. And she'll be ready for whatever bullshit Jacobsen tries to pull."

Duncan looked specifically to Brunelle. "Are you willing to work with her on this case, Dave?"

Brunelle thought for a moment. *Am I willing to work with a 40-year-old divorcée who can kick the lead defense attorney's ass?*

"Yeah, I'm willing to do that."

CHAPTER 12

The King County Prosecutor's Office was indeed large, with well over a hundred attorneys and twice as many support staff, spread across several skyscrapers in downtown Seattle. Luckily, most of the criminal division was in one building, so Brunelle only had to go down three floors to introduce himself to Gwen Carlisle. He should have taken the stairs, but they were those ugly cement-and-metal emergency type, hidden behind fire doors at the end of the hallway. Much farther away than the elevator bank right outside the main lobby.

He stepped off the elevator onto the 23rd floor and set out for the burglary unit. The attorneys' offices circled the outside of the floor, each with its own door and views of the city. The legal assistants, on the other hand, sat in a communal cubicle maze in the middle. The legal assistants rotated between units more frequently, so after a while, Brunelle had gotten to work with most of them. The attorneys tended to stay longer in their units, and the burglary unit was one of the felony teams where the newest lawyers started, once they'd finished their initial rotation in misdemeanors. So Brunelle said his hellos to the familiar faces in the legal assistant farm as he passed, but didn't even recognize most of the names on the attorney doors until he got to the nameplate that read 'Gwen Carlisle.' And even then, he didn't recognize the woman inside.

Carlisle was facing away from the door, typing on her computer. On her desk were an open file folder filled with police reports, several printouts of case law, and an oversized coffee cup boasting the words 'World's Greatest Lawyer.' She was intent on her work and didn't notice Brunelle. He scanned her office further and found it to be neat and tastefully decorated, with framed nature photographs joining the obligatory diplomas on the wall. No photos of significant others.

Gwen Carlisle herself matched the décor. Simple and stylish. A black suit coat was hung on a set of hooks near the door, and Brunelle could see her toned arms under her white blouse as she typed. She had thick, blonde hair cut just above her shoulders and only a gold necklace for jewelry. No rings.

Brunelle knocked on the doorframe. "Hi, Gwen. I'm Dave Brunelle." He gestured vaguely upstairs. "I work in homicides. Do you have a minute?"

Carlisle stopped typing and spun to face her visitor. "Hi, Dave. I know who you are. We've nodded to each other in the elevator a few times."

Brunelle smiled to cover up the awkwardness of someone remembering prior contacts that he didn't. "Right. I thought you looked familiar," he lied. "So, uh, you got a minute?"

Carlisle pushed her keyboard away and gave her full attention to Brunelle. "Of course. What can I do for you?"

Brunelle already liked her professionalism. It would play well in front of the jury. Jurors wanted their prosecutors to be professionals. Defense attorneys could be colorful, but prosecutors were supposed to be the adults in the room. Gwen Carlisle was clearly an adult. "I'm looking for a second chair on a new murder case and I was wondering if you might be interested."

Carlisle sat up a bit straighter and began nodding. But Brunelle interrupted her acceptance. "Actually, Duncan suggested you," he told her. She should know that. Not that Brunelle didn't want her on the case; but the big boss did want it. It was true, and real adults told the truth. He'd recently been reminded of that.

"Oh," Carlisle replied. "Well, that's very flattering. And yes, I'd very much like to work on the case. Thank you."

"Done," Brunelle announced. He finally sat down in one of the two guest chairs crammed into the small office. "So, do you want to hear a little about the case?"

"Of course," Carlisle replied. "And then I'll read the discovery tonight."

Brunelle grinned. "Uh, I think there's already like five hundred pages of reports. We'll get another two thousand or so before we're done."

"All the more reason to get started," Carlisle smiled back. "I'm not afraid of paper."

Spoken like a true civil attorney. Brunelle hated paper, unless it was photographs of the crime scene or ballistics reports matching the defendant's gun to the bullets extracted at autopsy.

"Yeah, Matt mentioned you were in civil for a while," Brunelle said. "In fact, that's why he recommended you. The lawyer for the shooter is Ron Jacobsen."

Carlisle let out a light laugh. "Ron? Oh, God. Yeah, I know Ron. He's not afraid of paper either. Shit, I think he must own stock in a paper company, the way he cranks out the motions."

Although surprised by it, Brunelle kind of liked the s-bomb Carlisle dropped. It was real. Adult and authentic. Perfect partner.

"Yeah, well, there are six different attorneys we're going to have to deal with," Brunelle went on. "I want Jacobsen to be the last one standing, then you and I can take him down together."

Carlisle's eyebrows raised. "Six attorneys? So, six defendants? What happened? Did a gang beat somebody to death?"

Brunelle shook his head. "Not exactly. One guy shot another guy for being a snitch, and the rest helped him out, each in a different way."

Carlisle nodded thoughtfully. Then she turned back to her computer and grabbed the mouse. "What's the shooter's name?"

"Hernandez. Elmer Hernandez."

Carlisle raised an eyebrow at Brunelle. "Elmer?"

"He goes by 'Burner,'" he explained. "He's a drug lord in North Seattle. Lake City."

"So yeah, Elmer doesn't fit that," Carlisle agreed. "Although there's probably a glue joke in there somewhere. We should keep an eye open for that."

Adult, authentic, and a sense of humor, Brunelle thought. *Jackpot.*

"Okay, here we go," Carlisle said, her eyes again fixed on her computer screen. "Elmer Hernandez, Nathan Wilkins, Samantha Keller, James Rittenberger, and Lindsey Fuller." She'd already pulled up the case. "That's only five codefendants. You said there were six."

"Uh, right," Brunelle answered. "The sixth is uncharged. She came forward right away, before we even knew who she was. She gave us the info we needed to be able to charge Hernandez, so we already cut her a deal."

That eyebrow of Carlisle's raised again. "Before the investigation was complete?"

"The investigation wouldn't have been complete if we hadn't agreed to talk to her. We had no evidence at that point. Well, we had a dead body and a mostly incoherent statement by Josh Rittenberger while he was still high as a kite. Not enough to charge at that point. The problem is that the only witnesses were also participants. We have to cut deals with some of them in order to get the others."

"But how do you know which ones to give deals to?" Carlisle questioned.

Brunelle frowned. "You try to cut the deals to the ones who are least culpable so you can get the ones who are most culpable."

"But if the only witnesses are the defendants themselves," Carlisle asked, "and they all want a deal and have every reason to blame the others, how do you know who to believe? "

Brunelle nodded. "Welcome to my world." He raised an eyebrow of his own. "You still want in on this case?"

Carlisle only had to think for a moment before returning the smile. "Fuck, yes."

CHAPTER 13

The next morning, Brunelle decided to swing by Carlisle's office, just to check in. He doubted she'd actually read all the discovery, but she'd probably started. Maybe they could begin discussing strategy over a cup of coffee. But when he arrived, he realized they'd be spending the morning in her office.

Carlisle had removed all the frames and diplomas from one of her walls and replaced them with a large sheet of butcher paper. Taped to the sheet were the five booking photos of the charged defendants, along with a copy of Amanda Ashford's driver's license photo, and an old booking photo of Derrick Shanborn. Below each photo was the person's name, known aliases, date of birth, and any prior violent felony convictions. Above each photo was a one-word description of each defendant's role in the murder. Hernandez got 'Shooter.' Keller got 'Girlfriend.' And Brunelle's immediate favorite: Ashford got 'Siren'—although Fuller's 'Harpy' was a close second. Each defendant's name was written in a different color ink, but the labels were in black, in quotation marks, and followed by different numbers of colored circles, some filled in, some not.

"So you read the discovery?" Brunelle deadpanned.

Carlisle had been standing in the center of the room, chin in hand, examining her chart. She turned to Brunelle and laughed lightly. "Yeah. I was here pretty late last night." She gestured to her handiwork. "I'm kind of a visual person. I need to see the relationships."

Brunelle nodded approvingly. Cleaned up a little and mounted on a foam board, the diagram would make a hell of an exhibit for closing argument. "So what do the colors mean?"

"Yeah, isn't that cool?" Carlisle enthused. "Each defendant has his or her own color. Hernandez is the killer, so he's red."

"Of course," Brunelle agreed.

"Wilkins is like his business manager," Carlisle went on, "so he's green. Keller is like Hernandez's queen, so she gets purple. Rittenberger is weak so he gets orange. I hate orange. I made Fuller brown because she's a piece of shit. And that leaves blue for Ashford."

"Because she's a siren rising out of the ocean?" Brunelle ventured.

Carlisle scrunched up her face at him, then laughed. "No, because that was the last color left over. But very poetic."

Brunelle sighed. "Yeah, I'm routinely accused of being poetic."

He was joking but Carlisle met his gaze and smiled. "There are worse things to be."

Brunelle felt a rush from the eye contact. He hadn't noticed before, but she had bright green eyes. Not hazel, but truly green. They were striking; he was surprised they hadn't caught his eye the day before.

"Uh, yeah, I suppose," he stammered. "I'll try not to give my closing argument in sonnet form."

"That'd be a pretty short closing," Carlisle responded. "I

mean, longer than a limerick, but still, just fourteen lines."

Brunelle put his hands in his pockets and nodded. "Yeah, I have no idea how long a sonnet is."

"Fourteen lines," Carlisle replied. "I just told you. And yeah, that's not surprising."

"You think I'm not cultured?"

"I think you're a dude and a lawyer," Carlisle answered. "You majored in beer and the only thing you read is closed captions."

Brunelle was taken aback. And a little hurt. "There's more to me than that."

Carlisle put her hand on her hips and smiled. "Oh yeah? Well, we'll see. In the meantime, I need to talk with that dude and lawyer." She pointed to Amanda Ashford's photo. "Would you do her?"

"Um," Brunelle managed to respond after a moment. "What?"

"Ashford," Carlisle gestured again at her photo. "Would you do her?"

When Brunelle still didn't answer the question, Carlisle rephrased. "*Fuck* her. Would you fuck her?"

"I know what you meant," Brunelle replied. "I just— I mean... Why would you ask me that?"

Carlisle crossed her arms and cocked her head to look across the room at the photo of Amanda Ashford. "She claims Hernandez used her as a fuck toy. But I don't know. She looks pretty skeezy. I don't know if I'd put my dick in that. I mean, if I had a dick."

Brunelle was speechless.

"You have a dick, right?" Carlisle prodded.

"Uh, right."

"So would you stick it in that?"

Brunelle hesitated, but only for a moment. Then he gave up. He looked at Ashford's picture. She was attractive enough, although no one looked good in a booking photo. Well, almost no one. And he'd seen her in person too. "Well, I am a dude, as you say, but I'm an upstanding, honorable, sensitive kind of dude. But absent that... Yeah, I'd probably have sex with her."

"Have sex?" Carlisle asked with a grin. "Not 'stick your dick in'? Aw, that's nice. You're adorable, even for a guy."

Brunelle straightened himself up a bit and tried to move past his adorableness. "Okay. Great. Glad I could help somehow. It seemed credible to me from the start, but probably because I'm a dude. And because I wanted to believe her since her story is what we based the charges on."

"I know," Carlisle answered. "Which is why I was testing that. But even if she's telling the truth, she doesn't give us enough. See those colored circles?"

"Yeah. I was going to ask about those."

Carlisle explained. "Every defendant has a color, right? Well, the circle after the defendant's label tells us which witnesses said what. Look at the circles after the word 'Shooter' above Hernandez. The orange circle is filled in because Rittenberger—he's orange, right?—Rittenberger said he saw Hernandez pull the trigger. But the blue circle has an X through it because Ashford said she wasn't there so she can't say who actually pulled the trigger."

Brunelle nodded approvingly. "Good system. What about the other circles? Green, purple, and brown? Those are empty. What do those mean?"

"Those mean we don't know yet what those people will say," Carlisle answered. "But we need to find out. Every circle we fill in is another witness against Hernandez."

"And another deal with the devil," Brunelle sighed.

"No," Carlisle said. "Hernandez is the devil. We'd be cutting deals with his henchmen."

Brunelle chuckled at that. "The devil's henchmen are still demons."

Carlisle laughed too. "I suppose so."

Brunelle shrugged. "Well, who would know better what happens in hell than the demons?"

"The victims," Carlisle answered after a moment. "The damned."

Heavy, Brunelle thought.

"But our victim is dead," he said. "So that just leaves the demons. So let's try to use as few of them as possible, and the ones with the least blood on their hands."

Carlisle and Brunelle both stared at Carlisle's diagram for several moments. Finally, Brunelle stepped forward and tapped on one of the photographs.

"Lindsey Fuller," he said. "We start with her."

CHAPTER 14

Lindsey Fuller may not have been the least culpable of the five defendants. Then again, she might have been. They were still low on details. Hernandez pulled the trigger—that much seemed certain—which left everyone but Hernandez in the running for the least culpable award. What tipped the scales in favor of Fuller wasn't anything she'd said or done. To the contrary, screaming at Rittenberger to not cooperate was definitely a check in the negative column. But she had one thing the others didn't have: Nick Lannigan as her attorney.

Rittenberger had Barbara Rainaldi. A fine attorney. She'd do him well. Too well. Before she let her client talk, she'd want every possible assurance, benefit, and favor, all in writing and witnessed by two priests and a rabbi. All Lannigan would need was a promise he wouldn't actually have to go to trial.

"I noticed all five of the defendants are set for pretrial this morning." Carlisle asked as they reached The Pit, the large meeting room where all the criminal attorneys, prosecutors and defenders, meet every day to make the sausage of plea bargains and deals that kept ninety-five percent of criminal cases out of trial courtrooms, lest the system be completely overwhelmed. "Are we going to keep them together for all of the court dates? I heard what happened at the arraignment."

"After this, we'll start scheduling them on different dates," Brunelle answered. "But I want them to see each other today, going from the jail to court, then get split up while they talk to their individual attorneys. I want them wondering if someone else is talking. Nothing encourages you to snitch like thinking somebody else might snitch you out first."

He opened the door to The Pit and they both stepped inside. There were at least twenty attorneys inside. Most were sitting at tables, holding two-, three-, or even four-way conversations. Defender A talking with Prosecutors B and C about two different clients, while Prosecutor B was also talking with Defender D about a third defendant and Prosecutor C was showing pictures of his kids to Defender E and Prosecutor F. It was all very congenial. Crimes were committed, deals were made, pleas were entered, next. At least, that's how Brunelle hoped the morning would go with Lannigan. If it did, then Jacobsen, Edwards, and Rainaldi would just have to wait. And Robyn Dunn too. But Robyn wasn't very good at waiting.

"Hello, Dave." Robyn emerged from the crowd to greet him before he was even two steps inside. She cast an appraising glance at Carlisle. "Is this your sidekick?"

The sidekick smiled and extended her hand. "Gwen Carlisle. Pleased to meet you."

Robyn shook her hand without hesitation. "Nice to meet you too." She tipped her head toward Brunelle. "Be careful of this one. He's slippery. You never know what he's really going to do."

Brunelle straightened up a bit at the statement, but before he could protest, Robyn added, "It's not his fault. He has trouble deciding what he wants. You should double-check his decisions to make sure they're really the best thing for the case."

Carlisle smiled. "Okay. Thanks for the advice."

Brunelle didn't like being talked about as if he weren't there. He glanced past Robyn into the throng of attorneys behind her. "Is Nick here? I want to talk to him first."

"Of course you do," Robyn replied with a laugh. "Why do you think Jessica assigned him to Lindsey Fuller?"

Brunelle paused for a moment to consider Edwards anticipating his decisions and stacking the deck against him before they even got started. Before he could consider it too much though, Robyn handed him a stack of papers. "I know there's no point in talking deal with you today, so here's our motion to sever Ms. Keller's trial from her codefendants, and a scheduling order setting the argument for two weeks from today. I imagine the other attorneys will all piggyback my motion. Well, all except Nick." She turned and looked to a back corner of The Pit. "He was the first one here this morning. I know because I was second. He's waiting for you."

Brunelle took the pleadings from Robyn. "Thanks. So, I guess that's all we need to do on your case for today?"

Robyn smiled, making that one dimple pop again. "For today, Davey. But you know there's lots more coming. If you decide you'd like to talk to my client, let me know, but I'm not going to come to you hat in hand. You know I don't beg."

Brunelle had managed to keep his mind on business up to that point. But the purr in Robyn's voice as she said that last sentence sent his heart racing again. "Right," he forced himself to say. "Great. We'll be in touch. Or whatever."

Carlisle and Robyn exchanged goodbyes as Brunelle pushed into The Pit to talk to Lannigan. By the time he reached Lannigan's hiding spot at a table in the back corner, Carlisle had caught up to him.

"Hey, Nick," Brunelle said. "How's it going? This is Gwen Carlisle, my co-counsel."

Lannigan stood up and greeted Carlisle warmly. They shook hands and then Lannigan got right to it. "My client is interested in making a deal." He looked around the crowded room. "Is there somewhere private we can go to discuss it? I don't think she'd like me talking about a deal for testimony out here where anyone could hear."

Brunelle could understand that, although it would all come out in the end. Prosecutors had to hand over any statements made by witnesses in the case prior to trial. That included giving snitch statements to the non-snitch defendants. Still, until and unless the statement actually happened, Brunelle was willing to give Lannigan whatever assurances he needed to turn Lindsey Fuller from a codefendant with the right to remain silent to a cooperating witness testifying against Hernandez and the others.

"What about one of the conference rooms you guys use to talk privately with your out-of-custody clients?" Brunelle suggested.

Lannigan nodded. "Yeah, that will work. Perfect." He scooped up his file and almost ran through the crowd and out of The Pit. The conference rooms were a series of glorified closets off the main hallway. By the time Brunelle and Carlisle got out of The Pit, Lannigan was already halfway down the corridor, holding the door to one of the rooms open. "Over here, guys," he called out, as if they couldn't just see him standing there.

Once inside, Lannigan practically collapsed into one of the two chairs jammed inside the room. Brunelle and Carlisle both remained standing.

"I'm glad Ms. Fuller wants to cooperate," Brunelle started.

He didn't get any further.

"Yeah, well, I'm not sure I can say that just yet," Lannigan interrupted. "But I think I can get her there. I mean, if the offer is good enough."

Brunelle raised a pained hand. "Wait. You just said she was interested in making a deal. Not two minutes ago, Nick. You just said that."

Lannigan surrendered a nervous laugh. "Well, yeah, I guess I did say that. What I meant was, I think she should cut a deal for testimony, and I think I can talk her into it, if the deal is good enough."

"That's a pretty big difference," Carlisle observed.

Lannigan shrugged. "I dunno. We end up in the same place either way."

Carlisle disagreed. "No, if she's ready to cooperate, we're at our destination. If you need to talk her into it, then we're just looking at ticket prices."

Brunelle liked the metaphor. "She's right, Nick. If your client wants to be first in line to cut a deal, we're willing to make that happen. But if she's not ready yet, we'll talk to whoever is. And if, after we talk to Rittenberger or Keller, we don't need your client anymore, well, then she will have missed her opportunity and she can sit next to Hernandez at the trial. And you can sit next to her."

Brunelle knew the last thing Lannigan wanted was to have to actually try a murder case. He wasn't ready for that.

"Okay, okay." Lannigan held his hands up in a surrender gesture. "I get it. But you gotta understand. She's not some normal person who got a DUI on the way home from the office Christmas party. She's a street-toughened drug addict. I can't talk her into it just because it's the right thing to do. She's gonna want something in return."

"Of course," Brunelle huffed back. "That's why it's called a deal for testimony."

"So what's the deal?" Lannigan asked. "Make it good and I bet I can get her to do it."

Carlisle looked to Brunelle, but Brunelle closed his eyes and pinched the bridge of his nose. "That's not how it works, Nick. You know that. Or maybe you don't. I don't give deals to snitches in advance. I need to hear what they have to say, and how they say it. I agree not to use it against them at trial if we don't reach a deal, but I'm not binding myself into a deal before I know what they have to say. If I knock it down to rendering criminal assistance and then she says she pulled the trigger, then I'm screwed."

"She didn't pull the trigger," Lannigan assured.

Brunelle sighed. "Yeah, I know that. But that's not the point. No deals until I hear what she has to say."

Lannigan looked down and chewed his lip for a moment. "Okay, and if you don't like what she has to say, the others don't find out she snitched, right?"

"Wrong." Brunelle shook his head. "I can drag my feet a little bit in releasing it to the others if we're in the middle of plea negotiations, but it's evidence in the case. I can't withhold it. If she talks, the others will know about it, whether we reach a deal or not."

Lannigan looked down again and shook his head. "She's not gonna like that."

Brunelle didn't have much sympathy. "Yeah, well, I doubt Derrick Shanborn liked getting three bullets to the chest."

Lannigan looked up. "Well, sure. But that's kind of irrelevant to my client. She just cares about herself."

Brunelle suddenly felt glad the negotiations had failed. "And that's the problem, Nick. Good luck fixing it." He put his hand on the doorknob. "I think we're done here."

But Carlisle added one more thought. "Tell Lindsey that Josh is ready to talk. First one who talks gets a deal, the other goes down for murder. It's a pretty easy decision, really."

Lannigan turned to Brunelle. "Is that true, Dave? Did Josh Rittenberger already offer to snitch?"

"He started to snitch when the cops first talked to him," Brunelle answered without answering. "He might as well finish it up."

Lannigan nodded. "Okay, okay. Give me a couple days. I'll have to work on her, but I think I can do it."

Brunelle nodded. "Two days. Then we take Rittenberger's statement and your client is out of luck."

"Deal," Lannigan responded. "I'll make it happen. One way or another, I'll make it happen."

The lawyers separated at that point and Brunelle and Carlisle huddled in the hallway.

"That didn't go quite like you said it would," Carlisle said.

Brunelle shrugged. "I may have underestimated Fuller's resistance to snitching. But I was right about Lannigan's fear of trial. He'll talk her into it."

"In the meantime, do we talk to Rittenberger's lawyer?"

"Rainaldi?" Brunelle shook his head. "Not yet. She's going to do the same thing Robyn did. File a motion to sever codefendants, and try to get some leverage against us."

"How do you know that?" Carlisle asked.

"Because she's a good lawyer," Brunelle answered. "And that's what any good lawyer would do."

CHAPTER 15

Sure enough, Rainaldi, Edwards, and Dunn all filed the same motion to sever. They had obviously worked together; the briefs were almost identical, down to the footnotes, with the only noticeable difference being the name of the defendant in the caption and the name of the attorney in the signature block. Jacobsen, on the other hand, had written his own brief. It cited most of the same cases, but also added three accusations of misconduct by Brunelle and/or his office and two demands for production of documents that either didn't exist or didn't exist yet, including statements of any cooperating codefendants. Lannigan didn't file anything. Although if all the other attorneys succeeded in severing their clients from the others for trial, Lannigan would benefit from that equally, without having to put a single fingertip to a keyboard.

"How do you want to respond to these?" Carlisle asked Brunelle at their next brainstorming session. "Do you want to split them up, you do two and I do two, or do you want me to just do all four, since the argument is basically the same?"

Brunelle voiced a third option. "Or I could write the responses to all of them myself."

"Oh," Carlisle replied. "Sure. If you want. I just figured, since I was second chair, I'd be doing more of the grunt work."

But Brunelle shook his head. "No, that's not how I work. We're partners. I just thought it might be easier for me to do since I've been doing criminal a lot longer than you. Have you even dealt with the issue of testifying codefendants and severance of trials before?"

"I'm familiar with the problems that arise from joint trials," Carlisle responded. "We had those all the time in civil. The plaintiff gets punched in the mouth by some homeless guy on a bus. He sues the homeless guy, but he also sues the county for letting him on the bus in the first place. Not because the county really can control everyone, but because the homeless guy doesn't have any money but the county does."

"I guess that makes sense," Brunelle answered. "But it's more complicated in a criminal setting. See, there are two constitutional rights in direct conflict. The right of one codefendant to confront the witnesses against him, and the right of the other codefendant—"

But Brunelle's law school lesson was interrupted by the ringing of his phone. He looked at the caller ID, but didn't recognize the number. If he had, he might have been able to determine whether he could let it go to voicemail. As it was, he couldn't tell if it was important or not, so he decided to go ahead and answer it.

"Brunelle. Homicides." Yeah, he liked that after all.

"Wow, Dave." Jessica Edwards laughed on the other end of the line. "That almost sounds menacing. Good thing I know you better."

"I can be menacing," Brunelle insisted. Carlisle cocked her head askance at him.

"Maybe to Nick Lannigan," Edwards replied, "but not to me."

"Nick Lannigan is an excellent judge of character," Brunelle said. "And an astute attorney with deadly instincts."

"He has no client control," Edwards returned, "and he'll never get Lindsey Fuller to cooperate with you."

"Who said I wanted cooperation from Lindsey Fuller?" Brunelle asked. He finally covered the mouthpiece and whispered, "Jessica Edwards," to Carlisle, who nodded in response.

"Everybody in The Pit saw the three of you leave to go cut a deal in the hallway," Edwards said. "By the way, who was that with you? I didn't recognize her."

"That, my dear Jessica, was the infamous Gwen Carlisle, late of the Civil Division of the King County Prosecutor's Office and hand-picked for this case to unleash purifying justice upon the wicked persons responsible for the tragic death of one Derrick Shanborn."

There was a pause, then Edwards asked, "She's right there with you, isn't she?"

"Yep," Brunelle confirmed.

"Put me on speaker. I'll save you the time of having to relay this to your wickedness vanquishing co-counsel."

"As you wish," Brunelle agreed, and he pressed the speaker button on the phone base. "Can you hear us?"

"Loud and clear," Edwards replied. Then, "Hi, Gwen. Nice to meet you. Just try to ignore Dave sometimes. We all do."

"Thanks for the advice," Carlisle responded. "I've already been doing that."

Brunelle gave her a 'What the hell?' expression, but Carlisle just smiled more broadly.

"Anyway," Brunelle said, "you didn't call to give my co-counsel advice on how to deal with me. What can we do for you, counselor?"

"It's not what you can do for me," Edwards replied. "It's what I can do for you. Or more correctly, what my client can do for you. He wants to talk."

Brunelle and Carlisle exchanged glances. Carlisle's was excited, but Brunelle's held consternation. Wilkins seemed to be the second most culpable, right after Hernandez. Brunelle wanted to work his way up the ladder. If it went the way he wanted it, Hernandez and Wilkins would be the last two standing to face trial, with the others all having taken deals in exchange for testimony. Wilkins wasn't the bottom of the ladder; they'd be skipping a rung or two, at least, to work with him.

"I don't know, Jess," Brunelle responded cautiously. "I'm waiting to hear back from some other attorneys. I'm not sure I want to start with your guy."

"Start?" Edwards repeated. "Okay. Good. That means you haven't talked to anyone else. And you won't need to either. My guy will give you everything you need on everyone you've charged, plus more maybe."

"More?" Brunelle asked. "Are you saying there were even more people involved?"

"I'm saying, you should talk to my guy. If you do, you won't need anyone else. I've talked to him. He's ready to spill."

Brunelle thought for a moment. Carlisle raised an eyebrow and gave an encouraging nod.

"What does he want in return?" Brunelle asked.

"I've already been through that with him," Edwards answered. "He knows how this works. You give him transactional immunity for the statement. It can't be used against him, unless he takes the stand and testifies differently at trial. He gets one shot at this. He has to tell you everything and he has to be believable. If you think he's holding back, or downplaying his own involvement, you won't want to work with him. And he knows that's the worst possible result: he rats out his buddies, they read every last word of it, but he doesn't get a deal because he pissed you off. I know the drill, Dave, and so does he. He's ready to give you Hernandez and all the others too. All you have to do is call Chen and schedule the when and where."

Brunelle paused to think. This wasn't how he wanted it to go. He looked up to Carlisle. Her smile was gone, replaced by a serious, thoughtful expression. Then she nodded.

"Okay, Jess," Brunelle said. "I'll call Larry. Then he'll call you. The when and where will depend on his schedule."

"Good call," Edwards answered. "You won't regret this."

But Brunelle frowned as he hung up the phone. He was experienced enough to know people only said that when they thought you probably would.

CHAPTER 16

"Are you sure about this?" Chen asked.

Brunelle and Carlisle were huddled in one corner of a conference room in the basement of the King County Jail, along with Chen and Jackson. Chen because he knew the case; Jackson because he knew Wilkins. Edwards and Wilkins were huddled in the other. Two corrections officers guarded the only door in or out of the room.

"Am I sure I want to cut a deal to one of the most culpable people involved? No, I'm not sure about that," Brunelle answered. "Am I sure he's the only one who's offered to talk to us so far? Yes. And am I sure I'm going to need at least one of these guys to turn on the others to have any sort of chance of winning at trial? Yeah, I'm pretty sure of that too. So, I guess we see what Mr. Wilkins has to say, and then go from there. One step at a time."

Edwards had been quick to the phone and almost quicker to the conference room. Once Brunelle put the call in to Chen, it was only a few hours before Chen and Edwards had scheduled the meeting for two days hence. In the meantime, no word from Lannigan. Also nothing from Rainaldi or Dunn. Jacobsen had filed another motion to compel something or other. Brunelle was pretty sure they'd already provided it, so he gave the motion to his legal assistant to figure out. That left just Nate Wilkins who was willing to talk to them. Well, him and Amanda Ashford.

"Amanda Ashford is a liar," Wilkins began, after they had taken their seats around the conference table, Chen and Brunelle up front next to Edwards and Wilkins, and Jackson and Carlisle hanging back at the other end of the table.

Right out of the gate with a problem for Brunelle. *Not the best way to start*, Brunelle thought. He needed Ashford's testimony to be believed, not undercut by another witness.

"She didn't go into the back bedroom when it all went down," Wilkins continued. "She was there the whole time, taunting Shanborn. 'You thought you were gonna get to fuck me, didn't you, Derrick?'" he mimicked a high-pitched voice. "'Didn't you? Well, you're the one who's fucked now, huh, Derrick?'"

Brunelle raised a hand. "Okay, okay. Let's not get carried away right at the outset. We'll decide who's telling the truth and who's lying. You just tell us what you know and we'll take it from there."

But Wilkins wasn't one to take direction that easily. "I'm just saying, she lied to you. She played you guys. And now I'm locked up because of her lies."

"Is that why you wanted to talk to us?" Brunelle asked. "To claim Amanda lied about what happened?"

"Look, man." Wilkins put his hands on the table. "I know I'm going to prison. Those drug delivery charges you booked me on were bogus. I can beat those. But a dead snitch? No, I know I'm going down. But I'll be damned if I'm the only one. And I'll be damned if it's because some bitch lied."

Brunelle took a moment to look at Chen. In truth, it wasn't a bad preamble. If Wilkins actually gave them some useful information, Brunelle and Carlisle would have to convince the jury to believe him. What he'd just said about not going down alone had the ring of truth about it. But it was also going to go to a jury of school teachers and retirees. "Let's try to avoid name-calling, okay, Mr. Wilkins," Brunelle cautioned him. "In fact, let's try to avoid cursing altogether. You seem like an intelligent guy. I bet you can articulate what happened without having to resort to swearing."

Wilkins leaned back and fought off a grin. "You are super uptight." He looked to his lawyer. "You were right, Jessica. Way uptight." Then he turned back to Brunelle. "Okay, Mr. Clean, I'll try not to cuss. I wouldn't want your ears to bleed."

Brunelle stood up, pushing out the chair behind him. "And we're done," he announced. "You had your chance, Mr. Wilkins. Good luck at trial."

But Edwards popped to her feet too. "Dave, wait. Give me a moment with my client. This is the first time he's ever done something like this. Let me remind him to be polite."

"Remind him what he's looking at," Brunelle responded. "And remind him that a jury is gonna believe Amanda Ashford a thousand percent more than him, especially if he cops that kind of attitude on the stand. I can't use a witness who's an asshole, and I'm not working with someone who disrespects me while he's sitting in handcuffs."

Edwards nodded. "Got it. Give me five minutes. Three. Three minutes. There's just a couple things I need to explain better. Three minutes."

Brunelle took a moment, then answered, "Take as long as you need. We're only doing this once. If you can't get through to him now, there won't be a later."

Edwards nodded some more. "Right. Got it. I only need

three minutes."

The two sides broke back into their separate huddles. Brunelle could hear Edwards saying something about 'thin skin' and 'prosecutors' egos.'

"I got other stuff to do too," Jackson said. "If this jackass just wants to posture, I say we cut it off now."

"This is the biggest thing on my plate, by far," Carlisle offered. "Whatever you need from me, I'm on it. I think we give him one more chance."

Before Brunelle could offer his thoughts, Edwards called out, "Okay, Dave. I think we have this worked out."

The prosecution team returned to the table and Edwards pointed to the voice recorder, which Chen had turned off before they'd broken back into their huddles. "That's off, right?" Edwards asked. When Chen nodded, Edwards continued, "Look, before we got here, I explained to Mr. Wilkins that whatever he said would go out to the other defendants. He was just trying to sound tough, for them. I explained why that was a bad idea. That his audience is you guys, and the jury, not his codefendants. I think he gets that now, don't you, Nate?"

Wilkins nodded, a bit stiffly. "Yeah. I haven't done this before. I'm not used to working with cops. But I get it now. I'll be polite."

"Polite is good," Brunelle agreed. "And honest is even better."

Chen turned the recorder back on, then looked Wilkins straight in the eye. "Who shot Derrick Shanborn?"

Wilkins held Chen's gaze. "Elmer Hernandez."

Brunelle nodded and glanced at Carlisle, who returned the nod.

But Wilkins wasn't done. "And Lindsey Fuller," he said.

Brunelle snapped back to look at Wilkins. Before he could interrupt, Wilkins went on, "And me. All three of us shot him."

Brunelle had too many questions running through his head to grab any one of them to pose to Wilkins. Luckily, Chen was more expert at interrogations. "You *all* shot him? What does that even mean? Who pulled the trigger?"

"Each of us did," Wilkins answered. "Burner shot first. Then he gave the gun to me and told me to shoot him. I did. Then he took the gun from me and gave it to Lindsey and told her to shoot him too."

There was a pause as Brunelle and his team tried to understand. "Why?" Brunelle asked. "Why didn't Hernandez just shoot him three times himself?"

"He wanted us all in on it," Wilkins answered. "So we wouldn't do what I'm doing right now, snitching him out."

Brunelle turned to Edwards. "Jess, I can't give a deal to one of the shooters. You know that."

But Edwards raised a calming hand. "Listen to everything he has to say, Dave. He didn't fire the kill shot. Hernandez did that. Nate fired into a dead body. That's not murder."

"Maybe not," Brunelle replied. "But how do I know he didn't fire a kill shot? Any of those wounds could have been fatal. And it's not like they initialed their individual entrance wounds. Of course your guy says he didn't fire the kill shot."

Chen stepped in. "Why don't we go ahead and start from the beginning? Let's hear everything he has to say. You can decide later whether to believe it."

"Sounds good," Edwards was quick to reply.

Carlisle added an agreeable shrug. But Brunelle wasn't so sure. Jackson was leaning back in his chair, arms crossed, staring straight through Wilkins.

Brunelle decided to defer to the judgment of his lead detective—and friend. "Fine. We'll do what Detective Chen says."

Chen nodded and turned his attention back to Wilkins. "Okay, tell us the whole story. From the top."

Wilkins nodded. "Okay. It's pretty simple. Burner is one of the biggest heroin dealers in town. Lake City is his territory. I help him with the operation. I keep track of the shipments and the sales and the inventory. I know what's coming in and what's going out. I know all the junkies and how much they spend and how long it's been since their last hit. He trusts me.

"You run an operation like that, you get to know lots of different people, especially junkies. Most of them are losers, but a few of them are cool and Burner might let them hang out with us. Especially if they were girls. Burner likes pretty girls. He liked Amanda and he liked Lindsey. Lindsey and Josh were kind of boyfriend-girlfriend, so Burner put up with Josh too. And Sammy is Burner's old lady. She put up with Burner looking at the other girls because she liked being important. Nothing more important than being queen to the king.

"Derrick was another user that Burner liked to keep around. I don't know why. He didn't have a hot girlfriend or anything. Burner just liked him. He thought he was funny, I guess. And whatever, he was cool enough. But then we found out Derrick had turned snitch. The cops were always trying to catch Burner. Part of my job was to make sure that didn't happen. They'd do surveillance on us, but I'd do surveillance on them too. And then one day I saw Derrick talking with a cop. He was doing a controlled buy for him. I watched the cop give him some cash, then he went into one of the local drug houses. He came back out a few minutes later with a baggie of drugs and gave them to the cop. Classic method. And I knew that cops would have their informants do two or three controlled buys to establish credibility before sending the snitch after the real target. It didn't take a brain surgeon to know the real target was Burner.

"I told Burner right away. And it was pretty obvious what needed to be done. But it wasn't enough to just kill him. Burner wanted to send a message. He wanted everyone to know what happened to anyone who even thought about selling him out.

"But Derrick wasn't totally stupid either. He musta known Burner might find out. So instead of Burner inviting him over, we had Amanda do it. Everyone knew he wanted to fuck Amanda. He was always talking about how hot she was. And she loved it. She liked being the pretty girl. So she called him, told him Burner and Sammy were out and we were partying at Burner's place. He came running.

"But when he walked inside, Burner was waiting for him. I locked the door and then it was on. Amanda was telling him how stupid he was. Lindsey was laughing at him. He dropped to his knees and tried to explain. He said the cop was helping him get clean and sending him off to Wyoming or something. But he said he was just leading the cop on, he was never really gonna turn Burner in. And Burner just stood over him, staring at him, not saying anything. Josh was in the corner, high as a kite, laughing like crazy. And Sammy was standing right behind Burner, just shaking her head.

"When Derrick finished explaining, he just started begging for his life. He was like, 'I swear, Burner. I'd never snitch you out. I just need to get clean and that cop said he'd help me. But I was never gonna turn on you. Never, Burner. You gotta believe me.'

"But Burner didn't say anything. He just put his hand out like this," Wilkins extended a hand, palm up, "and Sammy went and got his gun. Derrick started crying and begging. Amanda was yelling, 'Shoot him! Shoot him!' And Josh was still laughing like a lunatic. Burner told him to stand up. Derrick did. He started to beg again. 'Please, Burner, please.' And then Burner just shot him in the chest.

"He fell against the wall and slumped to the floor. Burner handed the gun to me and told me to shoot him too. So I shot him once in the stomach. Then he gave the gun to Lindsey too. I don't know why her. I guess 'cause she was the closest one standing there. Josh had stopped laughing, but he was way too high to give a gun to. Burner told Lindsey to shoot too. She did. I don't even know where. And then it was over.

"Burner told Amanda and Lindsey and Josh to clean up. We waited 'til it was really late, then me and Burner loaded the body down to my car, and we dumped it behind the gas station.

"Everybody knew Derrick and everybody would know what happens to anyone who turned snitch on Burner."

Brunelle nodded. "Like you just did," he observed.

Wilkins shrugged. "Like I said, I know I'm going to prison. But I'll be dammed if I go because Amanda fucking Ashford was smart enough to go to the cops first. And I didn't kill him. Burner did. I'll plead guilty to what I did, but what I did wasn't murder."

There was a long silence as everyone considered the story that had just been presented. Finally, Edwards spoke up. "Well? What do you think, Dave?"

Brunelle leaned back in his chair, took a deep breath, and ran his hands through his short, graying hair. After several moments, he exhaled and leaned forward again. "As long as we're all supposed to be honest here. I don't know what to think."

CHAPTER 17

"It's just like Murder on the Orient Express!" Carlisle enthused after the proffer was over and Edwards and Wilkins had departed.

Brunelle thought for a moment. "I'm trying to remember that episode."

"Episode?" Chen practically spat. "It's a book."

"I know it's a book," Brunelle defended," but they also made a series for PBS."

"It was for the BBC," Carlisle corrected. "PBS just aired it in the American market."

Chen shook his head and placed a hand on Brunelle's shoulder. "I'm sorry, Gwen," he said. "Dave comes across as cultured and refined, but it's all for show. He doesn't even read books."

"When did I say I didn't read books?" Brunelle demanded as he pushed Chen's hand off his shoulder.

"When you said Murder on the Orient Express was an episode," Carlisle joked.

Brunelle took a moment to ground himself. "Fine. Excuse me

for enjoying quality television. Luckily, I prefer to watch TV alone, because I can assure you I'm never going to invite either of you over to enjoy the dulcet tones of David Suchet's fake Belgian accent."

"Now, don't be hasty, David," Carlisle said. "I can be quite the Masterpiece Theatre maven. I would add to the experience, I assure you."

Brunelle forgot all about David Suchet. He wasn't sure what to say. Chen knew to step in.

"Murder on the Orient Express," he said. "Twelve suspects, each with motive and opportunity to kill the victim. Impossible to exclude any of them."

"Because, it turns out," Carlisle continued, "they all stabbed him. One after another."

"All of them were guilty," Chen said.

"So in a way, none of them were," Carlisle concluded.

But Brunelle was still feeling petulant. "Bullshit. They were all guilty. I would have charged them all."

"I'm not sure you'd have jurisdiction in Belgium," Carlisle quipped. "Or whatever country they were passing through."

"Still, it's stupid," Brunelle groused. "Spreading the blame doesn't eliminate it. It's just more people to put in prison."

Carlisle exchanged a concerned glance with Chen. "It's just a story, Dave."

Brunelle nodded, trying to force his mood to lift, but not trying too hard. "So was Wilkins' proffer. Just a story. And not any more believable than a train full of people conspiring to murder some old bastard they all hate. We can't call Wilkins as a prosecution witness. Not only won't the jury believe him, but they'll think we're idiots for buying it. How do we explain cutting a deal to Wilkins but not Hernandez when the only difference between them is who shot first?"

Carlisle didn't have an answer ready.

Jackson did. "There is no difference. They all shot him, so they all go down. Don't put Wilkins on the stand."

Brunelle nodded. He knew the decision was ultimately the lawyers' decision, not the detectives', but he couldn't disagree with Jackson. Still, it wasn't that simple. "We're still short on eyewitnesses," he pointed out.

"Better too few eyewitnesses," Jackson responded, "than one who's a liar."

They fell silent for a few moments as they each considered the situation in their own heads. Finally, Chen spoke up.

"I'd love to stay and discuss strategy," he said, glancing at his watch. "but it's after five and Mrs. Chen has plans for me this evening. She signed us up for a cooking class at some new kitchen supply store in Belltown."

"That sounds like fun!" Carlisle said. Brunelle just shrugged.

"Evie thinks so," Chen said. "And that makes it fun for me too."

Carlisle smiled at that. Brunelle didn't. But he did manage to say, "Thanks for your help today, Larry. You too, Tim. Gwen and I will talk it over and let you know how we want to proceed."

Chen offered a "Sounds good" and departed with Jackson, who was already teasing him about going to a cooking class instead of the bar after work. When they were gone, Carlisle looked at her own watch. "Hey, why don't we talk it over while it's still fresh in our heads? It's basically dinner time. I'm not looking for a cooking class, but there is this new Vietnamese place I've been wanting to try. What do you say?"

Brunelle wasn't sure what to say. He had planned on wallowing a bit longer. But dinner with Gwen...?

"I promise I won't tease you about your reading habits," she promised. "Or anything else. I forgot, men don't like being teased by women. I should have known better. Detective Chen started it, but you guys are both dudes and have obviously been friends for a long time. I should have stayed out of it. Sorry."

Brunelle frowned slightly. There was a lot in that outburst of words. He wasn't sure he understood or agreed with it all. But he decided he didn't need to. What mattered was the spirit in which it was offered. "Apology accepted," he said. "And your invitation is accepted too. Dinner sounds great."

They headed for the door. As Brunelle turned off the lights in the conference room, he asked, "So where's this Vietnamese place?"

Carlisle smiled broadly. It didn't produce a dimple in her cheek, but a twinkle flashed in her eye. "Lake City."

CHAPTER 18

Brunelle drove. But mostly so Carlisle could look for a restaurant on her phone.

"There's no Vietnamese restaurant in Lake City, is there?" Brunelle asked.

"I dunno. Probably," Carlisle answered. "I'm still looking."

"I mean, the dinner invitation. That was just a lie to get us out to Lake City so we could look at the crime scene, right?"

"I prefer the term 'ruse,'" Carlisle grinned.

Brunelle laughed. "Yeah, that's what the detectives call it when they tell the suspect they have his DNA and fingerprints all over the crime scene, when really they don't have shit. If they had his DNA and fingerprints, they wouldn't be working so hard for the confession."

"Just like our case," Carlisle observed.

"I suppose so," Brunelle admitted with a shrug. Then he changed the subject. "Does it matter if it's Vietnamese?"

"Uh, I guess not," Carlisle answered. "I just kind of had a craving."

On the 'guess not,' Brunelle turned suddenly into a tiny,

unevenly paved parking lot. His car bounced as he completed the turn and pulled into the one open parking stall in front of the run-down store front. "This Thai place doesn't look like much, but the food is pretty good," Brunelle explained. Then he pointed to the gas station across the street. "And we have a great view of where the body was dumped. That *is* why we're here, right?"

Carlisle smiled. "That's part of it." Then she opened the car door and stepped out.

Brunelle took a moment, then followed suit.

* * *

The food wasn't all that good after all, and the tables were almost as sticky as the glasses, but the prices were cheap and they managed to get some food in their stomachs before heading out into the night to explore the crime scene. The sun hadn't quite set yet, so the increasing darkness was being held at bay by both the glow on the horizon and the streetlights that had just turned on. A light rain had started as well, but not enough for a Seattleite to bother with an umbrella. Brunelle turned up his overcoat collar. Carlisle just put her hands in her pockets.

"So that's where they dumped the body?" Carlisle asked as they walked past Brunelle's car and toward the crosswalk a few storefronts away. Lake City Way was too busy of a street to risk jaywalking, especially in growing dark and rain.

"Yeah, there's a ditch behind the parking lot," Brunelle answered. "It was pretty obvious he'd been rolled down the hill, probably straight out of somebody's trunk."

"That's great that you got to see it in person that night, instead of just looking at photographs later," Carlisle said. "Wish I could have been here too."

Brunelle supposed that would have been good. "Well, I bet you'll be doing more homicides soon enough. Then you can get a two a.m. phone call and have to trade a warm bed for a cold body."

Carlisle chuckled. "Beats sharing a bed with a cold body. Been there done that. A rainy ditch might be preferable."

Brunelle took a moment to decide whether to follow up on that bit of too-much-information. It wasn't that he wasn't interested in who had been sharing her bed, or why he was so cold. It was more that he was enjoying her company and working with her. For some reason, he didn't want to rush into ruining that just yet. Maybe he was protecting the case. Not a good idea to co-chair a case with someone he was sleeping with. Even worse if it went sideways fast and he had to co-chair the case with an ex-lover. And if it went that bad that fast, it would have been something really terrible, probably embarrassing, maybe involving broken furniture and industrial solvents.

"Dave?" Carlisle's voice pulled him, mercifully, from the spiral his thoughts were descending into. "Hello?"

"Uh, sorry," he stammered.

"No, I'm sorry," she responded. "That was T.M.I. We're colleagues, not friends."

Brunelle cocked his head at her. "We can be both," he assured. "But if you start mentioning beds and bodies, I might need a moment."

Carlisle laughed. "Fair enough. We can all use more friends. And I'll keep my bed thoughts to myself so you can concentrate."

The crosswalk signal turned white and the two prosecutors hurried across the busy street. They had to walk almost the same distance back down Lake City Way to get to the gas station across from the restaurant. It was that typical gas station busy: cars coming in and out for gas, splashing through small puddles, as pedestrians and motorists ducked into the store just long enough to give the clerk some cash, or buy a pack of cigarettes, or get the key for the restroom that was outside and around the back. Itinerant travelers and local ne'er-do-wells intersecting just long enough to hold the door open for each other or hand off the bathroom key in the light rain of a Seattle twilight.

Brunelle and Carlisle walked through the puddles and the people to the back corner of the lot where Brunelle had stood with Chen on a darker, wetter night.

"Right there." He pointed down to where Derrick Shanborn's body had been lying, bullet-ridden and bloody. There was absolutely no evidence left that it had ever been there. The city had healed itself of the affront; the residents had forgotten it. Mostly.

"Huh." Carlisle shrugged. "Looks like a ditch. I guess those crime scene photos are useful after all. Nothing to see here, folks."

Brunelle nodded. "Yeah, it was more impressive when the body was still here and there were cop car lights flashing. Everybody knew it was a big deal. Now there are just two people, way overdressed from their day jobs, standing at the edge of a dirty gas station parking lot."

"I suppose so," Carlisle answered. "But it is helpful to see how this place is actually laid out." She turned around and scanned the area. "They probably drove in right there." She pointed to one of the driveways. "It leads straight past the pumps to right here. Although I wonder how they even knew this ditch was here. I mean, who hangs out at the edge of a gas station often enough to realize you could dump a body there?"

Brunelle pointed at the used syringes littering the asphalt near the dumpster and the restroom door. "Drug addicts. And their dealers. This is probably a well-known place for scoring heroin. And the bathroom is right there, so no need to wait 'til you get home to get your fix."

Carlisle nodded. "I suppose." She took a step toward the

building. "I wonder what's around back."

Before Brunelle could answer, Carlisle stepped through the discarded needles toward the back of the gas station, past the restroom into the dark shadow cast by the streetlights which had been abandoned by any further glow on the horizon. Night had settled in. The rain was picking up too.

"Wait," Brunelle cautioned, but weakly. Carlisle didn't hear him, or didn't care to heed him. She disappeared into the shadow. He sighed and followed her.

It was about as interesting as one would expect—which was, not very. More trash, probably syringes, but hidden in the dark. No smoking gun connecting Hernandez or anyone else to Shanborn's murder.

Brunelle was about to ask, 'Are we done back here?' when they heard voices from around the far corner of the building.

"This shit is almost twice what Burner was charging," a man was saying, "and it's total shit. It ain't doing shit for me."

That's a lot of shit, Brunelle thought. But rather than say anything, he raised a finger to his lips to urge quiet. But Carlisle was looking toward the voices, not at him.

"I know, I know," responded another man. "But hang in there. Nate knows what he's doing, man. I heard he's got a whole fucking master plan. Burner's going away, man, but Nate's gonna beat it. He always took care of us, right, man? Everything'll be cool again when Nate's running shit. He was running shit anyway, but now we won't pay extra so Burner can take his cut."

"Yeah, but in the meantime we're paying twice as much 'cause Burner ain't here to keep things under control. They're fucking gouging us, man."

Carlisle finally turned back to Brunelle. Her wide eyes were visible even in the dark. She nodded toward the voices, her expression asking, 'Did you hear that?!'

Brunelle nodded. He had. And it pissed him off. That was just the type of info he needed to get Edwards to realize Wilkins was playing her. It was probably too late to use Wilkins—lying in a proffer kind of burned his credibility—but still, it could help knock out that bullshit Murder on the Orient Express story. Brunelle wondered if Chen or Jackson could get down there before the men attached to the voices disappeared into the night. He reached into his pocket for his phone. But when he pulled it out, Carlisle grabbed his wrist and whispered, "They'll see the light!"

Brunelle knew that, but didn't get a chance to whisper-yell back. When Carlisle grabbed his arm, it threw his balance just slightly and he took one half-step backward. Right onto a glass syringe.

Crack-tinkle!

Fuck, Brunelle thought.

"Hey!" one of the men yelled. "Who's there?"

Nothing like a vein full of heroin combined with secret complaining about the drug dealer who murdered snitches to make an addict paranoid. Before Brunelle or Carlisle could even react, both men came barreling around the corner. Paranoid and reckless. For all they knew, Brunelle and Carlisle could have been armed drug dealers. They weren't, of course. They were two lawyers in suits and out of their element. And the only person who was armed was the junkie brandishing his pocket knife as he came around the corner.

"It's cool, man," Brunelle tried, but he didn't get a chance to say anything else. It all happened too fast. The man extended the knife and came at them. Brunelle stepped in front of Carlisle and instinctively reached out to stop the man. The man slashed at Brunelle, slicing down the length of Brunelle's right palm. Brunelle yelled in pain and pulled his hand back to his body.

The man was stunned for a moment at the success of his attack. So Carlisle pushed Brunelle aside and punched the man squarely in the nose. A loud crack filled the darkness and the man shrieked. He dropped the knife and ran back the way he'd come. His friend ran away too and a moment later, Brunelle was on one knee, his suit pants stained from the dirty water and his suit coat stained from the blood pouring out of the hand he held clutched to his chest.

"Are you all right?" Carlisle leaned down and helped him to his feet. "Come on, let's get you out of here."

Brunelle wasn't about to argue. Carlisle led him back into the main part of the parking lot. "We need to call 911," she said.

But Brunelle shook his head. "No, I'm okay. We can drive to the emergency room."

"That was a crime," Carlisle protested. "We need to report it."

"That was a mistake," Brunelle argued. "We should forget it. No need to add insult to injury. They'll never catch whoever it was anyway."

"He dropped the knife," Carlisle pointed out. "There may be fingerprints on it. And his nose is broken, so he might go to the emergency room too. They might very well catch him."

"Maybe we can share an ambulance," Brunelle quipped.

Carlisle put her hands on her hips. "Is this because I punched him? Are you embarrassed that you were saved by a woman?"

Brunelle thought for a moment. "No. Actually, I'm grateful. I'm just in a lot of pain and acting like a baby. I'm sorry. Thanks for breaking his nose. Very impressive."

Carlisle shrugged. "I used to get into fights a lot when I was younger. I learned how to defend myself."

Brunelle looked at her. "Huh. I guess there's a lot I don't know about you yet."

Carlisle laughed. "You have no idea." Then she tugged on his good arm. "Let's go."

Brunelle didn't argue. Instead, he looked at his injured hand. The bleeding had slowed, but definitely not stopped. He supposed he was lucky—there were no arteries in his hand. He'd live.

But he was pissed.

CHAPTER 19

Brunelle burst through the door of the law offices on the third floor of the Maynard Building. It wasn't a law firm—not like Jacobsen, Moneybags & Jerk. It was just a conglomeration of solo practitioners, each independent, but sharing a receptionist and a conference room. Brunelle ignored whatever protest the startled receptionist shouted after him and stormed down the hall to the last office on the right. The smallest one. With the view of a brick wall next door.

Nick Lannigan's office.

Lannigan was sitting at his computer, back to the door, and surfing the internet. The latest Hollywood gossip from the looks of it. Brunelle slammed a sheaf of papers on his desk with his good hand. "We need to talk, Nick," Brunelle barked. "Now."

Lannigan spun around, clearly startled. His wide eyes landed on Brunelle even as his hands skittered across his desk like two crabs, unsure whether he needed to hide anything from his unexpected visitor.

"Dave! Hey, great to see you," tumbled out of his mouth.

"Geez, what a surprise. So, uh, what brings you by unannounced?"

Brunelle flashed his eyes at the stack of papers on Lannigan's desk. "New discovery on the Hernandez case," he snarled.

Lannigan laughed nervously. "I like to think of it as the Fuller case."

Brunelle didn't react. Lannigan shifted uneasily in his chair and rubbed the back of his chubby neck. Then his eyes landed in Brunelle's hand. "Oh wow, what happened, Dave?"

"Your client happened," Brunelle growled. He raised his hand slightly to look at the bandage covering the palm and most of the fingers on his left hand. The wound was seeping blood again. Hell of a place to get stitches.

Lannigan cocked his head. "Lindsey happened? I, I don't understand. Did you get into some sort of fight with her? You didn't go see her without me, did you?"

Brunelle allowed a dark laugh. "No, Nick. I learned my lesson about that."

Lannigan shrugged. "Then what happened? I don't understand."

Brunelle stayed standing, fairly menacing Lannigan over his desk. "I was in Lake City, looking at the crime scene, when I got attacked by some drug addict behind the gas station."

Lannigan waited a moment, clearly expecting more. "Was Lindsey there or something? I mean, I'm pretty sure she's still in the King County Jail. I guess I could see if she bailed out without telling me, but I don't—"

"No, Nick," Brunelle snapped. "She wasn't there. That's not the point. The point is, I shouldn't have been there either. This case should've settled out with a bunch of pleas weeks ago. I shouldn't be looking for new leads at a crime scene trying to figure out which snitch I need to court the hardest. I should be at my desk, prepping for a trial against Elmer Hernandez, and endorsing your client as a witness, not a codefendant."

Brunelle took a deep breath. Lannigan's helpless expression was hard to stay angry at. "Damn it, Nick. This is ridiculous. As long as this case is pending, it's dangerous to be me. Your client can help me end it. If Hernandez sees everyone else is lined up against him, he'll probably just plead guilty and go off to prison. Your client gets a reduced sentence and I get back to not being stabbed behind gas stations."

Brunelle finally sat down in one of the guest chairs. Lannigan offered a tentative smile.

"Look, Dave. I don't disagree with you," Lannigan admitted. "I think it's in her best interest to take a deal to testify. But I've talked to her about it, more than once, and she'd adamant. No deal for testimony. Nothing's changed."

"Wrong," Brunelle replied. He tapped the discovery on Lannigan's desk. "Everything's changed."

Lannigan looked at the papers, but didn't reach for them. "What is it?" he asked, as if afraid to look for himself.

"Nate Wilkins' proffer," Brunelle answered. "He says your client shot Shanborn."

"That's not true!" Lannigan practically shouted.

"I know, Nick." Brunelle leaned forward. "That's why I'm here."

"But, but he's lying," Lannigan protested.

"Of course he's lying!" Brunelle almost laughed. "But he said it and he's ready to testify to it. And not just against Hernandez. Against everyone, including Lindsey Fuller."

Lannigan thought for a few moments. He still didn't reach for the discovery. "What did he say, Dave?"

Brunelle sighed. The problem with his gambit was that Wilkins' story was a self-serving lie. He knew it. And Lannigan, even as limited as he was, would see it too. But there was no way around it; Wilkins had said what he said, and it was on tape. So Brunelle leaned forward and related everything Nate Wilkins had told them: the good, the bad, and the bullshit.

When he'd finished, Lannigan leaned forward too. "Ooh, just like 'Murder on the Orient Express'!"

Brunelle pinched the bridge of his nose. "Yes," he admitted. "Just like 'Murder on the Orient Express.'"

Then Lannigan leaned back again. "But that's not what really happened."

Brunelle raised his gaze again. "What did really happen, Nick?"

Lannigan started to answer, but then caught himself. "I'm sorry, Dave. I can't say. Attorney-client privilege and all that."

Brunelle sighed again. He rubbed his good hand over his shortly cropped hair. "Look, Nick. I get it. I understand your position. But you need to understand mine. I have one witness who claims she wasn't present for the shooting. I have another witness who was too high to remember what was going on. And I have one witness who says your client shot Derrick Shanborn. If I don't get more, if I don't get different—if I don't get *your* client's story—then that's what I have. And that's what I'll go forward on. And if I do, your client is looking at going down on murder one."

"Even if it's not true?" Lannigan asked, like a child first encountering the harsh realities of life.

"Even if it's not true," Brunelle confirmed. "Because, see, I wasn't there. I don't know what's true and what's not. But your client does. That's why I'm here, Nick. I can't let Hernandez walk. I know Wilkins' story is bullshit. So give me a better story."

Lannigan cocked his head. "A better story?"

Brunelle sighed one more time. "The truth, Nick. Give me the truth."

CHAPTER 20

Lannigan was taking too long to get back to Brunelle. If Lannigan had trouble standing up to a little bit of friendly pressure from a colleague, he was unlikely to exert much pressure himself over a hardened drug addict willing to suffer anything to avoid a snitch label. Too bad. Fuller was Brunelle's top choice. But she wasn't his only option.

He picked up the phone and dialed Robyn Dunn's number. As it rang, he stood up and looked out his office window at the Seattle downtown. He couldn't see the crime from so high up. But he knew it was still there.

"Law office of Robyn Dunn." She answered her own phone. A sign of either dedication to her business, or insufficient business to afford a receptionist. "How may I help you?"

"You can get Samantha Keller to talk," Brunelle answered.

There was the slightest pause. Brunelle hoped she was smiling. He imagined it, and decided to just tell himself she was. Her voice seemed to confirm it.

"Yeah, I got the new discovery this morning," she said. "It came by messenger. I must admit, I'm a little disappointed."

"Disappointed?"

"Hurt," Robyn corrected. "Nick got an in-person visit, but all I get is a phone call. What's the matter, Dave? Don't you miss me?"

Brunelle knew to ignore the question. "Nick's more of an in-person guy. You can get stuff done over the phone," he offered.

"I get stuff done in person too," Robyn reminded him.

Brunelle again ignored the comment. "And in all honesty, I went to him first because I wanted to turn his client the most and she had just gotten implicated."

"Honesty?" Robyn asked. "Are we doing that now?"

It dawned on Brunelle that he was actually being the professional one, avoiding and ignoring the double entendres and invitations to flirt and/or reminisce. He was sort of proud of himself. "But Lannigan's taking too long," he soldiered forward. "So you're next up the ladder."

"But my client didn't get implicated by Wilkins," Robyn pointed out, apparently willing to discuss the case after all. "So his proffer doesn't really change anything for us."

"Well, it means he might get a deal and do less time than your client, even though he's more culpable."

"That's on you," Robyn countered. "If you let one of the shooters get less time than my client, who by all accounts did nothing—"

"She fetched the gun for Hernandez," Brunelle pointed out.

Robyn laughed, unimpressed. "Good luck proving that. Or that she knew what Hernandez was going to do with it. Without prior knowledge, she's not an accomplice. She walks."

"A known snitch gets invited over to their house and he tells her to go get his gun?" Brunelle offered his own laugh. "There's no way she didn't know what was going to happen."

"You'll have to prove she knew he was an informant before

he was shot," Robyn insisted. "Up until then, he was just another drug addict who crashed at her place. For all she knew, he was coming over to shoot up and pass out."

Brunelle took a moment to gather himself. "Look, this is pointless. We can argue that shit to the jury. I'm trying to avoid having to do that. Do you really want to put your client's fate in the hands of twelve people too stupid to get out of jury duty? I don't want to go forward on Wilkins' story either. And Fuller won't help, apparently. Amanda Ashford says she wasn't there and Josh Rittenberger was too high to remember his name, let alone who shot Derrick Shanborn. That leaves your gal."

Robyn paused. "I know."

"I need her," Brunelle pressed.

"I know that too. I've known that since I read the first police reports. Wilkins actually makes you need her more."

"So make a proffer," Brunelle practically begged. "Tell me what happened. What really happened."

Robyn thought for a few seconds. Brunelle could hear her clicking her tongue. "If she does testify, what's the offer? Rendering criminal assistance? Credit for time served?"

But Brunelle shook his head. "No offer until after the proffer. I need to hear what she has to say."

"That's not gonna work," Robyn replied. "I need to go to her with some reason to do it, not just a kiss and a promise."

Brunelle was reminded of some of his own previous kisses and promises. "I'm sorry, Robyn. That's not how I do these. I always get the information first, then formulate an offer. I need to judge her credibility, see how she comes across, see if she's really going to be helpful. That's my standard operating procedure."

"Come on, Dave. This is me you're talking to," Robyn lowered her voice a half-notch. "I know you can do stuff you don't normally do. And I know you can like it."

Brunelle could feel his cheeks burn. He was suddenly very glad he had called her and not stopped by her office. "Look, Robyn..." he started.

"No, you look, Dave," Robyn interrupted, her voice suddenly strict. Brunelle felt the blush deepen. "Samantha has no criminal history. You cut her a rendering criminal assistance and a first time offender waiver and she's out by the weekend. You do that, and she'll talk to you. I guarantee it. But if not, well, you can stop calling."

Brunelle was taken aback. "I didn't know you'd become such a hard ass since leaving the public defender."

Robyn offered that smoky giggle of hers. "We both know my ass is neither hard nor soft. It's just right. The only question is: are you man enough to do anything about it?"

Brunelle had no reply ready.

"Think about it," Robyn said, not clarifying if she meant her proposal or her ass. "Call me if you change your mind."

Robyn hung up and Brunelle was left with the receiver in his hands and his gaze on the city, completely not seeing it in favor of the images rolling past his mind's eye.

After several moments he recovered himself and hung up the phone again. He returned to the window and focused on the peekaboo glimpse of Elliot Bay as he considered how to proceed.

His phone rang. He turned and wondered if it was Robyn calling him back with a new proposal. He almost hoped not. Almost. He was of a mind to accept whatever proposal she might make.

But it wasn't Robyn Dunn. It was Barbara Rainaldi.

"Mr. Brunelle," she got right to the point. "Josh Rittenberger is ready to talk."

CHAPTER 21

Brunelle and Carlisle walked over to the King County Jail together. The sun was out and it was only a few blocks away from their offices. Brunelle wasn't always the most social person—he could get caught up in his work or whatever else was occupying his thoughts—but he found he liked spending time with Gwen Carlisle. It was like he was still alone with his thoughts, but had a friend there too. It was almost like having a girlfriend, but without having all that extra girlfriend stuff.

"Dave," she said as they waited for a traffic signal to change, "we need to talk."

Or not.

"Uh," he replied slowly, "okay."

Which was what he usually said to his girlfriends when they started a conversation that way.

"I just wanted to say," Carlisle started, "that I've noticed you've been making some decisions and doing some things on the case without always checking in with me. And I wanted you to know I'm okay with that. You're lead, and I get that. That's all."

Brunelle nodded. That was way better than what usually

followed a 'we need to talk.'

"Sorry about that," he said. "If I'm doing stuff without consulting you, it's just that I'm not always used to working with another prosecutor. But I'm not lead. We're partners. Equals."

"Eh…" Carlisle responded as the light changed and they started across the street. "I'm not so sure about that. If you talk to lawyers or set up proffers without checking with me, that's cool. But if I did it without checking with you, not cool."

Brunelle wanted to disagree, but he couldn't. But he could show her some retroactive respect. "Do you think we shouldn't talk to Rittenberger?"

But Carlisle shook her head. "No, it's not that. Of course we should talk to him. If he's willing to tell us more, then great. But if it's good, maybe let's you and I meet to discuss it before we extend any solid offers to Rainaldi."

Brunelle smiled. She knew him pretty well already. "Okay. Deal."

Carlisle smiled. "And bring me along sometimes. I'd love to see Lannigan's or Robyn's offices."

"I didn't go to Robyn's office," Brunelle pointed out as they reached the entrance to the jail, located in the middle of downtown Seattle, just up James Street from the courthouse—and the tourists on the waterfront.

"Plenty of time for that, I'm sure," Carlisle replied with an enigmatic grin. "But come on, let's go see what Mr. Rittenberger claims to remember now."

Chen and Jackson were already waiting in one of the conference rooms on the lower level. They'd pulled Rittenberger from his cell. Rainaldi was there already too. Brunelle and Carlisle took their seats around the table and they were ready to begin.

Rainaldi started things off with an apology. "Sorry it took so long to get this set up." She rested a hand on her client's shoulder. "Josh got pretty dope sick when he was booked in. It took a while until he was well enough to talk with me about options."

Brunelle nodded. "Heroin withdrawal is a bitch," he agreed. "Are you feeling well enough to proceed today?" he asked Rittenberger directly. Generally speaking, a prosecutor couldn't talk directly to a represented defendant. But this was different. Rainaldi was there, and the whole point of the meeting was for Rittenberger to talk to them. Plus, it was an ice-breaker; it communicated to Rittenberger that Brunelle cared about him, at least a little bit. That might help Rittenberger feel more at ease about opening up to a room full of prosecutors and cops.

But Rittenberger's nerves weren't going to be soothed quite so easily. He was sober enough to talk to them. That meant he was also sober enough to know who he was about to throw under the bus. And what happened to the last guy to do that. "I, I think so," he answered. "Maybe. I guess we'll see."

He looked like shit. Deep, dark bags still under his eyes and messy long hair. Plus his skin looked like it hadn't seen the sun in years, which it probably hadn't. If he still looked like that at trial, the jury would believe he was a drug addict at least. As for the rest of the story, well, it depended on what the story was.

"Let's get started then," Chen interjected. It was his show, after all. Brunelle (and Carlisle, he reminded himself) needed to be present to judge Rittenberger's credibility, but Chen (and Jackson, Brunelle supposed) were the expert interrogators. "Tell us what happened."

Brunelle smiled to himself. Quite the expert question. But it had a purpose: to get Rittenberger to start thinking about where he was then, and forget about where he was now.

Rittenberger took a deep breath. "Okay. I was pretty high.

I'd been on a bender, so the days kind of blur together. I was always high back then. I had a maintenance level. If I didn't keep it up, well, I'd get sick, real sick, like I did in here."

"Sure," Chen encouraged.

"I knew Derrick," Rittenberger went on. "He was a good guy. I mean, good enough, you know? I mean, he could be kind of irritating sometimes. He was always mooching. Food, money, drugs, whatever. You had to watch your stuff around him. I'm pretty sure he stole some of my stuff to trade for drugs. So yeah, that kind of sucked, but, you know, overall, he was a good enough guy."

"Did you know he was working as an informant?" Jackson asked.

Rittenberger shook his head, a little more than might be normal. "No way, man. Like I said, Derrick was a hardcore druggie, always stealing your shit and never paying you back. I never would have thought the cops—I mean, you guys—I never thought you guys would trust a guy like that to be an informant."

Brunelle nodded to himself. Good point. But then again, Rittenberger didn't know Jackson had coached Shanborn's little league team.

"So what happened that day?" Chen tried to get Rittenberger back on track.

Rittenberger thought for a moment, frowning. "I don't really remember Derrick coming over. I was pretty out of it. I was a little low on my maintenance level, so I took a bigger dose than normal. Burner and Sammy let me crash there sometimes when I tripped, so I was just crashed out on a mattress in the living room."

"And the living room is connected to the kitchen?" Chen confirmed.

"Yeah, it's all one big open room, except for the bedrooms in the back. And the bathroom. But I was out front, in my own little world."

"Then what happened?" Chen followed up.

"I heard some yelling," Rittenberger answered, frowning at the effort of remembering. "I looked up and I saw Burner yelling at Derrick. He was like pushing him back toward the wall and was right in his face, yelling something."

"What was he yelling?" Jackson asked.

Brunelle looked to see if Chen was getting irritated by Jackson interrupting with his own questions, but it didn't appear so. They had probably coordinated the good cop/bad cop thing before everyone else had arrived.

Rittenberger shook his head. "I don't really remember, man." He looked to Rainaldi and shrugged. "Sorry. But like I said, I was pretty out of it. I noticed how loud he was, and how angry he was, but his exact words? Yeah, I don't remember. But he was pissed. I'm not sure I've ever seen him that angry, and I've definitely seen him angry before."

"Was anyone else there?" Chen asked. It was his turn, apparently.

Rittenberger thought for a moment then nodded. "Oh yeah. But I'm not exactly sure who."

"Nate Wilkins?" Chen asked. So maybe he wasn't just trading off every other question with Jackson.

"Yeah, I think so," Rittenberger answered. "Yeah."

Jackson's turn. "Samantha Keller?"

Rittenberger thought for a moment. "Probably. Sammy was always there. Yeah, she was the one who let me crash there. So yeah. Unless she left."

Brunelle stifled an eye roll. He wasn't having any trouble believing Rittenberger so far, but he wasn't sure how helpful the proffer was going to be after all. All the guessing was unlikely to survive a speculation objection at trial.

"What about Amanda Ashford?" Chen's turn.

"Ya know," Rittenberger shrugged, "I didn't really know her that well. She was kind of a bitch to me. Like stuck up, you know. Everybody knew she was fucking Burner." Rittenberger looked around at the rest of the room, "I mean, she was his girlfriend, or whatever. So she kind of strutted around like she was important or something."

"So was she there?" Chen pressed.

Rittenberger thought again, then blew out a breath of air. "Fuck, I don't know, man. It seemed like she was always around. Sammy didn't like her, but she kind of liked that too, I think. So yeah. Sure, she was there."

Brunelle felt the need to interrupt. "Look, Josh," he said. "I don't want you guessing, okay? If you remember someone was there or something happened, fine. But guessing doesn't help anyone. You won't be allowed to guess in court, and if you guess wrong now, the other attorneys will use that against you."

Chen frowned at Brunelle. Whatever success the detective had had in getting the witness to think about the event, the prosecutor had just undone by reminding the witness that he was going to have to go into open court and testify against a murderous drug dealer. Rittenberger's body language said it all: he crossed his arms and retreated backward into his chair, eyes staring at the floor.

"What about Lindsey?" Chen tried to coax the heroin-addicted turtle back out of his shell.

"Lindsey?" Rittenberger replied without looking up.

"Lindsey Fuller," Chen confirmed. "Was she there?"

Rittenberger shook his downcast head. "Uh, no. Lindsey wasn't there."

Chen shot another glance at Brunelle. Jackson's expression echoed Chen's. Brunelle decided not to turn to see what Carlisle's looked like.

"Look, Josh," Chen tried to soothe him. "I know Lindsey's your girlfriend, but you can't protect her. You can't lie to protect her. That won't help anyone. If you lie, we can't help you, and if we can't help you, you can't help Lindsey."

Rittenberger didn't reply. He just stared at the floor. After a moment, Rainaldi put her hand back on Rittenberger's shoulder and held up a finger to the others. "Give us a minute, okay?'

Brunelle was quick to agree and a few moments later, Rainaldi and her client were huddled at one end of the room, with Brunelle, Carlisle, Chen, and Jackson at the other.

"You," Chen pointed at Brunelle's chest, "need to shut up. Tim and I have this."

Brunelle raised his hands in surrender. "Right. Got it. Sorry. But if he'd just gone on like Fuller wasn't there, his proffer would've been worthless."

"I know that," Chen replied.

Brunelle nodded. "And you would have brought him around."

"Yes, I would have," Chen answered. "And without this attorney-client intermission. If he lawyers up again, we have nothing to show for today's little field trip."

Before Brunelle could offer up any more contrition, Rainaldi called out, "Okay. I think we're ready to go again."

Once they were all seated again, Rainaldi confirmed they were able to go forward. "I spoke with Josh. He understands that Nate Wilkins claims Lindsey shot Derrick. He wants you to know the truth and he knows the best way to help Lindsey is to tell you the truth about what happened."

Brunelle let out a sigh of relief. It was one thing if Rittenberger had never agreed to talk to them in the first place. It was another if he—he and Carlisle—had to go to trial on Wilkins' story because he—not Carlisle—had screwed up Rittenberger's proffer.

"So," Chen led him back in, "Lindsey was there, wasn't she?"

Rittenberger let out his own sigh. "Yeah. She was there. But she didn't shoot anyone. She's not like that. She's not violent."

Brunelle recalled Fuller's display in the lobby of the police precinct on the day of their arrest. She seemed pretty capable of violence then, at least in Brunelle's estimation.

"Well, not like that," Rittenberger clarified. "I mean, don't steal her shit." He laughed lightly at some memory. "She's kicked my ass more than once. But no, she would never shoot anyone. That's hardcore shit. She wouldn't do that."

"So you didn't see her shoot anyone?" Jackson asked.

"She didn't shoot anyone," Rittenberger clarified.

"Are you sure?" Jackson followed up. "You just said you were pretty out of it."

Brunelle wasn't sure he wanted them to challenge Rittenberger on this particular point, but he supposed it wouldn't hurt if Rittenberger stayed consistent.

"She was there," Rittenberger repeated, "but she didn't shoot anyone. I would have noticed that. I may not have been paying a lot attention to what was going on, but I always paid attention to Lindsey. I always knew where she was. She was my anchor, man. I know she didn't shoot nobody."

"So who did?" Chen asked. "Who shot Derrick?"

Rittenberger took several moments to reply. Finally he shrugged. "It was either Burner or Nate."

"You're not sure?" Jackson asked

"I was really high, man," Rittenberger defended. "I know I was a dude and I know it wasn't me. That leaves Burner and Nate."

Brunelle ran a hand over his head. His right hand. The left had graduated to a smaller, adhesive bandage on his palm, but he had gotten used to favoring it. He knew he wasn't supposed to interrupt Rittenberger again, but he looked to Rainaldi. "Barbara…"

But Rainaldi raised a hand of caution. "Don't ask him who shot. Ask him what he saw. It'll make sense."

Brunelle looked to Chen, who shrugged in reply. "What did you see?" the detective asked.

Rittenberger looked to Rainaldi for encouragement, then nodded. "Like I said, I was really high. At first, I didn't even notice Derrick was there. I didn't notice anyone. Except Lindsey. She was checking in on me. But then I realized someone was yelling. That kind of brought me to the surface and I looked over toward the yelling. Burner and Nate were in the kitchen with Derrick, right by the door."

"What about Sammy or Lindsey or Amanda?" Jackson asked. "Where were they?"

Rittenberger thought for a moment. "Lindsey was checking in on me, but I'm not sure where she was right then. She wasn't in the kitchen though. It was just the guys. They were really angry. I mean, you could tell there was gonna be a fight or something. The only reason a girl would've been there was to try to break it up, but nobody would try to break up a fight with Burner."

'So what happened?" Chen encouraged.

"So okay, I heard yelling. When I looked over, I realized it was two people yelling: Burner and Derrick. Nate was just standing there, next to Burner, but Burner was the one yelling. And Derrick was yelling back, but it wasn't angry yelling. It was scared yelling. Screaming more like. Like he was begging for his life."

"Did you hear that?" Chen asked. "Did you hear Derrick begging for his life?"

But Rittenberger shook his head. "No, man. It was just, it was the tone, you know. Plus, he got down on his knees and was just like scream-crying up at Burner."

"Do you remember what Burner was yelling?" Chen tried.

"No," Rittenberger answered. "Like I said, it was just really interesting—probably 'cause I was high—but I wasn't trying to follow exactly what was going on. I mean, shit, I didn't know they were gonna shoot him. I just figured he got caught stealing something and they were gonna beat his ass or something. Nothing serious."

An ass-beating for stealing something, Brunelle thought. *Nothing serious. Welcome to the underworld of the drug culture.*

"Right," Chen affirmed the sentiment. "So what happened next?"

"Well, I was just kinda staring at Derrick. It was so weird, man. He was just, he was just on his knees, and he looked so scared, man. It was trippy. I was tripping. It was all, just, whoa."

Brunelle could imagine his closing argument: 'Ladies and gentlemen of the jury, the murder of Derrick Shanborn was all, just whoa.'

"And then," Rittenberger went on, "it was just like, Bam! He got shot. And Bam! Bam! again. And I was like, Holy shit! And I just totally freaked out. I think I started screaming too 'cause Burner just started yelling at everybody to shut the fuck up. And Derrick is just lying there, man, dead. Blood fucking everywhere. And Burner is telling everyone to shut the fuck up."

"So what did you do?" Chen asked.

"I shut the fuck up, man," Rittenberger answered. "Man with a gun tells you to shut the fuck up, you shut the fuck up, man."

"So he had the gun in his hand?" Jackson interjected.

Rittenberger thought for a moment. "Yeah, I guess so. Yeah."

Brunelle smiled internally. That was huge. *Good job, Detective Jackson.*

"Then what happened?" Chen followed up.

"He told us all to clean up."

"Did you?"

"Hell, yes," Rittenberger answered. "He'd just killed Derrick, man. He was begging for his life and they just shot him. I didn't know what they'd do to me. I was a witness. I thought I might be next. So yeah, I helped clean up."

"What did you clean up with?" Jackson asked.

"Shit, I don't know." Rittenberger shrugged. "Whatever they gave me. Bleach or some shit."

"Then what did you do?" Chen asked.

"After I was done cleaning?" Rittenberger clarified.

"Yeah."

"I got high, man. Really fucking high. And I stayed as high as I could until you guys arrested me."

Brunelle had no trouble believing that.

"Did you ever talk about it with Burner or Nate?" Jackson asked.

Rittenberger shook his head strenuously. "Nope. Nobody."

"Not even Lindsey?" Jackson inquired.

"Nope," Rittenberger assured. "No. Body. I got as high as I could and stayed that way."

Chen nodded and looked to Brunelle. Brunelle was satisfied, for the moment anyway.

"Okay, thanks, Barbara," he directed his comments back to

the attorney, rather than the client. "Let me consider this—" He caught himself and smiled at Carlisle. "Let *us* consider this, and we'll get back you."

Rainaldi nodded. "Okay. Thanks, Dave. Call me if you have any follow up questions." She turned to her client. "So that's all for now, Josh. I'll come visit you later today and we can talk more about what you said and what happens next."

Rittenberger nodded to express his agreement with his lawyer's proposal. He didn't really have a choice.

But Brunelle did. Brunelle and Carlisle. Once they were back out on the street, Brunelle started the conversation.

"So what do you think?"

"I believe him more than Wilkins," Carlisle replied.

"Me too," Brunelle agreed.

"But he didn't actually I.D. the shooter. It could have been either Hernandez or Wilkins."

Brunelle nodded. "That is a problem."

"And Ashford says she wasn't in the room," Carlisle recalled.

"So neither of them can contradict Wilkins directly."

"I guess that means they could all be telling the truth," Carlisle offered.

"More likely, they're all lying," Brunelle opined with a frown. "And we're running out of time."

CHAPTER 22

The omnibus hearing was scheduled four weeks prior to the trial date. That was supposed to give the lawyers enough time to get their preparation complete by the omnibus, and the trial judge enough time to set new deadlines after yelling at them for not getting it done by then after all.

The judge in question was the Honorable Susan Quinn. She'd been a judge long enough to see through the tricks the attorneys tried to pull on her. And before that, she'd been a lawyer long enough to have pulled all the tricks herself, so she didn't get upset about it. The lawyers had a job to do, and so did she. Sometimes those jobs came into conflict. It was the nature of the system. She was a hard-ass without being a jerk about it. That was about the best a lawyer could hope for.

Brunelle and Carlisle arrived at Quinn's courtroom together. Brunelle had taken Carlisle's criticism to heart and had swung by her office on his way to the courtroom so they could enter as a team.

When they did, Team Jacobsen was already there. He had two suited underlings seated behind him in the first row of the gallery. And there was a stack of motions waiting on the prosecutor's table.

"Good morning, Mr. Brunelle, Ms. Carlisle," he greeted them from the defense table as they walked in. "I must admit, I'm a bit hurt. You never called me to see if my client wanted to talk with you. Everyone else got to play."

"Everyone else doesn't represent the actual killer," Brunelle replied.

But Jacobsen shrugged off the reply. "I suppose it depends whose statement you believe. Mr. Wilkins said there were three killers."

"Mr. Wilkins said your guy shot first," Brunelle replied. "And anyway..." But he trailed off. He was about to say they weren't planning on using Wilkins, but that exact decision hadn't been made yet. The plan was to see how the omnibus hearing went, then make final decisions. But it would take some sort of unforeseen disaster for Nate Wilkins to supplant Josh Rittenberger on the state's witness list.

"It all sounds very confusing," Jacobsen opined. "In fact, it sounds remarkably like reasonable doubt. Are you sure you don't want to speak with Mr. Hernandez? I could probably talk him into pleading no contest to a misdemeanor in exchange for his testimony."

Brunelle offered a saccharine smile but didn't reply. He turned his attention to the stack of pleadings on his table. They were undoubtedly new motions, just filed by Jacobsen, to be argued at yet another pretrial hearing. Brunelle decided not to look at them just then. They were there for the motion to sever. Five motions to sever actually, one filed by each defense attorney. The only appreciable difference was the name of the defendant in the caption and the name of the attorney in the footer.

He looked again at the stack of papers on his table. "I don't suppose those are just additional copies of old motions?"

Jacobsen offered a grin. "Exactly the opposite, actually. Originals of new motions. And I expect to have more when those are done."

Brunelle had expected as much. Jacobsen was being paid by the word, so he made sure there were lots of them, and multisyllabic to boot. But the rest of the defense attorneys were being paid by the office of the public defense. At a fixed rate. It wasn't cost-effective to file frivolous, harassing motions.

The motion to sever wasn't frivolous. In fact, it probably would have been malpractice not to bring it. But regardless of the defense attorney who signed the brief, the issues raised were basically the same for all of them. Each defendant was worried they'd be painted with a broad brush and the jury would have difficulty separating the evidence against one of them from the evidence against the others. And they were right. Which was why Brunelle would fight the motion.

The other defense attorneys began to arrive for the hearing. The defendants were all in custody, so they had been brought *en masse* by the jail guards and seated in the jury box, with at least one seat on each side separating them all from each other. Looking at the collection of jail-garbed accused murderers in the box, Brunelle was reminded of Daniel Webster's jury. He wondered whether he'd be able to summon the same articulateness when it came time for him to argue his case to the true jury of teachers, retirees, and others who could afford to be off work for the weeks and weeks a multiple codefendant trial was sure to last.

The first attorney to approach Brunelle was Rainaldi. She leaned down and whispered into Brunelle's ear. "So, do we have a deal?"

Brunelle nodded, but also shrugged. "I think so. I'll send

you a formal offer this afternoon."

"I kind of need to know now," Rainaldi responded. "If we don't have a deal, then we need to note up the motion to sever."

Brunelle nodded again. "Understood. Let's go ahead and note it for two weeks out. We can always strike it if—I mean, when—we work out the deal."

Rainaldi frowned slightly but agreed. "Okay. Is that what you're doing with the others too?"

Brunelle smiled. "What others?"

Rainaldi surrendered her own, less enthusiastic smile. "Fine. Just send me that offer this afternoon. I need to know if I'm really going to trial. If not, great. But if so, I have a lot of prep to get started."

Brunelle understood that. Absent a plea of guilty by all five of them, he was going to have to do his own prep. He considered whether it would help to read that Daniel Webster story again...

Brunelle was about to respond with some comment about his own trial preparation or whatever, but that's when Robyn Dunn walked into the courtroom. He couldn't help but notice.

"Excuse me," he said to Rainaldi, with a lesser gesture in the direction of Carlisle, who had been sitting quietly next to him at the prosecutor's table. He stood up and headed for Robyn.

"Hey," he greeted her, although it was a bit awkward that he did so. He wasn't the *maître d'* for the courtroom.

"Uh, hey,' Robyn replied. "Did you come to escort me to my table?"

Brunelle just shook his head. "No. I just wanted to say that I appreciate your representation of your client."

Robyn waited a moment. When Brunelle didn't say anything more, she replied. "Okay. A compliment from the prosecutor about how to be a defense attorney. I guess I'll accept it in the spirit it's offered."

Brunelle gave a lopsided smile. "Thanks. It's just too bad we can't work together on this."

Robyn didn't smile back. "We would never work together, Dave. Even if my client agreed to testify, I wouldn't be working *with* you. I would be representing my client's best interests. It's possible that those interests might align with yours, but we wouldn't be working together."

Brunelle's smile, such as it was, faded. "Well, I guess it would feel like we were working together. For me anyway."

"I guess that's what matters," Robyn replied coldly. "How *you* feel."

As Brunelle reeled slightly, Robyn stepped to the side to go around him. "Now, if you'll excuse me, Dave. I need to go talk to my client before Judge Quinn takes the bench."

Brunelle suddenly became aware of the room again. Carlisle, alone at counsel table after Rainaldi went to talk with her client, was staring at him. So were the two jail guards. Luckily, Jessica Edwards walked in right then, followed by Nick Lannigan. A study in opposites. Rather than greet them too, Brunelle returned to join Carlisle at their table.

"Are you going to be able to focus on the case?" Carlisle asked. Her voice was serious, not mocking.

Brunelle frowned. "Of course." He picked up a couple of the pleadings and tapped them on the table to straighten them. "We need her client to testify. I was just trying to butter her up a bit."

Carlisle raised an eyebrow, but let it go. "Okay. Sure." She looked around the courtroom. "So everyone is here. What's the plan?"

"The plan," Brunelle answered, an experienced eye on the shadow appearing in the doorway to the judge's chambers, "is to stand up."

"All rise!" the judicial assistant called out as Judge Quinn entered the courtroom. "The King County Superior Court is now in session, the Honorable Susan Quinn presiding."

"Please be seated," Judge Quinn instructed once she'd ascended the bench. "Are the parties ready to proceed?"

Brunelle, who had just sat down, stood up again to address the judge. "The state is ready, Your Honor."

This was followed by a disorganized series of 'yesses' and 'readys' from the various defense attorneys.

Quinn looked out at her packed courtroom and frowned. The defendants were all still in the jury box, guards within lunging distance and unwilling to risk the chaos that might occur if they were required to seat all of the defendants next to each other at a table in front of the judge. The defense attorneys were scattered. Edwards was sitting next to Wilkins in the jury box. Robyn was standing just outside the box, next to Keller, who had received an outside seat. Jacobsen was seated alone at the defense table, his client barely within his field of vision. Rainaldi was standing behind Jacobsen, apparently unsure where to sit. And Lannigan had just taken a seat in the gallery—the second row of the gallery.

Judge Quinn pursed her lips, then nodded to herself. "Okay. I'm just going to take over then. This is going to take forever if I let you folks direct the proceedings."

Brunelle had no problem with that. Quinn was right, and he had other things to do that day, just like everybody else. "Yes, Your Honor," he said, as if the judge needed his agreement. Carlisle remained quiet and the defense attorneys threw in another discordant chorus of 'yes your honors' and at least one 'sounds good.' Judge Quinn couldn't quite suppress an eye roll. Then she got started.

"Trial is scheduled for four weeks from today. Is anyone requesting a continuance of the trial date?"

All the attorneys answered in the negative.

"Has all discovery been provided by the state to the defense attorneys?"

All the attorneys agreed that it had.

"Pretrial motions were due by this morning's hearing." Quinn went on. "Have they all been filed?"

Brunelle patted the stack of papers on his table. "Yes, Your Honor."

"Is the state agreeing to any of the motions?"

Brunelle knew that he would eventually agree to sever the trials of any codefendants who turned into state's witnesses. But he hadn't made that final decision yet. He had been hoping Robyn might have changed her mind. He was still hoping she might. Agreeing to any severance at that point would tip everyone off as to who was going to turn state's evidence. "No, Your Honor," he answered.

Quinn sighed. "I was afraid of that. So we'll need to schedule a hearing on the motions to sever. The five different motions to sever," she added with obvious irritation.

"There are five motions," Brunelle replied, "but they're not really that different. I think it was so many cut-and-paste jobs."

Quinn frowned at him. "The law is the law, Mr. Brunelle. I don't need original prose. We're not giving out Pulitzers here."

Brunelle nodded contritely. "Yes, Your Honor. I just meant to say that the issues will be very similar for each defendant."

Quinn did an even worse job of suppressing her next eye roll. "I'm not sure your opponents would agree, Mr. Brunelle," she allowed. "We need to get these ruled on as soon as possible. Can we set them for next week?"

At that, Jacobsen stood up to address the court. "I would ask that the motions to sever be set over for two weeks so that the court can address Mr. Hernandez's additional motions in advance of that hearing." He nodded toward the stack of papers on the prosecution table. "We have filed several motions in addition to those filed by the other defendants."

Brunelle looked down at the stack of papers with the name 'Smith, Lundquist, Jacobsen and Brown' in the bottom right corner. "That's true, Your Honor."

"Any objection to hearing those motions next week, Mr. Brunelle?"

"None, Your Honor," Brunelle replied quickly. He'd anticipated the time table already.

The other attorneys all agreed to setting the severance motions two weeks out.

"Anything else, then?" Judge Quinn asked.

Brunelle looked at each defense attorney in turn. All of them offered a shrug or shake of the head to confirm there were no additional issues for that morning's hearing. "No, Your Honor," Brunelle answered. He hadn't looked to Carlisle before answering.

"All right then," Quinn exhaled. "Thank you for being on time and thank you for your efficiency this morning. If we can keep this up, we might get this case tried before the end of the year after all."

She stood up to leave and the judicial assistant barked out the "All rise!" order again. Once Quinn was out of the room, the defense attorneys went to the individual defendants to explain what had just happened and answer any questions their clients might have. Brunelle scooped up the defense motions and nodded to Carlisle, before the two of them exited the courtroom and turned toward the elevators.

But Carlisle stopped them after a few steps away from the courtroom doors.

"Don't take this the wrong way, Dave," she said, "but should I just skip the motions to sever?"

"What?" Brunelle lowered his eyebrows. "Why would you skip them?"

"You seem to have everything under control, I guess," Carlisle replied. "I mean, you didn't really consult me in there once the judge came out. I don't want to sound ungrateful, but I have lots of other cases that need work. I can't really afford to spend time coming to court if I'm just going to sit at the table and watch you answer questions about how the case should proceed."

Brunelle thought for a moment. He considered arguing with her. Instead, he said, "Sorry."

Carlisle's expression softened. "It's just... Well, it's kind of embarrassing. I'm an accomplished attorney and litigator. I don't want everyone thinking I'm just here to carry your briefcase."

"Of course you're not," Brunelle insisted.

"Then include me," Carlisle said. "Or let me go. It seems like you know your way around a murder case just fine."

"I do," Brunelle answered. "But you know Jacobsen, and he just dropped fifty pages of motions on me." Then he smiled, and Brunelle held out the stack of papers for Carlisle. "I mean, on *us*."

CHAPTER 23

Three days later, Carlisle was in Brunelle's office to discuss the motions Jacobsen had filed on them. On *her*.

"I counted thirteen different motions," Carlisle reported. "Although some of them kind of blurred into each other, or were repeated in a different pleading in a slightly different way."

"Sounds kind of sloppy," Brunelle remarked. It was another nice day. The sunlight streamed in the window and lit the edge of Carlisle's hair.

Carlisle smiled sardonically. "That's what you're supposed to think. But really, it's clever. It makes it harder for his opponent to respond. Make no mistake, he'll be crystal clear at oral argument."

"So what kinds of motions are they?"

"Mostly garbage, actually," Carlisle answered. She pulled the top pleading off the stack. "Lots of demands for things."

"Like what?" Brunelle took a sip from his morning coffee. Drip, black, extra hot.

"A bill of particulars, for starters," Carlisle replied. "He claims we haven't alleged the crime with sufficient particularity."

"His client murdered Derrick Shanborn," Brunelle said.

"How much more particular can we be?"

"Probably a lot more, to be honest," Carlisle admitted. "We aren't exactly clear on how he died."

"He was shot. Three times."

"Okay, okay, right." Carlisle held up her hands. "But we don't say who did it. Was it Hernandez acting as the shooter, or was he an accomplice to someone else?"

"It doesn't matter." Brunelle took another sip of coffee. "You get the same punishment whether you're the principal or an accomplice."

"Agreed," Carlisle responded. "But he's claiming he can't defend Hernandez if he doesn't know whether we're saying he's the shooter or just an accomplice."

Brunelle shook his head. "He knows whether Hernandez shot. Hernandez told him."

"I'm sure he did," Carlisle answered. "But we'll never find out the content of that communication. It's privileged. So it's kind of irrelevant."

Brunelle nodded begrudgingly. "I know. But it's stupid. It's not about what really happened, it's about what we can prove."

"And adequate notice to the defense attorney of what we're going to try to prove," Carlisle added. "Which brings me to kind of an important point. The other motions are similar. Basically complaining about a lack of notice as to what evidence we're actually going to put on at trial. We've given him transcripts of all the proffers to date—Ashford, Wilkins, and Rittenberger—but we haven't told anyone who we're actually going with. I can't really respond to these motions if I don't know what factual theory we're going with."

"Factual theory?" Brunelle repeated. "Our factual theory is the truth."

Carlisle sighed. "Whose truth? Wilkins'? Rittenberger's?"

"I dunno." Brunelle smiled. "But that sounded pretty good, didn't it? 'Our factual theory is the truth.' Yeah, nice."

Carlisle laughed a little. "You're in a good mood today," she observed.

Brunelle returned the chuckle. The sunlight was still lighting up Carlisle's hair, and accentuating the clean curve of her jaw. And his coffee was just the right degree of scalding. "I guess I am. It's good to know these motions are in the right hands."

"Mine?" Carlisle confirmed.

"Yes."

"So you're not going to help at all?"

Brunelle cocked his head. "I'm helping now, aren't I? And anyway, you said you wanted to play a more active role."

Carlisle laughed. "I'm not sure I meant writing all of the responses to thirteen different motions to compel and dismiss."

"How about closing argument then?" Brunelle asked.

Carlisle took a moment. "What?"

"Closing argument," Brunelle responded. "I think you should do the closing argument."

Carlisle took another moment. "You want *me* to do the closing argument on *your* murder case?"

"It's our murder case, remember?" Brunelle laughed. "And yes, I think you should do the closing."

"Why?" Carlisle asked. "I mean, don't get me wrong. I'm flattered. But why would you give me the closing? I thought I might do opening, or maybe you'd do both opening and closing."

"No, I'll do opening statement, but you should do closing argument," Brunelle answered. "Opening statement is just a story. Letting the jury know what the evidence is going to show. But closing is when you explain to the jury what the evidence did show, and why it adds up to murder."

"Isn't murder more your area of expertise?"

But Brunelle demurred. "It's not about murder, per se. It's about logic, puzzle solving, explaining. It's about taking all the disjointed testimony and exhibits, spread out over weeks of trial, and muddied and bloodied by cross-examination and inarticulate witnesses and jurors dozing off after lunch, and making it all make sense again."

Carlisle just looked at Brunelle.

"That's your strength. That's why you're on this case."

"Not because of Jacobsen?" Carlisle asked.

Brunelle shrugged. "It's related. Jacobsen represents the worst guy, and he's filed the most motions. He'll be the leader of the defense in the courtroom. You understand him. And you know how to clarify his disparate arguments—and destroy them. And that's closing argument."

Carlisle leaned back in her chair and smiled. "Yeah. I guess you're right. I'd love to do closing argument. Thank you."

Brunelle waived the thanks away. "Thank you for agreeing to do this case. I can take on one defense attorney, maybe two. But five? Six, if you count Welles. No way. I'd be overwhelmed."

But Carlisle narrowed her eyes. "You don't seem like the kind of guy who's easily overwhelmed."

Brunelle smiled. He was about to deliver a nice double entendre that he hoped might lead to dinner on Friday, but his parry was interrupted by a knock on his doorframe and the appearance of the short, stocky figure of Detective Tim Jackson.

"Hey, Dave," he greeted Brunelle. Then he looked to Carlisle. "Uh, hey…?"

"Gwen," Carlisle replied with a gracious, although still slightly irritated, smile. "Gwen Carlisle."

"Right," Jackson replied. "I knew that. Sorry. It's been a long day already."

Brunelle looked at his clock. "It's nine-thirty."

"I'm a cop, Dave," Jackson defended. "I get calls at two in the morning on a regular basis."

"Did you get one last night?" Carlisle asked.

Jackson laughed. "Well, no. But you know, it could have happened."

"You sound like a defense attorney," Brunelle joked. "So what brings you by, detective? Has there been a development? Somebody confess or something? Maybe video from a nearby business showing the entire murder on tape?"

Jackson grinned. "I wish. No, actually Chen told me there'd been developments on your end. Burner's lawyer filed a bunch of motions or something?"

Carlisle held up the stack of papers. "Yeah, he's bitching because we haven't told him our factual theory yet."

"Truth," Brunelle interjected. "Our factual theory is the truth."

Carlisle laughed at their inside joke. "Unless we can't figure that out. Then we're going with what Rittenberger and Ashford said."

"Not Wilkins?" Jackson asked.

"No, not Wilkins," Brunelle confirmed. Then he asked, "Why? Do you think his 'we all did it together' thing is actually true?"

But Jackson shook his head. "No. No way. I was just making sure you weren't buying it. He's the last guy we should cut a deal with. He needs to go away for a long time. As long as Burner."

Brunelle nodded. "Okay. Good. The only problem is, Rittenberger and Ashford aren't really that great of witnesses.

Ashford wasn't there and Rittenberger was too high to really be credible. I wish we had somebody else."

"What about Sammy?" Jackson asked. "I always thought she'd turn state's evidence."

"I think she's too loyal to Hernandez," Carlisle offered.

"Yeah, I talked with her lawyer," Brunelle added, "but she won't budge. So we're left with Ashford and Rittenberger. Hopefully, it's enough."

Jackson's eyebrows shot up. "Hopefully? You don't sound too sure."

Brunelle shrugged. "Like, I said, they aren't the best witnesses. But they're all we have."

"But if you got Sammy, you think you could definitely convict Hernandez and Wilkins?" Jackson asked.

Brunelle exchanged glances with Carlisle. Lawyers knew there were never any 'definitelys' in trial work. "I don't know about 'definitely,'" he said, "But it would help a lot."

Carlisle nodded up at Jackson. "A *lot*," she confirmed.

"So make another run at Sammy," Jackson suggested. "We want the case to be overwhelming."

But Brunelle shook his head. "It won't work. Believe me, I've tried."

Carlisle nodded. "Oh, he's definitely tried. Like the nerdy school boy asking the cheer captain to homecoming."

Brunelle shot a look at Carlisle. "Wow. Thanks. Nerdy school boy?"

Carlisle laughed. "So you don't disagree that Miss Robyn Dunn is like a hot cheerleader?"

Brunelle could feel his face begin to flush again. An image of Robyn in a cheerleader outfit flashed through his mind—of course. He couldn't find words.

Carlisle laughed. "He has it bad," she said to Jackson.

"I don't have anything bad," Brunelle protested. "I'm just done asking the cheer captain to prom."

"Homecoming," Carlisle corrected.

"Whatever!" Brunelle threw his hands up. "It's over. She won't talk."

"Make another run at her," Jackson insisted. "Tell her Detective Jackson wants to talk with her."

Brunelle's levity dropped a bit. "Why? Would that matter?"

Jackson nodded. "Yeah, I knew her back in the day, before she got involved with Hernandez. She was a drug addict, but she was a good kid. Like Derrick. She'll talk to me if it's just me."

"It won't be just you," Brunelle interjected. "I'm going to be there." Then he remembered to point at Carlisle and say, "We'll be there. And her attorney. And Chen, I would think."

But Jackson shook his head. "No. Just me. You all don't need to be there. Neither does Chen. Just me and her."

"Well, her lawyer will be there," Carlisle pointed out. "There's no way around that."

"Is that right, Dave?" Jackson asked. "Does her lawyer have to be there?"

"Oh yeah," Brunelle confirmed. "We can't talk to her without her lawyer present. We'd all get fired."

Jackson frowned for a moment. "Okay, just me and her and her lawyer. No one else. No recording. Just talking. I'll get her to tell us what she knows."

"Uh..." Brunelle raised a concerned finger. "I want it recorded. I'll need a transcript."

"No," Jackson answered. "That'll freak her out too. We need her as comfortable as possible. Extra people and digital recorders will just make her clam up."

Brunelle gave a concerned look to Carlisle, who returned it.

But Jackson assured them, "I know what I'm talking about. I interview people for a living. The best thing you can do is make them comfortable and forget they're talking to a cop. People are more forthcoming when they think things are off the record."

"But it's not off the record," Brunelle pointed out. "We'll need to disclose whatever she says to all the other attorneys. How do we do that if she's not recorded?"

"I'll take notes," Jackson answered. "And I'll write a report when I'm all done. You'll know exactly what she said and you can disclose it to every lawyer in town, for all I care. But if we don't do it this way, you won't have anything to disclose because she won't talk."

Brunelle thought for several moments. He looked to Carlisle. "What do you think?"

Carlisle pursed her lips. "It's worth a shot. If it doesn't work, we're no worse off than we are now. But if she talks, then we'll have that information and can make her a witness. That's a way better position than we're in right now."

"Robyn won't go for it," Brunelle opined. "No way."

"It's not her call," Carlisle reminded him. "It's her client's. Just get her to ask her client if she'll talk to Jackson one-on-one, no recordings. Say it's for old time's sake or something."

Brunelle frowned. "I don't think that will work."

But Carlisle leaned forward and smiled broadly. "Come on, Dave. Just turn on that Brunelle charm. Robyn Dunn will find you irresistible."

Brunelle considered that for a moment and sighed. *Exactly the opposite, actually*, he thought.

CHAPTER 24

Brunelle stepped into Robyn Dunn's tastefully appointed law offices, above a bookstore, and just a few blocks from the courthouse.

"This is really nice," he remarked. "A lot better than Nick Lannigan's place."

"I'm a lot smarter than Nick Lannigan," Robyn replied as she walked them from the reception area to her corner office in the back. "And prettier too."

There was no point in denying that, Brunelle knew. Especially walking behind her. When he didn't reply, Robyn laughed lightly. They arrived at her office and she gestured toward a guest chair and took a seat at her desk. It looked like an antique, with sloping legs and a leather writing surface. It matched perfectly with the collections of plants and prints in the office, and the view of the city out her window.

"I kind of miss you, Dave," she said.

Brunelle frowned slightly and nodded. "I kind of miss you too."

"So is this a social call?" she asked.

But Brunelle shook his head. "Afraid not."

Robyn clicked her tongue. "Pity."

"I know," Brunelle agreed.

"So what's up, then?" she asked, leaning forward and resting her hands on her desk. "I assume this is about the Keller case?"

Brunelle nodded. "I wanted to try one more time to convince you to get your client to cooperate."

"Cooperate with you, you mean?" Robyn barbed. "She's always been very cooperative with me."

"Yes, with me," Brunelle admitted. "With the state."

"With the prosecution?"

"Yes."

"Of her boyfriend?"

Brunelle shrugged. "That seems likely."

"Likely?" Robyn laughed. "Now that's the David Brunelle I know. Never willing to fully commit."

Brunelle ignored the comment behind the comment. "It's the lawyer in me, I suppose. But I say 'likely' because I just want her to tell the truth. If the truth is that Hernandez shot the victim, then yeah, I guess she'd be cooperating with the prosecution of her boyfriend."

"And why would she do that?" Robyn wondered aloud.

"I don't know," Brunelle replied. "I mean, he wasn't really that great of a boyfriend. He was cheating on her with Amanda Ashford."

Robyn gave an exaggerated nod and another few tongue clicks. "Yes. Tsk-tsk. That's the behavior of a scoundrel. It would be hard to forgive that."

Brunelle felt his stomach turn. Even their business calls were social calls somehow. He tried to push forward. "Well, I guess it depends on the person. I don't really care if she's forgiven him or she hates him. I just want to hear what she knows about him, and what happened that night."

Robyn tapped her fingers on her desk and considered her guest for several moments. "And what if Elmer isn't really the killer?"

"Then she would've talked already," Brunelle posited.

Robyn laughed. "Good point. You may be a crappy boyfriend, but you're a good lawyer."

"Uh, thanks?" Brunelle replied. "I guess."

"But why do you think she'll talk now?" Robyn asked. "I've already told you no twice."

"Maybe," Brunelle allowed, "but you didn't say the safe word, so I didn't know if you really meant it."

Robyn's cheeks betrayed the slightest blush. "Mr. Brunelle," she exclaimed. "I'm shocked. Shocked, I say." Then she lowered her eyelids ever so slightly and giggled. "You really can't help but flirt, can you?"

"Is it helping my cause?" Brunelle asked with a grin.

"Which cause?" Robyn returned. "Getting my client to talk, or getting down my pants?"

"You mean getting down your pants *again*," Brunelle quipped.

"Not cool," Robyn stiffened up a bit. "And not helping your cause. Either one."

Brunelle nodded. "Okay, then let me try this. Det. Jackson thinks your client is freaked out by ten people in a room and a tape recorder."

"*Tape* recorder?" Robyn interrupted. "Did you really just say *tape* recorder? Recorders haven't used tape in, like, a century or something. How old are you?"

"Too old," Brunelle joked. Then, "Maybe."

"Maybe," Robyn agreed. "Maybe not."

"Anyway," Brunelle kept playing it straight—mostly, "Jackson said he knows her from way back, before she met Hernandez. He thinks she'll talk if it's just him."

"Just him?" Robyn questioned.

"And you too, or course," Brunelle affirmed. "But no Chen. No me. No Gwen Carlisle."

"Ah, yes, Gwen Carlisle," Robyn almost purred the name. "Tell me what you know about her."

This time it was Brunelle's turn to feel a burn in his cheeks. "Uh, actually I don't really know her that well."

Robyn laughed. "Oh, Dave. You're adorable." Another laugh. "And I know you're telling the truth."

Brunelle wasn't sure what to say. Somehow, she could laugh at him in a way that just made him want her all the more. He needed to wrap it up.

"So, anyway," he started. "Yeah. Um, so maybe talk to your client. Samantha. Sammy. Ms. Keller. Tell her it'll just be her and Jackson. And you. And no tape recorder. Or whatever type of recorder. He'll just write up a report later."

Robyn nodded and gave him a small smile. "Okay. I don't think she'll go for it, but I'll talk to her. For you."

Brunelle offered a chuckle. "Yeah. We go way back."

Robyn smiled more broadly—a smile that reached her eyes. "A way back. That sounds nice."

Brunelle smiled back. "Yeah. It does." He stood up. "I can see my way out. See you later, Robyn."

Robyn didn't stand up. Instead she turned her chair so she could watch him leave. "See ya, Mr. B."

CHAPTER 25

Brunelle didn't want to arrive too early for the hearing on Jacobsen's motions. Early meant sitting in the judge-less courtroom, trying to make small talk with Jacobsen. That sounded terrible. It wasn't that Jacobsen was a defense attorney. Brunelle had plenty of friends who were defense attorneys, and he'd enjoyed plenty of pre-judge conversations with the likes of Jessica Edwards and Nick Lannigan. It was that Jacobsen was a jerk.

So he swung by Carlisle's office and the two of them walked to the courtroom together, timing it to arrive just as the clock struck nine. If he was going to have to engage in small talk, Brunelle would much rather it be with Carlisle than Jacobsen.

"So, I got a voicemail from Jackson," he informed her on the way. "He said the interview with Keller went well. No details though. And no word from her attorney yet either, so I assume everything went well."

"Yeah, 'her attorney,'" Carlisle replied with a grin. "Robyn something, right? What is up between you two?"

Brunelle considered denying anything between him and Robyn. In a way, he would have been right. But instead, he said,

"It's a long story."

Carlisle laughed. "I bet."

"Anyway," Brunelle pushed on, "I can't wait to hear what Keller said, but no report from Jackson yet."

"When do you think we'll get it?" Carlisle asked. They were almost to Judge Quinn's courtroom.

Brunelle shrugged. "Before next week's hearing on the motions to sever, I hope. Jackson probably has the report already. It's likely just waiting approval by a supervisor. Every report has to be approved by a supervisor before we see it. For new cops, that's important. For senior detectives, it's just so much red tape."

Brunelle opened the courtroom door for Carlisle and they entered the chamber. As expected, Jacobsen was already there, but his client was with him too, so there wouldn't be any small talk. It was just the two of them this time—no other defendants or defense attorneys. It almost felt lonely in the otherwise empty courtroom.

Before Brunelle and Carlisle had even reached the prosecution table, the judicial assistant asked them if they were ready. Brunelle stole a glance at the clock. It was 9:00 exactly. Quinn was punctual, he'd give her that. He'd also give her that she was a good judge, with reliable instincts based on years of experience. But right then, punctuality was front and center.

"We're ready," Brunelle confirmed.

The judicial assistant made a quick, mouth-covered phone call—to the judge's chambers, Brunelle knew—and a few moments later, the Honorable Susan Quinn took the bench.

"Is the state ready to proceed, Mr. Brunelle?" she asked once everyone had returned to their seats following the traditional bellow of "All rise!"

Rather than reply himself, Brunelle looked to Carlisle, who stood up and responded. "The state is ready, Your Honor."

Judge Quinn smiled. "Will you be handling the motion then, Ms. Carlisle?"

"Yes, Your Honor," Carlisle replied. She didn't need to mention that she'd also written the briefs. Quinn was a conscientious judge. Everyone knew she'd read the briefing, and it was Carlisle's signature at the end. For better or worse, it wasn't unusual for junior attorneys to have to write the briefs but not get to argue the motions. Hence Judge Quinn's assumption she would be hearing from Brunelle; and her apparent pleasure at learning she was wrong.

The judge turned to the defense table. "And I assume you'll be arguing for the defense, Mr. Jacobsen?"

Jacobsen stood and offered a polite laugh for the judge's little joke. "Yes, Your Honor. And gladly. We have raised some significant issues, I believe, and—"

"Okay, hold on, Mr. Jacobsen," Quinn interrupted. "I'm looking forward to your advocacy as much as anyone, but let's be organized about this. Which motion do you want to argue first?"

Jacobsen considered, but only for a moment. "Why don't we start with my motion to dismiss for governmental misconduct? If the court grants that motion, we need not address the others."

Brunelle would have rolled his eyes at Jacobsen's arrogance, but he appreciated the logic.

Quinn looked back to the prosecution table. "Will that work for you, Ms. Carlisle?"

"Yes, Your Honor," Carlisle was quick to reply.

"All right then," Quinn said. She adjusted the papers in front of her and got comfortable in her seat. "It's your motion, Mr. Jacobsen. Begin whenever you're ready."

Jacobsen thanked the judge, then stood up and organized the papers and notes in front of him as well. Once he was satisfied with their positioning and accessibility, he looked down to his client, nodded, then raised his face to the judge.

"Your Honor," he practically shouted. His voice echoed off the walls of the nearly empty courtroom. "This case presents a unique confluence of misconduct by the prosecutor's office. Misconduct which has deprived my client of his constitutional rights to confront the witnesses against him, to have competent and prepared defense counsel, and to have the fair trial demanded by the Due Process Clause of the United States Constitution and Article One, Section Twenty-Two of the Washington State Constitution."

Brunelle rolled his eyes, then looked down to take diligent notes, lest he roll them again and the judge see it. He understood advocacy required a certain amount of showmanship. He just hated having to sit through other people's showmanship.

Carlisle had her chin on her hand, focused attentively on Jacobsen as he went on.

"My client, Elmer Hernandez," Jacobsen gestured dramatically to the man seated next to him, "sits before Your Honor charged with the heinous crime of murder in the first degree. But his path to this courtroom today was not a simple one. No, the lengths and depths taken by the state to generate sufficient evidence to support, even if just barely, the charges against Mr. Hernandez are, quite frankly, astounding. And deeply, deeply troubling."

Brunelle frowned. The problem with someone else's showmanship arose when they were good at it. Jacobsen was good at it. Quinn would discount it, but the jurors could end up mesmerized by the tall, handsome man in the tailored suit, words dripping from his mouth like so much honey.

Hmm, Brunelle thought, *maybe I could use that in rebuttal...*

"For you see, Your Honor, when my client was first arrested for the murder of Derrick Shanborn—may God rest his soul—even the prosecutor's office had to admit they didn't have enough evidence to hold him. Rather than charge and arraign Mr. Hernandez, they had him held for two extra days while they flailed about for something, anything, that might implicate him. And they found it, barely, in the likes of one Amanda Ashford."

Jacobsen reached down and picked up his book of court rules. "Now, it's important to note, Your Honor, that under federal constitutional law a defendant's right to counsel does not attach until he or she has been charged with a crime, while under Washington law, that right to counsel attaches immediately upon arrest. Under Washington Criminal Rule 3.1, Mr. Hernandez had the right to an attorney as soon as he was placed in handcuffs by Detectives Jackson and Chen."

"Are you claiming some sort of Miranda violation?" Judge Quinn asked. "As I understand it, your client invoked his right to an attorney and all questioning ceased."

"Correct, Your Honor," Jacobsen replied. "All questioning ceased—as it should have—but Mr. Hernandez's constitutional right to prepared counsel did not."

Quinn frowned, but she nodded to him. "Go on."

"You see, Your Honor," Jacobsen continued, "the violation here came not from questioning Mr. Hernandez without his attorney present, but from questioning the witnesses against him without his attorney present."

"You wanted to be present during the interview of Amanda Ashford?" Quinn asked.

"It's not about what I wanted or didn't want, Your Honor," Jacobsen answered. "It's about what the Constitution requires."

"And your position," Quinn sought to clarify, "is that the Constitution requires a defense attorney be present anytime law enforcement interviews a witness? That seems a little unworkable,

Mr. Jacobsen. What are officers supposed to do in the middle of a bank robbery, or when they arrive at a murder scene? Wait for someone from the public defender's office to arrive before they proceed?"

"Or course not, Your Honor," Jacobsen answered. "And therein lies my point."

Quinn raised an eyebrow. "How so?"

"In those instances," Jacobsen explained, "the police are responding to the crime, protecting the public, trying to identify a suspect. No one has been arrested yet, let alone charged. But here, in Mr. Hernandez's case, the police had already made up their minds that he was the killer. He was arrested and booked into the King County Jail on suspicion of murder. And, as I mentioned earlier, under the court rules, his right to an attorney attached as soon as he was arrested.

"They would not have been allowed to speak to him without his attorney present. And similarly, they should not have been allowed to interview the witnesses against him without his attorney present. This was not the bank robbery or murder scene example Your Honor just gave. There were no exigent circumstances here, save the emergency for the state that they didn't have enough evidence to lawfully hold my client. They found a witness they could manipulate and prohibited me from being present while she was interviewed."

Quinn didn't mind a little showmanship, but she also knew how to call B.S. on something. "I'm not sure they prohibited you, Mr. Jacobsen. I don't know that you were even on the case yet. But it wasn't like you were standing in the precinct lobby, demanding admittance to the interrogation room."

"I can assure you, Your Honor," Jacobsen replied, "had I known what they were doing, I most certainly would have been in the precinct lobby demanding to be part of that interview. And the state should have wanted me there."

Quinn cocked her head at that. So did Brunelle. Carlisle was writing furiously on her notepad.

"Why would the state want a defense attorney present during the interview of a potential witness to a murder?" Judge Quinn asked.

"Why should they want anything different, Your Honor?" Jacobsen gestured toward Brunelle and Carlisle. "The prosecutors always claim that they just want the truth from the witness. They deny that they want a particular version that incriminates a known suspect. But we all know that's exactly what they want. If they truly wanted the truth, they would allow what happens here in open court when we want to figure out the truth: vigorous cross-examination. How much more information would the state have gotten, how much better would they be able to judge her credibility, how much more reliable would the entire interview have been, if I had been permitted to ask questions of Ms. Ashford myself? If I had been permitted to challenge her memory, her motives, her veracity? Perhaps she withstands the scrutiny. If so, we can all feel better that her word is believable. But perhaps she doesn't. Perhaps her story comes apart at the seams because there was someone there with a motivation to challenge it. How much better would we all be if a criminal defendant were not charged based on the unreliable and untested word of a co-conspirator looking for a deal?"

"And how does any of that implicate your client's right to confront witnesses?" Quinn challenged. "The witness will still have to come into court and testify. You'll get your chance to cross-examine her then."

Jacobsen smiled, like a salesman who knew he had his mark. "Ah, but will I? Will I truly get to cross-examine as effectively as due process requires? Or will I be hamstrung by the interview I was excluded from? You know what will happen if the witness deviates from their prior statement, Your Honor. The prosecutor will produce a transcript of the interview and for every little thing that's different, the prosecutor will be allowed to introduce the prior statement—the one I wasn't present for—to either refresh the witness's memory about what happened or to challenge their new testimony because it's inconsistent. Either way, that interview will make its way to the jury without Mr. Hernandez's lawyer ever having had the chance to bring out the real truth about the event in question."

Quinn took several moments to absorb Jacobsen's argument. Too many moments for Brunelle's comfort. The judge raised a hand toward Jacobsen. "I'm sure there's more to your argument, but I'd like to hear from the state at this point. Ms. Carlisle, can you explain to me why Mr. Jacobsen is wrong?"

Carlisle stood up sharply and tugged her suit coat back into place. "I would be glad to, Your Honor," she started. "First, let me begin by rephrasing the argument. This is not a question of whether a quest for the truth would be best served by giving all interested parties an opportunity to question that witness. The answer may or may not be yes. The question isn't even whether such questioning need take place at the time of the original interview, or whether that goal of truth-seeking can be satisfied by subsequent interviews by the defense attorney, which is the standard practice. No, the question is not what might be the optimal practice. The question is whether a murder defendant is entitled to have his murder case dismissed because the police followed standard procedure, rather than untested, never-used, pie-in-the-sky procedure devised by some defense attorney trying to help his client get away with murder."

Jacobsen stood up again. "I would object to that personal attack, Your Honor. I'm not trying to help anyone get away with anything. To the contrary, I'm trying to make sure the state doesn't get away with violating my client's rights."

Quinn liked showmanship, but not brawls. She pointed at Carlisle. "Rein in the personal attacks. The reason I asked you to respond now was because I think Mr. Jacobsen might have a point. Don't undercut your response by stooping to insults, even veiled ones."

Carlisle nodded contritely. "My apologies, Your Honor. I was trying to illustrate a point, perhaps too vigorously. But the point is valid. The question isn't, what are the best practices for witness interviews. The question is, whether anything done here justifies the dismissal of murder charges. And the answer is no."

"So what remedy then?" Quinn put to her. "Suppress the witness's statement? Prohibit the state from calling the witness at trial?"

"Well, Your Honor," Carlisle replied. "Discussing remedies presupposes a violation for which a remedy is needed."

"Oh," Judge Quinn smiled slightly at Carlisle, "I thought you were conceding the violation by moving directly to the remedy."

"No, Your Honor. Absolutely not," Carlisle assured. "It's just that the two concepts are interrelated. Remedies are fashioned to correct violations of the law. Even assuming a violation here, dismissal would not be appropriate. But we maintain that there was nothing wrong with interviewing Amanda Ashford without a defense attorney present. She was interviewed before Mr. Hernandez was charged."

Jacobsen stood up to say something, but Judge Quinn waved him off.

"Hm..." the judge said, stroking her chin in thought. "What about the interview of Josh Rittenberger? That was after Mr. Hernandez was charged. I believe Mr. Jacobsen had already filed his notice of appearance, communicating to everyone who cared to ask that he represented Mr. Hernandez regarding this very case, this very murder. Should he have been invited to the interview of Mr. Rittenberger?"

Carlisle hesitated, but only for a moment, and only long enough to process the question.

"No, Your Honor," Carlisle answered. "This is not open court and not the trial. There is a time for cross-examination, but it is not at the information-gathering stage. A defense attorney doesn't have a right to be present at a police interview any more that Mr. Brunelle or I would have a right to listen in on a conversation between Mr. Hernandez and his attorney."

Quinn narrowed her eyes at that. "I think that might also implicate the attorney-client privilege. You're not claiming some sort of witness-prosecutor privilege, are you?"

"Of course not, Your Honor," Carlisle began. "I just—"

"Your Honor," Jacobsen stood up again, "may I interrupt? There was one more point I wanted to make on this issue."

Quinn thought for a moment, then agreed. "All right, Mr. Jacobsen. Proceed."

"Thank you, Your Honor," Jacobsen said. "I just wanted to point out a policy argument in favor of the procedure which should have been used here, and quite frankly, should be used every time a witness is interviewed by the state after a defendant has been arrested. And that is this: if the witness were to suddenly go missing between the interview and the trial, their statement would be inadmissible as out-of-court hearsay. All that valuable information, lost to the state. And the jury. But if the defense attorney were present, then evidence rule 804 would allow the interview to be admitted into evidence even if the witness had disappeared. E.R. 804 allows for the admissibility of hearsay where the speaker is unavailable and," he looked down to read from his evidence handbook, "'the party against whom the testimony is now offered had an opportunity and similar motive to develop the testimony by direct, cross, or redirect examination.' You see? Even the Washington Supreme Court, who adopted our state's evidence rules, suggests a procedure whereby witnesses are subject to cross-examination when interviewed prior to trial."

Quinn frowned a little at Jacobsen. "I'm not sure this particular situation is what the Supreme Court had in mind when they adopted that rule," she said. "But that doesn't mean it wouldn't be applicable." She turned again to the prosecution. "What do you have to say to that, Ms. Carlisle? Doesn't it sound like a better procedure if it also means we could admit prior statements for witnesses who may be in the wind by the time the trial finally rolls around?"

"Again, Your Honor," Carlisle responded, "I don't think the court should be concerned with what procedure might be the best, or have advantages later on down the line if something else does or doesn't happen. Right here, right now, this defendant wants his murder case dismissed because of a completely standard, never before questioned practice of interviewing potential witnesses without a defense attorney in the room. Even if the court prefers the procedure suggested by Mr. Jacobsen, that doesn't mean the procedure used here was improper, and certainly not to the point of requiring dismissal."

Quinn narrowed her eyes and nodded. "So you're saying that I shouldn't go back and examine the procedures used to date, at least in part because it's never been challenged like this before?"

Carlisle shrugged her shoulders. "That's one of the things I'm saying, Your Honor, yes."

Quinn leaned back and sighed. She was clearly troubled by the issues raised in Jacobsen's motion. But she would also have been mindful that it was a murder case. In theory, a murder case was no different than a shoplifting case. In practice, not so much. The judge pointed at Brunelle. "Mr. Brunelle, I'm curious to hear your thoughts on the matter."

Brunelle looked at Carlisle, who mostly managed to mask her irritation at the judge's request to talk to her supervisor. He stood up slowly and addressed the court. "This really is more Ms. Carlisle's motion. I'm sure she can answer any questions you might have."

But Quinn shook her head. "I don't think so. The question I want answered is what you think of all this. You. I've known you for a long time now and I'm curious what your opinion is. I'd like to talk to you, not as a prosecutor, but as a lawyer. Not as an advocate, but as an intellect. One schooled and experienced in the criminal law."

Brunelle sighed to himself. That wasn't a road he wanted to go down right then. Especially not when Carlisle was supposed to be driving. He looked over at her to gauge her disapproval, but her expression was inscrutable. Or at least unexpected. Brunelle couldn't read what she was thinking. But she didn't wait long to let everyone know.

"Your Honor?" Carlisle interrupted. "If you're going to speak with Mr. Brunelle, may I be excused for a few minutes? There's a matter I believe I should attend to."

Quinn's eyebrows shot up. Attorneys didn't usually tap out in the middle of oral argument. But she acquiesced. "All right, Ms. Carlisle. If you believe you have something more important than this argument, I won't stop you from attending to it."

"Not more important than this argument," Carlisle insisted. "Just suddenly very time sensitive."

Quinn frowned, but not as deeply as Brunelle did. He would never have wanted to be abandoned in the middle of an argument, but it was all the worse after having to endure Carlisle's complaining about not being involved enough.

"I'll be right back," she whispered to him. He gave the slightest of nods in reply, but kept his eyes on the judge.

"Mr. Brunelle," Judge Quinn said as Carlisle slipped into the hallway, "what do you think of Mr. Jacobsen's argument that truth, and thereby ultimately justice, would be better served if he had been present when you interviewed Ms. Ashford and Mr. Rittenberger?"

Brunelle sighed. The judge wanted to talk to him as an intellect, not an advocate. That was a problem. In that moment, he had to do what the judge asked of him—that is, give her his candid appraisal of the arguments, independent of his role as counsel for the state. But it wouldn't change the fact that, after that moment, he would still be trying to put Hernandez away for murder.

"As a prosecutor," he made sure to begin, "I disagree strongly with Mr. Jacobsen's motion. But as a lawyer and an intellect," he almost groaned, "I have to admit, he has a point."

Quinn nodded. She clearly had expected that response. "Go on," she instructed.

Brunelle did as he was told. "Yes, had Mr. Jacobsen been present, he may have posed additional questions which could have fleshed out or tested the witness's account of the event. To that extent, Mr. Jacobsen's argument has merit. On the other hand"—he was glad to have an 'on-the-other-hand'—"the court should keep in mind that the witness may not be willing to talk at all if the lawyer for the man they're giving evidence against is right there, ready to pounce on them once they've finished telling their story. In that event, truth and justice would not be served because the information is never obtained."

Quinn nodded thoughtfully for several seconds. Then she turned to Jacobsen. "Anything more on this issue, Mr. Jacobsen?"

Jacobsen too thought for a moment. "I don't believe so, Your Honor. We would urge you to find a knowing violation of my client's rights under the Fifth, Sixth, and Fourteenth Amendments to the United States Constitution and the corresponding provisions of the Washington State Constitution, and grant our motion to dismiss the charges against Mr. Hernandez."

Quinn pursed her lips, and tapped her fingers loudly on the bench in front of her. She nodded slightly to herself as the words formulated in her mind. The lawyers knew enough to be patient and silent, even if the wait was killing them. Finally, Quinn leaned forward again and spoke.

"This is a very interesting issue," she started. "I have never heard of a defense attorney being present at the police interview of a witness against their client. Then again, this is an uncommon case. The witnesses against Mr. Hernandez are all also potentially accomplices to his alleged crime. As a result, each has a motivation to lie, or at least downplay their own roles. They may also, either by themselves or through advice from their own attorneys, be able to infer that the state is most interested in prosecuting Mr. Hernandez. As a result, they may inflate his relative level of culpability in order to curry favor with the prosecutor."

Brunelle frowned. But he also knew she was right. They usually did that, even when he told them not to.

"That all being true, I have to agree with Mr. Jacobsen that the preferred procedure would be for a defendant's attorney to be present to ask questions at any proffer made by a codefendant, at least after the primary defendant has been arrested and charged."

Brunelle kept his poker face. Quinn wasn't done talking. He really hoped the judge had her own 'on-the-other-hand.'

"On the other hand," Judge Quinn gave Brunelle his wish, "Ms. Carlisle raised the excellent point of whether this preferable procedure is in fact also the *required* procedure. That is, whether failing to follow this procedure sufficiently violates a criminal defendant's rights as to require dismissal of the charges against him. Dismissals for governmental misconduct—which is what Mr. Jacobsen is requesting here—are rare. The case law calls dismissal 'an extraordinary remedy.' One to be avoided if possible. So the question for this court is whether there is a remedy short of dismissal which will still protect the defendant's rights, or at least prevent further violations moving forward."

Brunelle closed his eyes. *Crap.* He knew what was coming. He looked at the courtroom door again. Where the hell was Carlisle? She needed to hear this too.

"Mr. Brunelle," Judge Quinn summed up, "I am not going to dismiss your case against Mr. Hernandez, but I am going to order that any further interviews must be conducted with counsel for the remaining accused present."

Brunelle cringed. "When you say, 'any further interviews,' do you mean *conducted* as of today or *turned over in discovery* as of today?"

Brunelle knew how important that distinction was. Jacobsen hadn't—until Brunelle asked the question. He jumped to his feet. "We would ask that it be any interviews turned over in discovery as of today. To date we are only aware of the proffers of Ms. Ashford and Mr. Rittenberger. Anything further—"

Carlisle burst through the doors at that moment and rushed

to Brunelle's side. "Sorry, Your Honor," she said without seeming to really mean it. Without waiting for any sort of acknowledgement from Quinn, she shoved a police report into Brunelle's hands. "It's Jackson's report. I got him to email me the unapproved version. Keller talked. She said Hernandez was the shooter."

Brunelle took a moment to process that he didn't have any more moments to bother reading the report. He turned and slammed it on Jacobsen's desk.

"No objection to the court's ruling," he announced. "We don't expect to interview any further witnesses."

CHAPTER 26

Brunelle and Carlisle went out for a celebratory lunch. Nothing special. The Mexican sort-of-fast-food joint down at Second and Union. But still, they deserved the victory meal. Quinn had granted some of the less important of Jacobsen's motions—providing a bill of particulars, which was going to be a snap now that they had Keller's version of the shooting—but they had dodged the dismissal bullet. And even the ruling about Jacobsen being present for future interviews was a hollow victory for him. They wouldn't be interviewing any more of the codefendants.

And, as a bonus, Brunelle would get to work with Robyn after all. Regardless of how she wanted to describe it.

Or maybe not.

Brunelle had barely returned to his desk when Robyn stormed into his office.

"What the hell is wrong with you?" she shouted at him.

"Uh," was all Brunelle could manage at first. She was really angry. Her flushed cheeks almost matched her red locks. He'd never seen her that angry—and he'd seen her angry before. "I, I was just going to call you. Looks like we're going to get to work together after—"

"No!" she snapped. "No. We are *not* working together. Ever. Certainly not on this case. And if this is how you're handling your cases now, not on any case ever. I need to be able to trust someone I'm working with."

Brunelle thought for a moment. "Is this about what happened between us at that club? Because, I kinda thought we were past—"

"Arggh!" Robyn threw her hands up in the air. "Why do you always have to be so dense? God, it never stops. No, Dave, I don't care about what happened between us at that club. I don't care what happened between us anywhere. What I care about is, you lied to me. You and that asshole Jackson lied to me and now I'm fucked. Or more accurately, my client is fucked, which is a million times worse. She was counting on me, Dave. God damn it, she trusted me. And you lied to me. And now she's fucked."

Brunelle was only sure of one thing right then: he had no idea what she was talking about. Well, that and the fact that she was really upset.

"Robyn, I'm not entirely sure what you're talking about," he said in as soothing a voice as he could manage, "but I want to know." He pointed to his guest chairs. "Let's sit down and start from the beginning. Obviously, you know something I don't. I just got the unapproved version of Jackson's report this morning. I haven't had time to do more than skim it. It looked like Samantha cooperated, but maybe I missed something. So let's figure this out."

Robyn's face was still flushed, her jaw still clenched, but her eyes softened. "Damn it, Dave," she said in a lower voice. "I trusted you. Why did I trust you?"

Brunelle considered a cute quip, maybe something double entendre-y. He thought better of it. "What happened?"

Robyn sighed, then finally threw herself into the chair. "Jackson lied, Dave. His report. It's not what Samantha said. He made it all up."

Brunelle's eyebrows shot up. "What?"

"Jacobsen sent me the report after your hearing," Robyn said. "He said you won most of the motions and he congratulated me on working out a deal with the devil."

"And I'm the devil?" Brunelle confirmed.

"Presumably," Robyn answered with a reluctant grin. "But don't ask me if I agree with him. You're looking pretty devilish to me right now."

"In a bad way?" Brunelle ventured.

But Robyn was in no mood. She raised a palm. "Don't. I'm still mad at you."

Brunelle nodded. "Right. Okay. So, Jackson got your client's statement wrong?"

Robyn laughed darkly. "You prosecutors. You think cops are all above reproach. No, Dave, he didn't get it wrong. He lied. What he put in his report, that's not what Samantha said. It's not even close. I should have known. That's why he didn't want it recorded, so he could write down whatever he wanted."

That was a pretty big accusation, Brunelle knew. He also knew Robyn's judgment could be clouded by her loyalty to her client. He needed to walk a fine line.

"So what exactly did he get wrong?" When Robyn shot him a scowl, he corrected it to, "What did he lie about?"

Robyn pulled her copy of the report from her purse. It was half-folded, half-wadded, obviously shoved in there in a fit of anger. Brunelle pulled his copy out of the Hernandez file, still resting on the corner of his desk.

"What didn't he lie about?" Robyn started. "Let's see. Well, yes, the interview did take place in the conference room of the jail. And yes, Detective Jackson, Samantha Keller, and Ms. Keller's attorney, Robyn Dunn, were all present. After that, it's pretty much a fairy tale."

Brunelle looked at his copy of the report. It was actually a pretty short report, Brunelle noticed. Just over a page and a half. It didn't have any verbatim quotes, just summaries and paraphrases by Jackson.

"Can you be more specific?" Brunelle asked.

"Where he wrote that Samantha said she saw Hernandez shoot the victim. She never said that?"

"Never?"

"Never," Robyn confirmed. "In fact, she was insistent that she didn't see the shooting."

Brunelle looked down at the report. Jackson was crystal clear: 'Keller stated she saw Hernandez produce the gun, point it at victim Shanborn's chest, and fire three times.'

Brunelle shook his head. "I don't understand."

Robyn laughed again, with even less mirth. "Of course you don't. You're a prosecutor. You think everything in a police report is gospel. You've never sat down with a client and had them tell you the cop was lying. And you've never had to tell them that it doesn't matter because the prosecutor will always believe the cop, and the judge will always believe the cop, and the jury will always believe the cop."

Brunelle frowned. "Well, between a cop and a criminal…"

"They're only a criminal because the cop said so!" Robyn shouted. "Don't you get it? A cop says somebody did something, then they did it. And if the person says they didn't do it, well, that's exactly what a criminal would say. There's no way to win. And if you guys even begin to suspect that maybe the report is, quote, 'not accurate,' unquote, then do you confront the cop? No, you cut a deal to make the case go away. I have to advise my clients to take the deal even if they're innocent because you have to take a deal for credit for time served over the risk of two or five or ten years in prison. And the fucking cop walks away, knowing he can do it again and again and again. Because he's a fucking cop and you're a fucking prosecutor."

Brunelle crossed his arms. "I'm not sure how true that is."

"Well, I'm sure your cop lied. Samantha never I.D.'ed Hernandez as the shooter. She wasn't there. She didn't see it."

She shook her head and pointed at him. "Here's the bottom line, Brunelle." She never called him 'Brunelle.' "You fucked me over. I was going to put my client on the stand at trial to testify that she had no advance knowledge of what was going to happen and wasn't present when it did happen. But now I can't. That fucking report is going out to every other attorney on this case. Not just you and Jacobsen, but Jessica and Nick and Rainaldi. Even that pompous ass Welles. And when Samantha testifies differently from what's in the report—which she will because the report is a fucking lie—then every attorney in the room will make her look like she's changing her story when she isn't. And the jury will conclude she's a liar. And she'll get convicted. Of fucking murder, Brunelle. *Murder.* All because I was stupid enough to trust you."

Brunelle was speechless.

Robyn stood up. "Well, don't worry. I won't make that same mistake again."

Brunelle stood up too.

"Well, you may not trust me," he said, "but I still trust you. I'll talk to Jackson."

CHAPTER 27

Jackson walked into Chen's office to find both Chen and Brunelle waiting for him. Brunelle wasn't about to accuse a cop of lying—a detective, and falsifying a police report, no less—without a witness. And backup. Chen was perfect. Brunelle trusted him. So did Jackson.

"Oh, uh, hey," Jackson started when he saw Brunelle. "What's going on, Larry? You didn't tell me Mr. D.A.-man would be here."

"Hey, Tim," Brunelle greeted the detective.

Chen shrugged. "Yeah, well, this meeting was Dave's idea. He just wanted..." he thought for a moment, "...to do it here at the precinct. So I volunteered my office."

Jackson nodded slowly, then sat down in the one guest chair that was unoccupied. "Geez, you're a terrible liar, Larry. How do you ever get anyone to confess?"

Chen chuckled. "Personal charm, I guess."

"He's not lying, Tim," Brunelle interjected. "I did want to do it here. It's sensitive. I thought it would be better if we did it on your home turf."

Jackson frowned and jerked a thumb toward the door. "My home turf is down the hall. This is Larry's turf. What the hell is going on?"

Brunelle hesitated, looking to Chen for guidance.

Chen just shook his head lightly and gestured toward Jackson. "Just tell him, Dave. No games. We're all grown-ups here."

Jackson looked back to Brunelle and raised an expectant eyebrow.

Brunelle took a breath then exhaled. "Robyn Dunn said you lied in your police report. She said Keller never said she was there for the shooting and never identified Hernandez as the shooter."

"Are you kidding me?" Jackson sat forward in his chair. "Are you fucking kidding me?" He looked to Chen. "Is he fucking kidding me?"

Chen shook his head. "I don't think he's kidding you, Tim."

"I'm not kidding you," Brunelle confirmed. "That's what she told me. She got a copy of your report from Jacobsen and then stormed into my office."

"My unofficial, unapproved report?" Jackson asked indignantly. "The one I emailed to your partner without question when she said she needed it immediately? The one that isn't supposed to go out until it's been approved? The one I violated policy to get to you because you needed it because that's what you do when someone on your team needs help? That report? That fucking report?"

Brunelle managed a tight smile and a nod. "Yeah, that fucking report."

Jackson crossed his arm and leaned back again in his chair. He looked away. "Nice. That's what I get for doing someone a favor, I guess."

"Does it matter that it wasn't approved?" Brunelle asked. "Is that why there's a disconnect between what you wrote and what Robyn told me?"

"Robyn, huh?" Jackson turned back to Brunelle. "Not Ms. Dunn, but Robyn. Nice. No, there's no disconnect. What I wrote in that report was the truth, the absolute truth. Having some fucking lieutenant approve it doesn't change what's in it. I know what Sammy said and she said Hernandez was the shooter."

"Did she say she saw it?" Brunelle followed up.

Jackson narrowed his eyes at Brunelle. "What does my report say?"

Brunelle didn't need to look at a copy of it. He'd memorized it before daring this. "It says she saw it."

"Then she saw it," Jackson growled through clenched teeth.

Brunelle wasn't sure where to go next. It wasn't like he'd expected Jackson to admit fabricating a police report. Then again, he wasn't really sure what he'd expected. And he didn't want to make an enemy of Jackson.

"Okay." Brunelle raised his palms. "That's all I needed to hear. The defense attorney told me something I had to follow up on. I followed up on it. We're done. Thanks."

Jackson's expression softened too. He relaxed his body. "No worries, Dave. I get it. We both have jobs to do. But I take my job just as seriously as you do. I want to put the bad guys away. Why would I risk that by lying about some penny-ante snitch we don't even really need?"

Brunelle wasn't sure they didn't really need Samantha Keller. But he supposed he was going to find out, because there was no way in hell Robyn was going to let her testify for the state.

"Yeah, I don't know," Brunelle replied. "Like I said, a defense attorney tells me something like that, I gotta follow up on it. But now I've followed up and we're good."

But Jackson continued to defend himself. "I took detailed notes. Everything in that report is one hundred percent accurate. I told you she'd talk if it was just me and her and no recorder, and she did. Now, she reads the report and realizes Burner's gonna know she sold him out, so she tells her attorney that wasn't what she really meant. That's why she didn't want to be recorded. So she could change her story. She's just scared of Hernandez, that's all."

Brunelle nodded throughout. Then he asked the one thing he cared about from Jackson's soliloquy. "Where are the notes?"

Jackson cocked his head. "What?"

"The notes," Brunelle repeated. "Your notes of the interview. Where are they?" He could show them to Robyn. Get her to understand it was just a misunderstanding. Maybe she was misremembering the interview.

Jackson took a moment before answering. "I destroyed them."

"What?" Brunelle threw his hands up. "Why did you destroy them?"

"Standard procedure," Jackson answered. He glanced to Chen for support. "I put everything in my notes into the report. No need to keep the notes any more, so I destroyed them. That's Seattle P.D. policy."

Brunelle looked to Chen as well.

Chen shrugged. "The policy doesn't require that we destroy our notes. But it allows it. Once it makes it into an official report, we can destroy the notes. We can't keep every last thing we ever write down."

Maybe not every last thing, Brunelle conceded to himself. *But the interview of an eyewitness to a murder?*

"I wish you'd kept them," Brunelle said instead. "I could show them to Robyn."

Jackson's expression hardened again. "What? My word isn't good enough? You believe your girlfriend over me?"

Brunelle was taken aback. "She's, she's not my girlfriend."

"Not any more, maybe," Jackson scoffed. "But everybody knows you two hooked up."

Brunelle was speechless. He looked to Chen for support, but got none.

Chen just shrugged. "Seattle may be a big city now," he said, "but the cops and courts are still a small community. Word gets around."

Brunelle wanted to protest, but he couldn't. "Okay, fine. Maybe we did hook up. Once. A long time ago. Well, before this case anyway. But that's not why I wanted to talk to you. I just—"

"Sure," Jackson laughed. "That had nothing to do with it. Let me ask you this: would you be here if it had been Wilkins' attorney?"

"Jessica Edwards?" Brunelle confirmed. "I'd look into it too."

"What about the others?" Jackson pressed. "That Lannigan guy? Or Rainaldi?"

"Rainaldi?" Brunelle thought. "I don't know. Maybe, maybe not. And Lannigan? No. I'd just figure he fell asleep, or was texting during the interview."

"Jacobsen?" Jackson asked.

"Lying," Brunelle answered.

Jackson crossed his arms smugly. "So it does matter that it was a girlfriend?"

"It matters that it was someone I've come to trust professionally," Brunelle replied.

"More than a detective with nearly twenty years' experience?" Jackson demanded.

Brunelle thought for a moment. "No, I guess not."

Jackson nodded. "Thank you."

Brunelle thought for a few more moments. "Don't mention it."

CHAPTER 28

Brunelle wasn't sure whom he could trust. And that wasn't just the detectives.

Where it really mattered was the witnesses. The codefendants. The accomplices. The murderers. How could Brunelle decide which accomplices to murder deserved a break? And more importantly—although it probably shouldn't have been more important—which accomplices to murder could he trust when they took the stand at the trials of the other murderers? Even an accomplice who deserved a break wasn't going to get one if Brunelle couldn't trust what they might say or do when they got in front of the jury.

The motion to sever was two days away and he still hadn't made his final decision on which defendants to endorse as witnesses and split from the others. It was classic internal bargaining. He wanted to work with Keller and Fuller. But he was going to have to work with Rittenberger and Ashford. He was trying to avoid the decision he didn't want to make. And procrastination could lead to late nights.

"Hey, Dave." Carlisle knocked lightly on his open door.

"What are you doing here so late? It's after six. Shouldn't you be getting your beauty rest for the big hearing?"

Brunelle had been curled over his desk, head on his hands, staring at the hectic scribbles and arrows he'd been sketching out on his legal pad. He straightened up and rubbed his eyes. "I could ask you the same thing."

Carlisle put a fist on her hip. "You think I need beauty rest?"

Brunelle closed his eyes for a moment. Maybe he didn't miss having a girlfriend after all. "That's not what I meant. I—"

Carlisle laughed. "I'm just kidding, Dave. Geez, relax. I know women can be impossible sometimes, but not right now. And for the record, so can men."

"Okay," Brunelle answered. "So you stayed late to give me cryptic relationship advice?"

"No, silly," Carlisle laughed. "I stayed late because I have a full caseload of burglary cases, plus our little endeavor. I just stopped by to see if you were still here."

Brunelle glanced around his office. "Yep, I'm still here."

"What are you doing?"

"Trying to figure out some way to proceed that doesn't rely on Josh Rittenberger."

A chuckle from Carlisle. "And how's that going?"

Brunelle grimaced. "You know the case. What do you think?"

"I think…" Carlisle raised a thoughtful hand to her chin, "you should stop trying to figure everything out on your own. We're supposed to be a team, remember?"

"I know," Brunelle allowed. He ran a hand over his head. "I guess I just have trouble giving up control sometimes."

"Ya think?" Carlisle teased. Then she threw him a quick nod. "Is that what happened between you and Robyn? She doesn't seem like the type who would want to be controlled."

Brunelle wasn't ready for that direct of a question, or observation. "Uh, well, it was a little more complicated than that."

Carlisle nodded. "Yeah, women are complicated. Again, so can men be. But women? Yeah…"

Brunelle wasn't sure what to make of their conversation. He was usually ready to read flirting into almost any interaction with a woman. Somehow, though, it seemed to be missing just then despite the subject matter.

"So, you wanna figure it out over dinner?" Carlisle suggested.

"My relationship with Robyn?" Brunelle asked.

Carlisle shook her head. "No, dummy. Our case. Who to cut deals with, so we can convict the rest. Remember?"

"Oh, yeah. That," Brunelle answered. "Right. Uh, sure. Another imaginary Vietnamese place in Lake City?"

"Hey, that place turned out to be real," Carlisle defended. "I just didn't know that when we started. How about a real Mexican place on Capitol Hill? I'll drive."

Brunelle nodded. "Capitol Hill?" Where Robyn lived. Maybe she'd see them together. He sighed. "Sounds great."

* * *

"So," Brunelle started the shop-talk after ordering the enchiladas verdes and handing his menu to the waiter, "how are we going to discuss secret plans on an active murder case in a crowded restaurant?"

"Easy," Carlisle responded over her water glass. "We use my code names. Remember?"

Brunelle smiled. "Oh, yeah. I liked those. But I'm not sure I remember them all."

"Well, we start with 'Shooter,'" Carlisle reminded him.

Brunelle nodded. "Right, although Shooter already has a nickname."

"Right, but that nickname is what people actually call him," Carlisle explained. "So it's like it's his real name. We should stick with Shooter."

"Agreed," Brunelle said.

At that point, the waiter arrived with their drinks. A margarita for Carlisle and a whiskey, neat, for Brunelle. He was glad they hadn't said 'Burner' after all. For all he knew, the waiter used to get his drugs from Hernandez too.

"Who's next?" Carlisle asked, before taking a sip of her drink.

Brunelle thought for a moment. "Girlfriend. But that went sideways pretty bad. So I don't think that's going to work out." He took a drink of his own.

"Yeah..." Carlisle nodded. "Okay, moving on, what about Harpy?"

Brunelle thought for a moment. "You know, I almost think Harpy would have been our best witness, if only Lannigan—" He stopped himself. "Wait, can we use the attorneys' names?"

Carlisle considered for a moment, aided by another sip of margarita. "I vote no. It could compromise the identity of our targets. Let's just call them 'Harpy's attorney' and 'Junkie's attorney' and like that."

"Good call," Brunelle agreed. "Okay, so yeah, Harpy would probably have been the best. She wasn't high, at least as far as we know. And she doesn't seem to have any particular loyalty to Shooter."

"But her attorney is a weak sack of shit," Carlisle observed.

Brunelle cocked his head, then laughed. "Well, yes. I believe that sums it up."

"So that leaves Junkie and Siren," Carlisle said.

"And Manager," Brunelle reminded her. "He talked too."

Carlisle rolled her eyes. "That Murder on the Orient Express story? We should have called him the Fiction Writer."

"Yeah, if we give that story to the jury," Brunelle opined, "they'll acquit everyone just to get back at us for being stupid enough to believe him."

Carlisle's eyebrows shot up. "Do you think he'll take the stand at the trial and actually tell that same story?"

"I hope so," Brunelle replied before taking another sip. Mexican restaurants weren't usually known for their whiskey selection, but he'd had worse. "Then the jury will know he's lying."

"And if he changes his story," Carlisle observed, "we can impeach him with his crazy, Hercule Poirot fantasy."

"Exactly," Brunelle said. "Win-win."

"Which is why he'll never testify," Carlisle supposed.

"Probably not," Brunelle agreed. "And definitely not for us."

"So it's settled then," Carlisle declared. "We endorse Junkie and Siren as the state's witnesses and agree to the severance of Junkie's trial from the others."

"And we object to the severance of the remaining defendants from each other," Brunelle continued, "so we only have to try the case once."

Carlisle raised her glass. "Hear, hear."

But Brunelle didn't raise his glass to hers. He had fallen into his own thoughts. "I just wish we could have worked it out with Keller," he complained. "That would have been the best possible result."

Carlisle lowered her glass again and shook her head at him. "Because she would have given us the best testimony for the jury?" she asked. "Or because you would have gotten to work closely with

Robyn Dunn?"

Brunelle had sipped too much of the whiskey to be able to pretend she wasn't right. So he didn't reply at all.

"You seem like you're still pretty hung up on her," Carlisle observed. "I mean, if you don't mind my saying so."

Brunelle shook his head. He could hardly mind someone telling him the truth. Well, he shouldn't mind anyway. And for some reason he didn't mind it coming from Carlisle.

"Were you guys together a long time?" she asked.

"No, actually," Brunelle admitted. "In fact, the whole thing was pretty fleeting. A lot of buildup, but then it was over before I knew it. Maybe that's why it still bugs me. It didn't last long enough for us to get sick of each other."

"Yeah," Carlisle replied. Rather than meet Brunelle's little joke with a laugh, she gave it a nod. She took another drink of her margarita, and for the first time opened up to Brunelle about her own personal life. "I was with Chris for almost ten years. We finally got married last year, but I think we were just trying to save something we both knew was over. Six months later we filed for divorce. It was simple enough—no fight over the property, no kids—but it still hurt. It always hurts when something ends, even when you know it should."

Brunelle took a sip of his own drink. "Especially after ten years, I would guess." He'd never been in that committed of a relationship.

"Yeah," Carlisle answered. "And then you realize you'd put all of your emotional energy into that one person. When you emerge, you have to start all over. New house, new plans, new friends." She stopped for a moment, then raised her glass again at Brunelle. "It's nice to have a new friend to grab dinner with."

Brunelle smiled and this time raised his glass. "Yes, it is."

CHAPTER 29

"Are the parties ready on the defendants' motions to sever for trial?" Quinn asked from her perch above the courtroom.

Just like last time, she had taken the bench at the stroke of nine. And just like last time, there were five defendants, seven attorneys, and enough jail guards to keep everyone on good behavior. Unlike last time, however, no one was seated in the jury box. Quinn had made arrangements for extra tables to be brought in. The prosecution table was shoved almost against the jury box, with the five defendants having to share three tables set up in an L-shape. There was barely enough room. The gap between the prosecution table and the defense tables was less than two feet; Jacobsen was practically sitting on Brunelle's lap.

Brunelle was disappointed that Samantha Keller's attorney hadn't been given that place of honor, but he was glad for the arrangement. It meant Quinn was already making plans for a joint trial. She had to entertain the defendants' motions to sever, but it sure didn't look like she was planning on granting them.

"The state is ready," Brunelle announced for his side.

Each of the defense attorneys answered in turn as Quinn

pointed to them. She started with Jacobsen, then moved along the tables: Edwards, Dunn, Lannigan, and Rainaldi. Everyone was ready.

Quinn was too. "Mr. Brunelle. Ms. Carlisle." she started. "Is the state agreeing to any of the motions for severance?"

Translation: *Has the state cut a deal with any of the defendants and, if so, can we get them out of here?*

"Yes, Your Honor," Brunelle was relieved to report, as he stood to address the court. "The state has no objection to the severance of Mr. Rittenberger's case for trial. The state anticipates calling Mr. Rittenberger as a witness in its case-in-chief at the trial of the other codefendants. We would ask the court to grant Mr. Rittenberger's motion to sever and reschedule his trial for sixty days after the commencement of the joint trial."

A little cockiness at the end there, assuming the remaining cases would stay joined. But that was part of the fun of trial work: poking your opponent in the eye.

Quinn turned to Rittenberger's lawyer. "Ms. Rainaldi, any objection to Mr. Brunelle's proposal?"

Rainaldi stood up. "No, Your Honor. Thank you, Your Honor."

"All right then." Quinn nodded. "As to defendant Rittenberger, the motion to sever trial is granted. We will reschedule his trial date as suggested by the parties." She looked to the lead jailor. "As soon as Mr. Rittenberger has signed his scheduling order, he can be returned to the jail. We could use the space."

The jailor acknowledged the instructions, and Quinn pushed on even as Rittenberger was made ready to leave.

"Any others, Mr. Brunelle?" Brunelle frowned. He wished there were. But there was one small consolation. "No, Your Honor."

Jacobsen looked up at him, surprised, then quickly over at Robyn. That was the consolation: Jacobsen hadn't seen that coming. Everyone who read Jackson's report figured Keller was turning state's witness. But that was before Keller got cold feet, or buyer's remorse, or whatever, and backed out. Robyn didn't return Jacobsen's gaze. She had her game face on, waiting for her turn to argue for severance.

She wouldn't have to wait long. "Okay, then," Judge Quinn said. "Let's get started. I placed you in the order I want to hear from you. And I mean that for both today and at trial." She paused. "Assuming, I don't grant the motions to sever, that is," she managed to add, albeit unconvincingly at that point. "I'll hear first from Mr. Jacobsen on behalf of Mr. Hernandez."

Jacobsen stood up, buttoned his suit coat, and chanced one last glance at Robyn. She didn't look up from her note taking.

"Thank you, Your Honor," Jacobsen began. "I'd like to begin by pointing out the obvious. The state has decided that my client, Mr. Hernandez, is the person who shot and killed Derrick Shanborn. They have reached this conclusion, however, without a shred of reliable evidence. They have merely managed to convince three drug addicts to tell them about the event, and clearly they were able to communicate to these people two things. First, they wanted to hear that Mr. Hernandez was the shooter, and second, they were in a lot of trouble if they didn't say as much. Two of them suggested it without actually saying it, and the one who did say it also claimed responsibility for himself. The state then elected not to charge one of them, cut a deal to another, and ignore the one person who admits someone other than Mr. Hernandez shot the victim."

"And this is relevant to the question of separate trials how?" Quinn interjected.

My question exactly, Brunelle thought. He gave a glance to

Carlisle to communicate the thought, and she nodded in reply.

"It's relevant, Your Honor," Jacobsen answered, "because the state has no credible evidence against Mr. Hernandez and instead wishes to paint the defendants all together with one broad brush, hoping the jury will throw up their hands and simply convict everyone in the room. Unable to disentangle the evidence against one defendant, such as it may be, from the evidence against the others, the jury will be tempted to convict everyone, lest the real killer—whoever that may be—be acquitted.

"Mr. Hernandez deserves to have the evidence against him presented to his own jury so that jury can decide his guilt or innocence independent of any responsibility for the others more involved in Mr. Shanborn's death."

"More involved?" Quinn raised an eyebrow.

"Mr. Hernandez vigorously maintains his innocence, Your Honor," Jacobsen replied quickly. "So anyone else here who was involved in Mr. Shanborn's death would, by definition, be involved more than him."

"Hm," Quinn answered. "That's not how it sounded when you said it."

Jacobsen simply nodded to the judge.

"Anything further, Mr. Jacobsen?"

Jacobsen thought for a moment. "No, Your Honor. Mr. Hernandez deserves his own trial. That's enough."

Quinn looked to the next attorney. "Ms. Edwards. Would you like to argue your motion on behalf of Mr. Wilkins?"

Edwards stood up as Jacobsen sat down. "Yes, Your Honor," she said. "Thank you. As Mr. Jacobsen vaguely referenced, my client, Mr. Wilkins, is in the unique situation of having cooperated with the police, only to be told his cooperation wasn't really wanted after all. He gave a statement which the state may or may not seek to introduce at trial—"

Brunelle stood up. "We will not be introducing it."

Jacobsen stood as well. "We may seek to introduce it, Your Honor. If this is a joint trial, I mean."

"You're going to introduce a statement that your client shot the victim?" Brunelle asked incredulously.

"I'll introduce a statement that two other people shot him," Jacobsen countered. "And—"

Quinn slammed her gavel on the bench. "Counsel! This will not deteriorate into a roundtable discussion of trial strategy. This is a motion to sever. I will hear first from the moving parties, and only then will I ask to hear from the prosecution. Is that understood, Mr. Brunelle?"

Brunelle lowered his eyes. "Yes, Your Honor. I apologize. I was just trying to add information for the court."

"Do it when it's your turn," Quinn instructed. She looked to Jacobsen. "You too, counsel. Understood?"

Jacobsen added his consent. Quinn nodded again to Edwards. "Go on, Ms. Edwards."

Edwards thanked the judge and continued. "Apparently, the state doesn't like what Mr. Wilkins said, because it didn't fit their theory of the case. So now he sits here, willing to cooperate, but joined for trial with Mr. Hernandez, the man who intimidated everyone into being involved in the first place. The dynamic in the house that day will simply be repeated here in this courtroom."

Again, Quinn interrupted. "Don't worry, counsel. I will not tolerate any outbursts in my courtroom. I am aware of what occurred at the arraignment."

But Edwards shook her head. "I'm not talking about physical violence, Your Honor. I'm talking about psychological intimidation. I'm talking about Mr. Wilkins having to decide whether to take the stand in his own defense, worried about, not just the state mischaracterizing they tricked him into making, but also afraid to explain his actions with Mr. Hernandez in the room. A joint trial will have a chilling effect on my client's rights to due process and a fair trial."

"Thank you, Ms. Edwards," the judge said. She turned next to Dunn. "Ms. Dunn?"

Robyn stood up. She tugged her suit coat into place. She didn't look at Jacobsen or Brunelle or anyone. She looked up at the judge, right in the eye. "Ms. Keller not only deserves a separate trial, Your Honor, she deserves a dismissal."

Brunelle frowned slightly. He knew what was coming. He couldn't really blame her—she was just doing her job—but he had let himself hope she might not raise the whole allegedly falsified report thing.

"Ms. Edwards is partially mistaken," Dunn explained, "when she says only her client spoke to the police and was then rebuffed. Ms. Keller also spoke to the police, but rather than have her version of events rejected by the state, her version of events was never recorded in the first place. Instead, the detective misrepresented her statement in his report. And when I say 'misrepresented,' I mean, he lied. Now, Ms. Keller faces the prospect not just of being confronted with a prior statement like Mr. Wilkins, but being confronted with something she never actually said. This issue threatens to overshadow this entire trial. I certainly intend to make that happen. The issue is no longer who shot Derrick Shanborn, but rather, why would the lead detective lie about it?"

"Chen is actually the lead detective," Brunelle whispered to Carlisle, but she shushed him. He returned his attention to Robyn, who had clearly gotten the attention of the judge.

"You plan to put the detective on trial?" Quinn asked.

"Yes, Your Honor," Robyn replied. "And I expect to take a long time doing it. If you don't want the other defendants' murder charges to disappear into the morass that I expect will come of my questioning of Detective Jackson, then you should grant the motion to sever."

"Sever everyone?" Quinn asked. "Four separate trials?"

"I couldn't care less about the other three defendants, Your Honor," Robyn replied honestly, and brutally. The very things Brunelle liked about her. "I only care that Ms. Keller has her own trial so the issue of police, and prosecutor, misconduct can take its rightful place front and center before the jury."

Quinn nodded thoughtfully as Robyn sat down again. After a moment, she turned to the last attorney still seated at the table. "Mr. Lannigan?"

Lannigan had been doodling on his notepad. He looked up with a jerk, then glanced at his client. After a moment, he shrugged and stood up. "Uh, we stand on our briefing, Your Honor. I have nothing to add."

Quinn frowned. Fuller did too. Brunelle tried not to.

"Are you sure, Mr. Lannigan?" Judge Quinn asked. "I'd like to hear the circumstances unique to your client."

Lannigan shrugged again, then stood up. He didn't bother to straighten his suit coat. In fact, it wasn't even a suitcoat; it was a blazer that didn't even match his pants. "Well, Your Honor, that's kind of the point. Ms. Fuller never made any statement to the police and she didn't try to cut a deal with the prosecutor. So I don't have the same arguments as the other lawyers. Sorry."

Quinn shook her head. "Don't be sorry, Mr. Lannigan. But do please do your job. If you have an argument on behalf of your client receiving a separate trial, I'd like to hear it."

Lannigan nodded weakly and thought for a moment. "Well, Your Honor, if you're going to sever the other defendants, then you should probably sever Ms. Fuller too."

Quinn raised an eyebrow. "That's it?"

Lannigan shrugged yet again. "Like I said, Your Honor, we rest on our written brief. I trust you to do what you think is right, regardless of whatever I argue."

Quinn frowned. "All right then." She looked to the prosecution table. "Mr. Brunelle or Ms. Carlisle? Any response?"

Brunelle stood up. Carlisle had handled the Jacobsen motions. It was his turn.

"Yes, Your Honor, thank you," he began. "I understand the points raised by the defense attorneys, but they all fail when weighed against the advantages of a joint trial. It is well established, Your Honor, that the law favors joint trials. Judicial economy is best served by a single trial, rather than two, or three, or four separate trials. Four separate juries, but all hearing the same evidence, from the same witnesses. And I think that's the deciding factor in this case, Your Honor. The evidence isn't different for these defendants. The evidence against Mr. Hernandez is the same as the evidence against Ms. Keller, and the same against Ms. Fuller, and the same against Mr. Wilkins. There may be differing cross-examinations, but the core evidence is the same, and it is a waste of resources to require the state's witnesses to testify four times to the same thing."

"Especially if some of those witnesses are cooperating codefendants?" Quinn interjected knowingly.

It was Brunelle's turn to shrug. "In all candor, yes, Your Honor. It's hard enough to get a cooperating codefendant to testify once. Getting them to testify four times may prove impossible, no matter what arrangements are made in advance. And if our witnesses refuse to cooperate after one or two trials, then that means the last defendant or two to have their trials may get acquittals simply because they were fortunate enough to be scheduled after the others. That's not justice."

"Is it justice to trick a codefendant into giving a statement and then not using him?" Quinn challenged. "Or lying about what another codefendant said?"

Brunelle took a moment to answer, lest he actually take the bait. "Justice will arise out of the examination and cross-examination of the witnesses. That will actually be better served if one single jury gets to hear all of the defenses against the state's case. Let Mr. Hernandez's jury hear that Mr. Wilkins was left at the proverbial altar. Let Ms. Fuller's jury hear that Ms. Keller claims the detective is a liar. Let one group of twelve people hear it all, and then decide accordingly. And whatever they decide, that will be justice."

Quinn grinned. "You have great faith in our jury system."

Brunelle demurred. "We have nowhere else to put our faith, Your Honor. The system may not be perfect, but it's better than anything else anyone has tried. In my experience, they usually get it right. And they'll get it right this time."

Quinn chewed her cheek for a moment and leaned back in her chair. The lawyers shuffled their papers for the short time it took the judge to collect her thoughts and pronounce her ruling.

"I believe," the judge began as she leaned forward to address the lawyers, "that Mr. Jacobsen made the most salient point in today's arguments."

Brunelle frowned. That was an inauspicious beginning. Maybe the table setup really was just for today. He suddenly realized the tables could be put back to wherever they came from just as easily as they had been brought there in the first place.

"Mr. Jacobsen pointed out," Quinn continued, "that it would

be difficult, if not impossible, for a jury to disentangle the evidence in this case. There are five different defendants, at least one of whom is now also a witness for the state. But everyone who testifies will be testifying about the same event, that is, the shooting of Derrick Shanborn. No matter what anyone says, their testimony will be entangled with the testimony of everyone else."

Brunelle had to admit that was true.

"And that's why," the judge ruled, "I am going to deny the motions to sever. One jury should hear all of the evidence, and all the challenges to that evidence, from every corner. I'm not persuaded by the state's concerns about cooperating witnesses getting cold feet—that's the nature of making those sorts of deals. But I am persuaded that this case, like every case, should be decided by a jury that has as much information as possible. I don't believe that can be done piecemeal with four separate trials. Accordingly, I am denying the motions to sever. Are the parties ready to begin trial next week?"

Jacobsen, who had seemed pleased when Judge Quinn began her ruling, had returned to a stone-faced countenance. "Mr. Hernandez will be ready, Your Honor."

"Mr. Wilkins is ready," Edwards added.

Robyn stood up sharply. "Ms. Keller will be ready, Your Honor."

All eyes turned to Lannigan. He took a moment to realize it, then said, "Sure, Your Honor. We'll be ready."

Then Quinn looked to Brunelle. "Will the state be ready to begin trial on the scheduled trial date?"

God, I hope so, Brunelle thought, before answering, "Absolutely, Your Honor."

CHAPTER 30

It was a little after eight o'clock on the night before trial and Brunelle was still in his office. Usually, he spent the night before a trial in his apartment, alone, maybe sipping a little whiskey, and going over his opening statement in his head until it felt just right. But this trial was different. So was his partner.

And he had an idea.

He picked up his phone and called Carlisle on her cell phone.

"Hello?" she answered.

"Hey, Gwen. It's Dave." He spun in his chair so he could look out the window. Random office lights lit up the night skyline. "I've been thinking about our case."

"Well, that seems appropriate," she replied, "since we're starting the trial tomorrow."

"Exactly," Brunelle answered. "I think I have an idea to streamline things a little."

"That sounds like a good idea," Carlisle responded. "What are you thinking?"

Brunelle gazed out at the nightscape. "What if we go ahead

and cut a deal to Keller. Not in return for testimony; just to get her out of the courtroom. She pleads to rendering criminal assistance and heads off to prison. One less defendant in the courtroom, and less for us to explain to the jury."

There was a long pause on the other end. "You want to cut Samantha Keller a deal? No testimony, just because?"

Brunelle shrugged to himself. "I dunno. Maybe. The evidence suggests she really didn't do anything. We can focus on Hernandez and Wilkins, the real bad guys."

When Carlisle didn't immediately respond, Brunelle asked, "What do you think?"

"What do I think?" Carlisle was ready with a response this time. "I think you want to give your ex-girlfriend a deal so she won't stay mad at you, in case there's the slightest chance you two could get back together."

"What?" Brunelle spun away from the windows. "No! No, I just—I was just thinking one less defendant would mean that much easier of a case. And she's a bit player, at best."

"Look, Dave," Carlisle almost chucked. "I don't blame you. I've seen her, remember? She's gorgeous. You'd have to be dead not to want to get back with that."

Brunelle wanted to protest, but the words 'gorgeous' and 'get back with that' derailed his thoughts for just a moment.

"I can see it, Dave," Carlisle continued. "Everyone can. You can list as many reasons as you want for dumping Keller's case. You might even be right. But everyone will think you did it because of what I just said."

"I'm not sure you're right," Brunelle finally managed to defend himself. "And I'm not sure it matters what everyone thinks, if it's the right thing to do."

"If it were the right thing to do, Dave, you would have done it already."

Brunelle wasn't sure what to say to that.

"It's too late, Dave," Carlisle went on. "You gave her a chance. You gave her multiple chances. Now it's time for trial."

Brunelle took a moment, then admitted, "I guess you're right."

"Of course I am," Carlisle said. "But now that I'm about to climb into the foxhole with you, I need to know you're not going to pull any punches. Try the hell out of this case, Dave, and make Robyn Dunn realize what a mistake she made."

"You mean for turning down a deal?" Brunelle asked.

"You know exactly what I mean," Carlisle answered. "Now, are you with me?"

Brunelle smiled. "I'm with you." And he was glad for it.

CHAPTER 31

Judge Quinn had left the tables exactly as they had been set up for the motions to sever. With Rittenberger back in his jail cell waiting to testify, it freed up a little room. Ron Jacobsen was no longer on Brunelle's lap. Then again, neither was Robyn Dunn.

Four defense attorneys meant everything took more than four times as long. Five parties instead of two, plus the standard slowing down of anything that gets complicated. But after a while, everyone got into the rhythm. First the state—either Brunelle or Carlisle—then Jacobsen, Edwards, Robyn, and Lannigan. That also speeded things up a bit; Jacobsen made most of the arguments, Edwards added some refinements, Robyn adjusted for her own client, and Lannigan said, "Nothing to add."

It took a full day to go through preliminary motions, and three more to pick the jury. But on the fifth day, the jury was sworn and seated, and at nine a.m. sharp, the Honorable Susan Quinn instructed them, "Ladies and gentlemen of the jury, please give your attention to Mr. Brunelle, who will deliver the opening statement on behalf of the state."

Brunelle stood up and buttoned his suit coat. He nodded to

the judge, then stepped out from behind counsel table and positioned himself directly in front of the jury box.

Opening statement was supposed to summarize the story that the lawyer believed—or hoped—the evidence would show. It was the one opportunity for the lawyers to tell a cohesive, compelling narrative before the disconnected, whiplash-inducing procedure of 'question, answer, objection, repeat' began. Many a trial lawyer would insist that a case was won or lost in opening statement. Whichever lawyer told the better story already had a leg up with the jury as they descended into the uneven crevices of testimony. Brunelle's problem was, he didn't know the whole story. He barely knew any of it. His star witnesses were a drug addict and an absent girlfriend. He didn't know exactly what had happened in Hernandez's house that night. So he started with what he did know.

"Derrick Shanborn was a snitch."

Hardly the sanctifying of the victim they taught at the prosecutor conferences.

"He was a drug addict. He was a thief. And rather than stay loyal to the very few friends he did have, he snitched them all out to the cops."

Brunelle glanced over the faces of the jurors to see if he had them. He did. They seemed stunned, or at least surprised, as if they were waiting for the punchline. Brunelle was happy to oblige.

"And they murdered him for it."

That was the case in a nut shell. One of the advantages—the many advantages—of being the prosecutor was always getting to go first. Opening statement, calling witnesses, closing argument. The prosecutor gets to set the table. But Brunelle needed to put some food on the plates too. It wasn't like Jacobsen and crew were just going to sit on their hands when he finished.

So Brunelle would focus on the victim and his story. It

wasn't a very sympathetic story, but he didn't have much choice. The other story—what happened when he was shot and killed—Brunelle didn't have a clear version of that. Not clear enough to promise it to the jury. So this would be short and sweet, heavy on emotion and light on details. Then hope to survive the defense openings and start calling witnesses.

"Opening statement," Brunelle explained with a practiced gesture of open palms, "is an opportunity for the lawyers to tell you what they believe the evidence will show. It's not argument—we don't argue whether those facts equal a crime or not. Instead, it's a narrative—a story to help you understand the testimony of each witness as they parade through the courtroom one by one."

Brunelle took two steps to his right. He knew not to pace. Pacing was distracting at best, annoying at worst. But a slight shift in position kept him from looking like a tree planted in front of the jury box. And it signaled the slight shift in his presentation.

"But the thing about a murder story is, it's rarely simple. There are a lot of players, a lot of witnesses. The people involved, the first responders, detectives, doctors, experts. It can get pretty confusing. So like any complicated story, it's helpful to start with the cast of characters, like inside the playbill you get when you go to your kid's school play."

That pulled a smile from a couple jurors in the back. Brunelle wasn't a parent himself, but the ones who smiled—they liked being parents, and now they thought he was a parent too, so maybe they liked him a little bit more than when he first stood up. That was important. Ultimately, at the end of the trial, he was going to be asking them to trust him. They wouldn't really get enough information to make a perfect decision. But they had to make a decision anyway, and, subconsciously, they would give greater weight to the lawyer, or lawyers, they trusted.

He took two steps back and opened his body to the lawyers and defendants behind him. Time to introduce the players. He'd considered starting with Shanborn, but that would have been a mistake. For one thing, he'd already introduced Shanborn's name. For another, Shanborn's roles were responsive—dependent on the players. He was a snitch against someone. He was a victim of someone. And that someone was...

"Elmer Hernandez." Brunelle pointed to Hernandez. Even dressed in street clothes so the jury wouldn't know he was being held in custody pending trial, he looked large and menacing. Perfect. And now everyone on the jury was looking at him too. He shifted slightly in his seat. Brunelle waited another beat, then tagged him. "Drug dealer."

Jacobsen exploded to his feet. "Objection, Your Honor!"

Double perfect, Brunelle thought. Now the jury knew it was true. *Thy lawyer doth protest too much.*

Brunelle rotated his upper body to look up to the judge. "I expect the evidence to support that statement, Your Honor."

Quinn narrowed her eyes at him. "Stick to the facts, Mr. Brunelle. Not disparaging labels. You know how to describe a person without resorting to incendiary monikers."

Brunelle nodded at the ruling and thought for a moment as he turned back to the defense table—the first of several such tables. "Elmer Hernandez," he repeated. "Entrepreneur."

That pulled a few more smiles from the jury box. It might have seemed flippant to call him that initially, but with the objection and instruction from the court, it seemed like Brunelle had no choice. What a guy.

"Mr. Hernandez ran a substantial, uh, *delivery service* in the Lake City neighborhood of Seattle. A highly lucrative enterprise, but one that needed to avoid the notice of law enforcement to remain profitable."

Brunelle took another step back and gestured toward the next defendant. "Nate Wilkins. Mr. Hernandez's business manager. It was his job to make sure deliveries were made on time, and accounts were collected punctually."

That last bit was code for beating up junkies who didn't pay. The jury could decipher that, he hoped. Edwards didn't object to the description. The words were smarmy at worst, but not really objectionable. And she was smart enough not to underline Brunelle's remarks by calling attention to them. Instead, she kept her head down, calmly taking notes. She knew she'd get her chance to talk.

Next defendant.

"Samantha Keller." Brunelle softened his gesture just slightly as he reached the first woman defendant. Sexism was a terrible thing. It was also real. And it could go both ways. A large man in a crisp suit aggressively calling out a woman in extra clothes borrowed from the public defender's office might engender sympathy from the jurors, or some of them anyway, even if only subconsciously. But a muted gesture and slightly relaxed shoulders were both less confrontational and dovetailed perfectly with the description. "Mr. Hernandez's dutiful long-time girlfriend."

Still a sympathetic description. But Brunelle would have been willing to sacrifice a conviction against Samantha Keller to get Hernandez and Wilkins.

It had nothing to do with the way Robyn was glaring at him as she sat, cross-armed, next to her client. Really.

Brunelle paused for probably a second too long as he tried to ignore Robyn's… well, her everything. He took one more beat, then managed to refocus his thoughts.

"And Lindsey Fuller." He set his shoulders a little straighter for this one. Fuller was a woman too, but she was hardly the long-suffering wife type. She was just one tough bitch. "A loyal ally and hardened drug user who conspired to bring Derrick Shanborn to Elmer Hernandez's house to be murdered as payback for snitching out Hernandez to the cops."

Lannigan didn't object either. He also didn't ignore or glare. He did the one thing worse for a defense attorney to do than all those. He watched Brunelle in rapt attention, pen down and chin on fist, as if everything Brunelle had to say was too important to miss. God help Lindsey Fuller.

Brunelle stopped and turned again to square himself fully to the jurors. He'd identified the players. It was time to tell the story.

"Derrick Shanborn was exactly what every parent fears. A good kid who got hooked on drugs and threw his life away." Another tug at the parent-jurors' heartstrings. He had the moms with the school play reference. Time to grab the dads. "He was that skinny ten-year-old standing out in right field, trying to pay attention to the game and just hoping the ball didn't get hit to him."

Brunelle paused just long enough to count the head-nods he got from the men on the jury. Two in the back and one in the front. Good.

"But Derrick the Little Leaguer turned into Derrick the Teenager, and then Derrick the Young Twenty-Something. And instead of standing alone in a field of outfield dandelions, he was lying alone in a gutter, hopelessly addicted to heroin made from a Central Asian poppy field."

It was an awkward construction, but Brunelle liked the symmetry between dandelions and poppies. He considered working in that scene from *The Wizard of Oz* when Dorothy and her friends all fall asleep in the poppy field, but he couldn't figure out how to do it and still sound serious and intense. Maybe next trial.

"Actually, it wasn't really a gutter," he continued. "That's a cliché. In real life, few people end up in an actual gutter. That's too public. The good people of the world don't want to see that." A quick jab at the jurors' collective guilt.

"The truth is, heroin addicts like Derrick Shanborn end up in drug houses, flopped out on a mattress on the floor, bodies slack, eyes glassy, and souls dying."

Jacobsen stood up again. "Objection, Your Honor." He was calmer this time, but still officious. "This is opening statement. The prosecutor is supposed to be discussing the facts of this case, not giving a speech about the evils of drug addiction."

Judge Quinn raised an eyebrow at Brunelle. "Response?"

"The facts of this case *are* a speech against the evils of drug addiction," Brunelle said. He'd have to thank Jacobsen later for that particular softball. "And the location where Mr. Shanborn used his drugs is highly relevant to the facts of this case."

Quinn frowned at him. "Rein it in, Mr. Brunelle," she warned. "You can discuss the facts, but stay away from the public service announcements."

Brunelle provided a contrite nod. "Understood, Your Honor."

He turned back to the jurors. "In *this* case, Derrick Shanborn bought his heroin from Elmer Hernandez. In *this* case, Derrick Shanborn flopped on a mattress in Elmer Hernandez's living room. In this case," a dramatic pause, "Derrick Shanborn's little league coach was Seattle P.D. narcotics detective Tim Jackson."

Every good story has a twist.

"And one day, Detective Jackson ran into that ten-year-old right fielder turned twenty-something drug addict. And because of that, it looked like Derrick might end up being one of those few—precious few—success stories. Not just another statistic in the war on drugs. Detective Jackson did exactly what a good cop should do—what a good *person* should do. He reached out to Derrick and rather than arrest him for possession of heroin, he offered to help him kick it."

Brunelle nodded thoughtfully and took a small step to his right. "And Derrick Shanborn, twenty-something drug addict, well, he remembered that ten-year-old little leaguer too. He remembered his best friend's dad, Mr. Jackson. And he said, 'Yes. Please help me.'"

Brunelle paused again. He frowned and looked down solemnly. After a moment he looked up again and rested his gaze somewhere between two of the jurors in the back row. "I wish I could tell you that's where the story ended. That Derrick got clean—which he did—and moved to Montana to get a fresh start— which he planned to do. But that's not how the story ended. The story ends here, in this courtroom. Because Derrick Shanborn told Detective Jackson who his drug dealer was. And Elmer Hernandez found out Derrick had snitched him out. And no one snitches out Elmer Hernandez. So the defendants in this room hatched a plan to take their revenge on Derrick Shanborn. They lured him to Mr. Hernandez's house. They shot him to death. And they dumped his body in an open ditch, right behind a gas station on Lake City Way. A warning to everyone that you don't snitch on Elmer Hernandez."

Brunelle returned to his original spot, centered in front of the jury box, and clasped his hands earnestly, solemnly.

"That was the end of Derrick's story. But it isn't the end of the whole story. As I said, the story ends in this courtroom. After you hear the evidence, listen to the arguments, and deliberate on your verdict. Only then will this story finally end. And at the conclusion of this trial, we will stand up again and ask you to end this story with verdicts of guilty to the charge of murder in the first degree.

"Thank you."

Brunelle walked back to his seat and sat down again next to Carlisle who offered a whispered, "Good job." It had gone about as well as he could have hoped. He didn't have a lot of details, so he'd painted broadly. A watercolor landscape rather than an oil portrait. He hoped it would be enough. But that would depend on how well his opponents did.

Something he was about to find out.

"Ladies and gentlemen," Judge Quinn announced, "please give your attention to Mr. Jacobsen, who will deliver the opening statement on behalf of Mr. Hernandez."

CHAPTER 32

Jacobsen stood slowly from his seat and buttoned his coat as he navigated the narrow space between his table and the prosecution's. He nodded to the judge, then turned to face the jurors.

"That," he began, pointing at Brunelle, "was a very nice story. A little short on detail, but still, very dramatic." He turned and offered a sarcastic golf clap to Brunelle. "Bravo."

Brunelle frowned slightly. He couldn't ignore the jab completely, but he didn't have to take the bait either and object. If Jacobsen wanted to act like a jerk, that was fine. Jurors didn't like jerks any more than anyone else did.

"But," Jacobsen turned back to the jurors, "that's all it was. A story. A simple, almost fantastic story, filled with clichéd characters and simple motivations. Like a fairy tale. And just like a fairy tale, it has the momentary ability to entertain, but it is ultimately detached from reality. So disregard it. Ignore it. Forget it completely."

Jacobsen paused and started pacing. He chewed his cheek for a moment and nodded, as if to himself. "Now, I know what you're thinking. Or rather, I know what you're expecting. You're expecting me to tell a story. A better story. Mr. Brunelle just told you a story. And I just told you to throw it out like so much trash. So I must have a different story, right? A better story."

He stopped pacing and shook his head. "No. I have no story for you. Mr. Brunelle can get up here, call my client names, spin some fantastic yarn about little league and lost redemption, and when he's done everyone thinks they know what the case is about. So of course, I should get up and tell a different story. A 'competing narrative' is what they call it, I think. But why should I? Or rather," he pointed a challenging finger at the jurors, "why shouldn't I?"

He waited, as if the jurors might actually answer. After another moment, Brunelle began to worry one of them might. Trials weren't classrooms. There weren't question-and-answer sessions. If some juror shouted out a guess, it could mistry the case. He started to stand up to object, but Jacobsen continued before he, or any of the jurors, could say anything.

"The answer, ladies and gentlemen of the jury, is simple. In fact, it's so simple that it's in danger of being overlooked. The reason I shouldn't provide you with a competing narrative, with a different story of what, as the judge said, I expect the evidence to show is this: I don't expect the evidence to show anything. And I don't have to."

He pointed at his client. His large, scary-looking, drug dealer client. "Take a look at Mr. Hernandez. There he is. Seated in a courtroom. Not as a juror, or a judge, or a lawyer, or a spectator in the gallery. No, he sits here as a defendant. A criminal defendant. And as such, he is absolutely, positively, completely, one-hundred percent innocent."

Brunelle almost never objected. Objections just drew attention to the other side's point, whatever it was. He only objected if he was sure he'd win and keep out evidence the jury shouldn't hear. Or if it gave him an opportunity to make a point. He stood up.

"Objection, Your Honor," he said calmly. "That's a misstatement of law. Criminal defendants are *presumed* innocent, not necessarily innocent in fact."

Quinn frowned at both of the lawyers. "This is opening statement, not closing argument. We won't be arguing legal standards here. You made your point, Mr. Brunelle. Move on, Mr. Jacobsen."

Brunelle sat down again and Jacobsen nodded, "Only presumed innocent, the prosecutor says. Only. As if it weren't really all that important. And of course, Mr. Brunelle wants you to think it's not very important. Who cares about the truth? Who cares about process? Just tell us your story. The prosecutor called your client a drug dealer. Is he or isn't he? Did he really shoot Derrick Shanborn for being a snitch? Did he play little league too?"

Jacobsen snorted with practiced disgust. "No, you don't need to know if Mr. Hernandez is a drug dealer, or a drug user, or short stop for the Seattle Mariners. You only need to know one thing: he is presumed innocent. And the fact that you expect me to tell you a story about the case just goes to show why that presumption is so important.

"I don't have to prove anything. The prosecution has to prove everything, and beyond a reasonable doubt. They don't just have to tell you a story, they have to prove that story to you, beyond a reasonable doubt. And they will fail. Just like with any fairy tale. A goose that lays golden eggs isn't reasonable. Three bears eating porridge in a cabin isn't reasonable. And the story Mr. Brunelle just told you isn't reasonable. It will fall apart just as surely as any children's bedtime story."

Jacobsen crossed his arms and raised his chin to the jurors.

"The only thing that could possibly save Mr. Brunelle's story is if I told you a worse one. Or one that confirmed most of his story, but tried to thread some legal needle. Validate his claim that Mr. Hernandez is a drug dealer, and a violent man, and a troll that lives under a bridge, but he would never actually murder a boy who once played little league. And if I did that, do you know what you would do?"

Again, a pause for the jurors to answer. Brunelle would give it two more seconds. A second-and-a-half later, Jacobsen answered his own question. "You would stop listening to the evidence. Or rather, you'd never start. If I tell you, 'Yes, Elmer Hernandez drinks the blood of children for breakfast,' but no witness ever says that, you'll still believe it. Because I told you so. And I wouldn't say it if it weren't true because I'm his lawyer.

"So if I stand here and tell you a story, any story, then I am shirking my responsibility to hold the prosecution to its burden, to prove each and every element of the offense beyond any and all reasonable doubt. You want me to tell you a story? Too bad. I don't tell stories. Mr. Brunelle does. But you don't convict people of murder based on stories."

He pointed again at his client. "Mr. Hernandez is innocent as he sits here now. And at the end of this trial, when the prosecutor has failed to prove his entertaining but ultimately vacuous fairy tale, he will still be innocent. All without me telling you anything.

"Because that's how it works.

"Because that's justice."

Jacobsen spun on his heel and marched back to his seat next to Hernandez.

Brunelle looked to Carlisle, unsure whether Jacobsen's opening was brilliant or suicidal. Carlisle didn't seem to know either. Judge Quinn didn't seem to care; she had a trial to manage.

"And now, ladies and gentlemen, please give your attention to Ms. Edwards who will give opening statement on behalf of Mr. Wilkins."

CHAPTER 33

Edwards stood and took her turn in front of the jury. Brunelle watched her walk into the well. Her expression was inscrutable, but he knew the gears were grinding even as she thanked the judge and took that last deep breath before beginning. She had a choice to make. Double down on Jacobsen's challenge, or undercut him by actually telling the jury her client's story.

Brunelle could guess what she'd do.

"Nate Wilkins," she began. She glanced over at her client and smiled softly. "He's also presumed innocent. He's also charged with a crime. And he also has a story. But," she paused and looked back to the jurors, "his story doesn't include murdering Derrick Shanborn."

Brunelle frowned inside. Edwards was good. Direct and powerful. *Damn.*

Edwards clasped her hands loosely in front of her—an earnest gesture, practiced and designed to disarm. Brunelle had just used it himself. "Nate was born and raised right here in Seattle. In White Center. As most of you probably know, that can be a pretty tough neighborhood, and Nate couldn't wait to get out of there.

Especially with a drug-addicted mother and an abusive stepfather. As soon as he turned seventeen, he left home, quit school, and moved in with friends up in North Seattle. Maybe not the ideal start to his adult life, but we can't all have ideal lives, now can we?"

A dig at those school play moms and little league dads. The tech industry had made Seattle an interesting place. There was almost too much money flying around, and even more guilt. Brunelle had played to their pride; Edwards plucked at their shame.

"So instead of going to college or even trade school, Nate went to work. He needed to make money. He needed to eat, to have a place to sleep. He wasn't going to be another homeless youth in the University District, begging for handouts."

Edwards took a step to her right and opened her stance slightly toward her client. "Nate was a hard worker, and he always did well at the jobs he took. But there was a limit. You can only make so much as a grocery bagger or a short order cook. He never made enough to get out on his own, to get his own apartment, to start building a real life. He had to rely on friends. Friends like Elmer Hernandez."

Brunelle stopped taking notes and looked over at Hernandez, just like everyone else in the courtroom did. Hernandez was aware of the eyes on him, but just sat there dumbly. Jacobsen, ever aware of the jury, took the opportunity to pat him affectionately on the shoulder. Jurors loved that shit.

"Now, the prosecutor called Mr. Hernandez a drug dealer," Edwards went on. "Maybe he was, maybe he wasn't. I don't know. And neither did Nate. Nate just knew that Mr. Hernandez had a place he could stay when he needed it, and odd jobs to do if he didn't ask too many questions. And growing up the way Nate did, he'd learned long ago not to ask too many questions."

Brunelle wondered, almost absently, whether Edwards

planned on calling any witnesses to support this 'terrible home life' line she was feeding the jury. Probably not. But they were hearing it. And absent some evidence to the contrary, they'd believe it.

"Deliveries here. Pick-ups there. A couch to crash on and pad thai from up the street. It wasn't permanent, but it was real. It was just another chapter in his life. He knew it would end soon enough and he'd start another. But he had no idea that next chapter would begin here in this courtroom, his destiny in the hands of twelve people he can only pray will understand his situation."

Brunelle mentally rolled his eyes. Another appeal to the guilty, liberal Seattleites in the jury box. The use of 'pray' was nice too, he thought. It suggested Nate Wilkins was a religious person, a choir boy perhaps. He probably hadn't been to church since he was kicked out of Sunday school in third grade for smoking.

Edwards took a moment and cast her eyes down solemnly. It almost looked like she might cry. Brunelle knew better of course, but he was impressed by the showmanship. After another moment, she looked up again.

"Nate knew Derrick Shanborn," she offered with a nod. "You wouldn't say they were friends exactly. But they knew each other. Derrick would crash at Mr. Hernandez's house sometimes too. And Nate knew—just like everybody who knew Derrick knew—Derrick had a drug problem. A bad one. He was addicted to heroin. And you're going to hear during the course of this trial that heroin is one of the hardest drugs to kick. The withdrawals are so bad, there's an FDA-approved synthetic heroin replacement that lets addicts basically keep taking the drug during rehab so they don't die from withdrawal."

Brunelle wasn't sure that was exactly accurate, but it would resonate with the jurors. At least some of them probably binge-watched crime dramas on Netflix. Edwards didn't have to be accurate; she just needed to dovetail her story with the jurors' own knowledge base. Nothing rings truer than confirmation of our own biases.

"Derrick Shanborn was a heroin addict. Nate didn't know where he got his drugs, and he didn't want to know. He wasn't interested in starting down that path. All he had to do was look at Derrick—pale, scrawny, dirty, strung out—to know he wanted no part of that. So whenever Derrick showed up, Nate found an excuse to leave."

Edwards paused again. She wanted that last point to have a few moments to sink in. Pauses in oratory give the listener a chance to reflect on what they just heard, and they'll always reflect on whatever they heard last. A skilled orator will use pauses to emphasize the points she wants the listener to remember. Unfortunately for Brunelle, Edwards was a very skilled orator.

"The day Derrick died..." She stopped and corrected herself with a nod. "The day Derrick was *murdered* was no different. No different from all the other days Derrick came over high and looking to get higher. Derrick laid down on the mattress, and Nate stood up to leave. He had no idea what was about to happen, and even less idea why."

Brunelle looked up from his note taking. Was Edwards really going to claim Wilkins left before the shooting started? After he'd told the cops he was one of the shooters? They couldn't introduce that statement to the jury—that was the deal. With one exception: if Wilkins took the stand and testified differently. But if he didn't take the stand, how in the world was Edwards going to establish Wilkins left the house before the murder?

But Edwards sidestepped it masterfully. After suggesting, strongly, that her client had departed the house before Derrick Shanborn departed our mortal plane, she left it alone, allowing it to solidify from suggestion to assertion without actually asserting it. Instead, she did what every good entertainer does: she left them wanting more.

"Derrick Shanborn is dead. There's no doubt about that. Murdered. Shot three times in the chest, and dumped right off Lake City Way here in Seattle. Again, no doubt about that. But Nate Wilkins guilty of that murder?" She shook her head. "No, there's nothing but doubt about that. Nothing but reasonable doubt, and a whole lot of it. And at the end of this trial I'm going to stand before you once again and ask you to return a verdict of not guilty."

CHAPTER 34

Edwards turned and sat down again. She too put a hand on her client's shoulder. They learned that in defense attorney school. Really. All attorneys were required to take continuing legal education courses, and the ones for criminal defense attorneys stressed ways to communicate to the jury that your defendant wasn't really all that bad. Obviously avoiding speaking with or even touching your client might inadvertently communicate to the jury that he was exactly the reprobate psychopath the prosecution was making him out to be.

As Edwards sat down, Robyn Dunn stood up, even before the judge instructed the jurors, "Now please give your attention to Ms. Dunn who will deliver the opening statement on behalf of Ms. Keller."

Dunn didn't look over at Brunelle, but he couldn't help but watch her as she took her place before the jury. He noticed Carlisle looking at him looking at Robyn, but he ignored her. Dunn started.

"Samantha Keller didn't like Derrick Shanborn."

Another thing they taught at defense attorney school—and prosecutor school too for that matter—was to start opening statement with what was called an 'attention grabber' or 'hook.' Admitting that your murder defendant client didn't like the murder victim was something guaranteed to grab attention. An excuse to keep watching. Brunelle set his pen down. He was as bad as Lannigan. He didn't care.

"She didn't like Nate Wilkins," Dunn continued. "She didn't like Lindsey Fuller, Josh Rittenberger, or Amanda Ashford. She didn't like any of them. And she still doesn't."

Brunelle glanced quickly at the other defendants. *Awkward.*

Dunn pointed at Jacobsen's table. "And Elmer Hernandez? She doesn't like him either." Another attention grabber, but more predictable—at least for Brunelle. "She *loves* him."

Despite the tired 'I don't like it, I love it' cliché, Brunelle couldn't help but smile. *Nice introduction,* he had to admit to himself. He picked up his pen again to finally take notes as she continued.

"In fact, that was part of the reason she didn't like Derrick Shanborn, and why she still doesn't like any of the rest of the drug addicts, and losers, and hangers-on that Elmer let crash at their home all hours of the day and night."

She held up a finger to the jurors. "But," she said, "she didn't kill Derrick Shanborn. And she wasn't involved in any plan to do so."

Brunelle looked up again at his one-all-too-brief-a-time girlfriend. Brunelle had told a story to the jurors, like they said to do in trial lawyer school. Jacobsen had defiantly refused to tell a story. Edwards told a story, but she labeled it as such. Now that it was Dunn's turn, it would have been easy for her to follow either Jacobsen's or Edwards' lead and weave the meta-theory of story-telling into her narrative. But her instincts were better than that. It suggested she was already exceeding the very estimable Jessica

Edwards in her trial skills. Calling a story a story weakened its power. The difference between, 'I'm telling you she didn't shoot Derrick Shanborn' and simply 'She didn't shoot Derrick Shanborn' was only three words, but was immense in its persuasive effect.

"Elmer supported Samantha. He paid the bills, put food on the table, and kept a roof over their heads. She didn't ask how, but, in all honesty, she knew. Computer programmers and aeronautical engineers don't have drug addicts crashing on mattresses in their front rooms. Now, we could have a lengthy conversation about the wisdom and morality of criminalizing drugs, but that's not the question before you. And let me make that perfectly clear—"

She leaned in toward the jury and challenged them with a schoolmarm stare.

"This is not a case about drug dealing. This is a case about *murder*. Murder. And the case against my client, Samantha Keller, is separate and distinct from the cases against everyone else in this room, even her boyfriend, Elmer Hernandez.

"The question before you is not whether anyone in this room was involved in selling or using drugs. The question is not even whether anyone on this room was involved in the murder of Derrick Shanborn. The question regarding Ms. Keller, the only question I care about, is this: Will the state *prove*, beyond *any reasonable doubt*, that Ms. Keller *herself*, committed the crime of *murder*?

"And I will tell you right now: they won't do it. Because she didn't."

Again, Brunelle admired, *direct and forceful*. He sighed. He really missed her.

"So let me repeat," Dunn straightened up to her full height again, her cropped red hair framing her stern face perfectly. "Samantha Keller didn't like Derrick Shanborn, but she was in no way involved in his murder."

She relaxed her posture slightly and paced a few steps as she continued. "The night Derrick Shanborn died was like any other night at their home. Derrick came over to shoot up heroin. Lindsey Fuller and her boyfriend, Josh Rittenberger, came over to shoot up heroin. Amanda Ashford came over to look pretty and make Elmer feel young and attractive again. And Samantha Keller went to her bedroom to get away from all of those people. She didn't talk to Elmer beforehand, but she planned to talk to him afterward. Another argument about parasitic drug addicts and loose-moraled groupies. But that argument never happened."

Dunn turned and paced back to her starting place. "Samantha fell asleep watching T.V. She woke up to the sound of gunshots. When she went out front, she saw Derrick Shanborn on the floor, bleeding. She screamed. She cried. She yelled at Elmer. And when she was done screaming and crying and yelling, and the body was taken away, she cleaned the blood off the floor of her home and tried to go on with her life."

Dunn paused for a moment. "Now, Samantha's not an idiot. She knew the cops would be coming. And they did. But in the meantime, she never talked to Elmer about what happened, and she didn't talk to anyone else either. When the police arrested her, she was cooperative. She knows Derrick Shanborn was shot to death in her home while she slept, but she doesn't know who did it."

Dunn took a half step back and raised a thoughtful hand to her face. "I suppose I could spend time discussing whether the state even knows who really shot Derrick Shanborn, whether they'll be able to put on enough evidence to let you know who did it. But I'll leave that to Mr. Jacobsen, and Ms. Edwards, and Mr. Lannigan. Instead, I'll simply tell you: Samantha didn't murder Derrick Shanborn and she doesn't know who did. And at the end of this trial, the twelve of you will know beyond any doubt that Samantha Keller is innocent of murder.

"Thank you."

With that, Dunn returned to her seat next to an obviously grateful Samantha Keller. It was a good opening statement. Clean, forceful, and it began the all-important task of separating Keller from Hernandez in the jury's mind.

Brava, Ms. Dunn, Brunelle thought.

Then all eyes turned to Nick Lannigan.

CHAPTER 35

Judge Quinn looked to the jury and gave her well-practiced introduction one more time. "Ladies and gentleman, please give your attention to Mr. Lannigan who will deliver the opening statement on behalf of Ms. Fuller."

Lannigan stood up, but didn't step out from behind his table.

"Your Honor," he said politely, "at this time I'd like to reserve opening statement."

Quinn blinked at him. "Reserve?" she nearly stammered.

Brunelle looked over too. So did Carlisle, and the defense attorneys. And the defendants. Even the corrections officers guarding the exits.

A defense attorney could reserve opening statement until after the prosecution had presented all of its evidence and rested its case. Theoretically, it enabled a defendant to wait and see all of the evidence against him and then tailor his story to fit the evidence. But that was exactly what the tactic looked like, so defense attorneys almost never reserved opening. It made the defendant look guilty. Besides, the jury was dying to hear what the case was about, what your side of the story was. So you tell them. As soon as you can.

"Yes, Your Honor," Lannigan confirmed. He didn't say anything else.

Judge Quinn stared at him for several seconds, then dropped a sympathetic glance at Lindsey Fuller. Finally, she turned away and nodded to Brunelle and Carlisle.

"All right then," she said. "State, call your first witness."

Carlisle stood up. "The state calls Detective Larry Chen to the stand."

CHAPTER 36

Brunelle fetched Chen from the hallway bench where he'd been waiting while the lawyers made their opening pitches. It was pretty normal to start a homicide case with the lead detective. It helped frame all the rest of the witnesses' testimony, and there was a familiar whodunit vibe to a cop telling the story of finding a bullet-ridden body in a ditch.

As Chen made his way to the front of the courtroom to be sworn in by Judge Quinn, Brunelle returned to his seat. Carlisle was going to do the direct. They had jointly decided that. For one thing, Brunelle had given the opening, so it was important that Carlisle appear to the jury as an equal partner. For another, they were striving for an even split in number and importance of witnesses. Carlisle would do the medical examiner and Brunelle would do the ballistics expert. Brunelle would do Josh Rittenberger and Carlisle would do Amanda Ashford. And Carlisle would do Chen so Brunelle could do Jackson.

"Please state your name for the record," Carlisle started. Good place to start.

"Larry Chen," came the practiced response.

And they were off. Questions and answers to tell the story of finding Derrick Shanborn's body behind the gas station. Brunelle knew the story already. Hell, he was there. He tried not to let his mind wander, but Carlisle was doing fine and he didn't feel the need to monitor every exchange. He forced himself to focus again on the direct exam.

"...how long have you been investigating homicide cases?"

"I was assigned to the homicide division six years ago, but I assisted on several homicide investigations while I was still in the major crimes unit..."

Still on the preliminaries. Brunelle glanced around the courtroom at his opponents, counsel and client, to see if they were paying attention. Of course they were, at least the lawyers; they still had to cross-examine him.

Another look up to Carlisle and Chen.

"...what happened next?"

"I walked to the back of the gas station parking lot and...."

And looked into the ditch and saw a body, Brunelle knew the answer.

The problem with Chen's testimony was that it was necessary to establish the murder, but he couldn't point the finger at any of the defendants. Not personally. Anything a witness like Amanda Ashford or Josh Rittenberger told him was hearsay. He couldn't tell the jury what those people said—they had to come into court themselves and tell the jury themselves. The only exception was when a defendant said something. A cop could always testify to what a defendant told him. They were serious about that 'anything you say can and will be used against you' stuff.

But Hernandez and Fuller had refused to talk and Wilkins and Keller only did so after a promise not to use their statements against them. Chen wasn't even allowed to tell the jury that they had all initially lawyered up. They had a constitutional right to remain silent and so the exercise of that right couldn't be used against them. As a result, all Chen could really tell the jury was he found a body in a ditch, it had been shot several times, and it was later identified as Derrick Shanborn.

"Thank you, Detective." Carlisle picked up her notepad and binder and looked up to the judge. "No further questions, Your Honor.

She returned to her seat and Brunelle gave her a 'good job' nod, as if he'd been paying close attention the entire time. She returned the nod with a subtle smile then turned her gaze to the first of the attorneys to cross-examine her witness. Jacobsen.

Brunelle watched too. He was curious what tack each attorney would take. In his experience, shorter cross-examinations were often more effective. Rather than rehashing everything the witness had already said on direct examination, the skilled defense attorney focused on the one or two areas that most benefitted their client—then sat the hell down.

By all indications, Jacobsen was a good attorney, but he was also a showman. And he loved the sound of his own voice. He stood up and delivered his first question from behind counsel table, pointing an accusing finger at Chen.

"You're a detective, is that right?"

Chen thought for a moment, as if there might be a trick imbedded in the simplicity of the inquiry. Then he answered, "Yes, sir."

Jacobsen came out from behind his table then, but kept the finger wagging at his witness.

"You solve cases, right?"

Chen shrugged and looked to the jury. "I try to."

Good, thought Brunelle. *Self-effacing*. A few of the jurors smiled at the reply.

"It's like solving a puzzle, isn't it?"

Chen considered the comparison. "I suppose. Sometimes."

"Sure it is," Jacobsen encouraged. "You look for patterns, deduce what isn't there, and try to figure out what really happened. That's solving a puzzle."

Chen waited for a question, but there really wasn't one. "Okay," he replied.

"For example," Jacobsen raised his voice and gestured toward the ceiling, "a body dumped in a public place is a warning. Isn't that what you said?"

Chen nodded slowly. "It can be."

"Well, I think you said it was. That when you found Derrick Shanborn's bullet-ridden body in a ditch just yards from Lake City Way, you knew it was a warning. Isn't that what you said?"

"I'm not exactly sure what I said," Chen admitted, again turning to the jury. "But when I found Derrick's body in that ditch, I considered the possibility that it was meant as a warning because usually people try to hide bodies, not dump them right next to main thoroughfares."

Jacobsen jabbed his finger several times toward Chen. "Yes, yes, yes. Exactly. So," he grinned at the detective, "if I wanted to kill my business partner to steal his money and run away with his wife, I should dump the body next to Lake City Way, or Aurora Avenue, or Alaskan Way, and you'll think someone else did it to warn people not to become a lawyer, correct? You'll never even think to look at the classic motives and money and jealousy because I out-thought you and made you think it was a warning."

Chen thought for a moment before answering. He sat up a bit straighter in his chair. "Well, I think there would be more evidence than that. If the firm's accounts were drained into yours and you and the widow flew off to Hawaii for two weeks immediately after the funeral, I might find that suspicious as well."

Brunelle smiled. He never had to object with Chen.

Jacobsen, though, frowned. Still, he wasn't about to let the witness off the hook. "Well, yes. But now you're introducing facts into my hypothetical. Absent those additional facts, you will conclude from the mere fact that a body was dumped near a main road that the killing was likely a warning."

Chen again considered. "It would be one of my first hypotheses."

Jacobsen's frown deepened at the careful reply. His animated hand dropped to his side. "Fine. One of your first hypotheses. And that's because you look for patterns when you solve your puzzles, right? Because a dumped body equals a warning. Just like one plus one always equals two."

"Usually," Chen answered, again looking to the jury. Another smile or two greeted him.

"Usually?" Jacobsen practically gasped. "One plus one *usually* equals two? When does it not, sir?"

"When there's another explanation," Chen replied.

But Jacobsen shook his head. "No, no, no. Please answer my question. One plus one equals two, correct?"

"Usually," Chen repeated.

"No," Jacobsen shot back. "Always. One plus one always equals two, doesn't it detective?"

Chen hesitated, unsure what he was really being asked.

"Set aside metaphors and analogies, detective," Jacobsen instructed. "And remember, sir, you are under oath. One plus one always equals two, correct?"

Chen took several moments to answer. But setting aside metaphors and analogies and remembering he was under oath, there was only one answer. "Yes, sir."

Jacobsen spun triumphantly on his heel. "No further questions," he announced and returned to his seat.

Judge Quinn watched after Jacobsen, then gave the slightest shake of her head before saying, "Ms. Edwards. Any questions?"

Edwards stood up. "Yes, Your Honor." She took the time needed to come out from behind her table and take up a position at the bar in front of the witness.

"You were the lead detective on this case, correct?" she started.

"Yes, ma'am," Chen agreed.

"That means you decide what needs to be done and assign those tasks to others to complete, correct?"

Chen thought for a moment, then nodded. "Yes, ma'am, I think that's a fair description."

"And these other people—be they patrol officers, forensic scientists, or other detectives—they write up reports and send them to you for review, correct?"

Again a nod. "That's correct."

"So you yourself don't actually *do* anything, right?"

Chen frowned at that characterization. "I don't think that's exactly accurate," he defended.

"You didn't do the autopsy, correct?"

"No, ma'am," Chen admitted.

"And you didn't do the ballistics examination on the bullets, did you?"

Again, Chen admitted, "No, ma'am."

"Photographing the scene, collecting the evidence, transporting the body to the morgue, you didn't do any of that, correct?"

Chen frowned. "Correct."

"You get the call out, see the body, and come up with a theory of what happened," Edwards said. "Then you collect any evidence that fits that theory and ignore the rest, correct?"

Chen straightened up in his seat. "I wouldn't say that."

"Oh, really?" Edwards responded. "Well, I would." She looked up to the judge. "No further questions, Your Honor."

Robyn was next. The same order as the opening statements. The same order as the defendants would put on their own cases, and the same order as closing arguments. She straightened her suit and took her place at the bar.

"You've been a homicide detective for six years, is that correct, sir?"

Chen nodded. "Yes, ma'am."

"And you were a detective in major crimes for ten years before that, correct."

Another nod. "Correct."

"And before that, four years investigating property crimes and drugs and the like?"

"Yes, ma'am."

"And in all of those twenty years as a detective, or in your eight years before that as a patrol officer, did you ever have any occasion to investigate my client for anything? Anything at all?"

Chen thought for a moment, but only a moment. He knew the answer. "No, ma'am. Not until this case."

Robyn nodded herself. "No further questions."

She returned to her seat and it was Lannigan's turn.

He squeezed out from behind his table upon the judge's invitation to question the witness. He stood awkwardly in the middle of everything, not quite at the bar, but not back with his client either.

"Detective," he started, his voice a bit too loud, "did you see

Lindsey Fuller shoot Derrick Shanborn?"

Chen cocked his head at the question. Then he shook it. "No."

Lannigan turned to look up at the judge. "No more questions, Your Honor," he said, and returned to his seat.

The courtroom was filled by a moment of dumbfounded silence. Then Judge Quinn raised her eyebrows and looked down at Carlisle. "Any redirect examination?"

Carlisle shot to her feet. "Yes, Your Honor."

Brunelle wasn't sure it was a good idea to ask Chen any more questions, but he was Carlisle's witness. She made her way to the bar.

"One plus one equals two, right, detective?" she began.

Chen gave an uncertain half-smile. But he trusted the prosecutor in front of him. "Right."

"And one plus one plus one equals three, right?" she continued.

Chen nodded. "Right."

"And," Carlisle raised a professorial finger in the air, "a police informant, plus a drug dealer, plus three gunshots, plus a body dumped for all to see, equals these four defendants are guilty of murder, right?"

Before Chen could answer, Jacobsen sprang up. "Objection!" he shouted. "The question calls for an opinion on the ultimate issue."

Brunelle frowned. That wasn't necessarily a valid objection, he knew. Witnesses gave opinions all the time on the ultimate issue of a defendant's guilt or innocence—or at least came close. One DUI trial with a cop saying the *driver* was falling down *drunk* proved that. But Brunelle was glad for the objection. And he hoped Quinn sustained it.

The judge frowned. She also must have known it wasn't really a valid objection. But it was a dangerous question. "I'll sustain the objection as to the form of the question," she said.

Jacobsen hesitated, then sat down again. Carlisle grinned. She'd made her point. The question was what mattered, not the answer. "No further questions, Your Honor," and she returned to her seat as well.

Chen's examination was over. Brunelle breathed a sigh of relief. Carlisle's question had been dramatic, but the answer would have been catastrophic. Chen was a detective, but he wasn't there when Derrick Shanborn was murdered; he couldn't say for sure what happened that night. And he was honest.

He would have answered, 'I don't know.'

And that would have equaled reasonable doubt.

CHAPTER 37

The next witness was Det. Jackson. Brunelle was doing the direct exam. He decided to keep it focused solidly on little Derrick Shanborn.

"Please state your name for the record," he began.

"Timothy Jackson," the detective replied.

"And how are you employed, sir?"

"I'm a detective with the Seattle Police Department."

And they were off. A few more of the name, rank, and serial number questions, and the jury knew that Tim Jackson had been a narcotics detective with Seattle P.D. for going on a dozen years.

"Did you know Derrick Shanborn?" Brunelle asked.

Jackson took a moment before answering. He frowned and lowered his eyes. "Yes."

"How did you know him?"

Jackson nodded then looked up to the jury. "He was my son's best friend when they were kids. I was his little league coach for three years. He was a good kid."

The jury nodded sympathetically. They already knew the

story of course—Brunelle had told them—but there was something about hearing it from the horse's mouth. Or the detective's.

A few more questions about Derrick's time as the skinny awkward kid who got stuck playing right field but who made all the boys laugh after the game at the ice cream shop and Brunelle jumped the narrative forward.

"Did you have occasion to run into Derrick again as an adult?"

Jackson nodded and took another moment before telling the jury, "Yes. I arrested him for drug possession. Heroin. I didn't even know it was him at first."

Brunelle made a gesture toward the jury box. "Please tell the jury what happened that day."

Brunelle knew the story. He'd heard it that first day he'd met Jackson. So he was surprised that Jackson didn't seem to remember the story very well himself.

"Well, it was a while ago," he started, looking toward the ceiling. "I remember I was doing standard narcotics enforcement up in Lake City when I ran across him. He was obviously a heroin addict; one look at him told me that. I stopped him on the sidewalk. He was tripping so bad I figured he might have some on him. I patted him down and found a used syringe with some brown liquid in it, so I arrested him for possession of drug paraphernalia."

Brunelle cocked his head slightly. "Did he also have drugs on him? Or anything like baggies or a scale, like drug dealers use?"

Jackson thought for a moment. "Well, I didn't write a report, so I may be forgetting some of the details. But I remember arresting him and then I remember recognizing him."

Well, okay, thought Brunelle. *That was the important part.*

"What happened when you recognized him?"

"Well, at first, I was like, 'Derrick? Is that you?'" Jackson related. "I mean it had been ten years. He'd grown up. And he looked really bad from the drugs. All gaunt and yellowy. But in a way, that was kind of how I recognized him. He was always a skinny little kid. And thanks to the heroin, he was still skin and bones."

Brunelle took a moment to steal a peek at the jury. A few of them looked genuinely moved. It was working.

"So what did you do?" Brunelle continued.

Jackson shrugged and turned again to the jurors. "I really only had two choices. The first was to book him for drug possession. But I knew that wasn't going to solve anything. He'd do some time, but not much, and go right back on the street again, right back to the heroin. The other choice was to offer to help him. But he'd have to help me too."

A little ominous, Brunelle thought. He needed to soften it up a bit. "Help you how?"

"By helping me catch some of the dealers in the area," Jackson explained. "I can arrest drug users all day and it won't stop the problem. But if I can put some of the dealers away, well, it's a start."

"And did you have a particular dealer in mind that you wanted Derrick to help you get?" Brunelle asked.

But Jackson just shrugged again. "No, not really. I didn't know who his supplier was. I didn't care either. I just wanted to get him, whoever it was."

Brunelle frowned slightly. "Was Mr. Hernandez a specific target for Derrick?" Brunelle half-asked, half-reminded the detective.

But Jackson shook his head after a moment's thought. "No. I mean, I was aware of Mr. Hernandez's criminal activities, but I don't think I knew Derrick was buying his dope from Hernandez."

Before Brunelle could figure out how to follow up that unexpected answer with another question, Jacobsen stood up. Thank God.

"I'm afraid I must object at this point, Your Honor," Jacobsen said. "The witness should not be allowed to testify to just general alleged criminal activities by my client, or anyone else for that matter. This case involves the alleged murder of Derrick Shanborn. The witness's testimony was that he was unaware of any specific criminal activity involving my client and Mr. Shanborn. That should be the end of the inquiry."

The judge looked at Brunelle. "Any response, Mr. Brunelle?"

But Brunelle could only shrug. Hernandez was on trial for murder, not drug dealing. What mattered was the connection to Shanborn. Apparently, Jackson wasn't going to give him any more on that issue.

However, before the judge could rule on the objection, Jackson spoke up. "If I may, Your Honor, I think I remember now that Derrick mentioned Mr. Hernandez as one of the people he bought heroine from."

"Objection!" Jacobsen nearly spat. "The witness needs to wait for a question before saying anything."

Quinn didn't wait for any input from Brunelle. "Detective Jackson," she instructed, "you are only to respond to questions, not volunteer information. Is that understood?"

Jackson nodded contritely. "Yes, Your Honor."

Judge Quinn frowned as she considered the state of affairs. "I will sustain the objection," she began. "Anything not related to both Mr. Shanborn and Mr. Hernandez is irrelevant." She sighed slightly and threw an irritated glance at Jackson before turning back to Brunelle. "That being said, you may ask another question, Mr. Brunelle."

Brunelle nodded. He knew what question to ask. Everyone in the courtroom did. "Do you recall now, detective, whether Derrick mentioned buying drugs from Mr. Hernandez."

Jackson nodded. "Yes," he answered. "I remember now that Derrick said he bought drugs from several different dealers. One of those was Mr. Hernandez."

Okay. Brunelle exhaled. He'd gotten what he needed. But he was uncomfortable with how he'd gotten there. Ideally, they should go through the formal arrangement between Shanborn and Jackson, exactly what information he'd provided, what benefit he'd been provided or promised. But Brunelle wasn't confident he knew what Jackson would say. And there was that old lawyer's axiom: never ask a question you don't already know the answer to. He'd connected Shanborn and Hernandez. That was enough.

"No further questions," Brunelle announced, and quickly returned to his seat.

Carlisle gave him a quizzical glance, but he ignored it. Or rather he deflected it. "I'll explain later," he whispered.

Quinn took a moment to realize the direct exam was over. She looked at Jacobsen. "Cross examination, counsel?"

Jacobsen smiled as he stood up. "Why yes, Your Honor. Thank you."

He sidled up to the witness. "So there was no particular emphasis on my client, is that correct?"

Jackson thought for a moment. "Not really, no."

"Just turn in anyone who might be dealing drugs?"

"Well, not turn in, exactly," Jackson corrected. "Just give information."

"So you didn't direct Mr. Shanborn to inform on Mr. Hernandez specifically?" Jacobsen led the detective.

"No, sir. Just any information he had about anyone involved

in the trade."

"Did he provide other names?" Jacobsen inquired.

"I'm sure he did," Jackson replied. "In addition to Mr. Hernandez's name."

"Who were those other names?" A legitimate question, Brunelle had to agree.

But Jackson shrugged. "I don't remember."

"You don't remember?" Jacobsen repeated, exaggerating his astonishment. "Did you keep any notes?"

"No, sir," Jackson replied. "I don't keep notes about my interactions with informants."

Jacobsen raised an accusatory eyebrow. "So you're hiding things."

"No, sir," Jackson replied quickly. "I'm protecting people. Protect and serve, that's what I swore to do. It wouldn't be safe for them if I wrote everything down."

"Wouldn't it be safer if you knew who they were interacting with?" Jacobsen asked.

"No, sir," Jackson repeated. "Criminals have gotten very sophisticated. Our department gets hundreds of public record requests every year from prisoners in the Department of Corrections. They ask for our home addresses, our dependents' information, and the names of anyone who's cooperated with law enforcement. I don't want to risk that kind of information getting out to a man like Elmer Hernandez."

Brunelle suppressed a grin. He wasn't sure he agreed with Jackson's policy, but he admired how the detective brought it back around to Hernandez.

Jacobsen, not so much.

"A man like Mr. Hernandez," Jacobsen mimicked. "Did he ever send you any sort of public records request like that?"

"No, sir," Jackson answered. "He murdered Derrick Shanborn."

Yeah, Brunelle thought, *don't ask a question you don't know the answer to. And don't give the witness an opportunity to answer a question you didn't even ask.*

"You don't know that," Jacobsen challenged.

"I deduced it," Jackson countered.

"Even though you have absolutely no evidence that Mr. Shanborn ever actually informed on Mr. Hernandez?"

"I wouldn't say 'no evidence,'" Jackson answered. "I remember it."

Jacobsen sneered. "But nothing in writing?"

"No, sir," Jackson admitted.

The sneer deepened. "No further questions."

Brunelle imagined Jacobsen probably did have quite a few more questions planned, but he was smart enough to realize each such question would be an opportunity for Jackson to rogue again.

Edwards was next.

"You're a detective?" she started when she'd reached the bar.

"Yes, ma'am,' Jackson answered.

"But not a homicide detective?"

"No, ma'am. Narcotics."

"And you weren't the lead detective on this case, were you?" Edwards continued.

"No, ma'am."

"In fact," Edwards said, "you weren't even a formal assistant detective on this case because you're not a homicide detective, isn't that correct?"

Jackson thought for a moment, chewing his cheek and shifting his weight back and forth in thought. "I don't know if I'd say that exactly. I assisted with some interviews. Detective Chen came to me."

"Because you were working the victim, Derrick Shanborn?" Edwards clarified.

"Right."

"But you didn't attend the autopsy?"

"No, ma'am."

"Or send the ballistics off to the crime lab?"

"No, ma'am."

"Or process the crime scene?"

Again, "No, ma'am."

"You just knew the victim, and helped with some interviews?"

Jackson considered for a moment, then answered, "Yes, ma'am."

Edwards nodded. "Thank you, detective. No further questions."

Then Robyn stood up. She asked her questions from behind counsel table.

"Mr. Shanborn gave you information about Mr. Hernandez, is that your testimony?"

Yes, ma'am," Jackson nodded.

"But he never once said he bought drugs from Ms. Keller, did he?"

Brunelle's eyebrows knitted together. That was a dangerous question. What if Jackson said he had given information on Samantha Keller? Anything was possible with no notes and a convenient memory.

Jackson considered for several moments. Finally, he answered slowly, "No, ma'am. I don't believe he ever did."

Robyn smiled slightly. "I thought you'd say that. No further questions."

When she sat down, Quinn looked to Lannigan. "Any questions, counsel?"

Lannigan stood up and thanked the judge. Then he took that same awkward spot in the middle of everything.

"Detective Jackson," he asked, "did you see Lindsey Fuller shoot Derrick Shanborn?"

Jackson shook his head. "No, sir."

Lannigan nodded. "Thank you. No further questions." And he returned to his seat.

Judge Quinn then looked back to Brunelle. "Any redirect examination?"

No way in hell, Brunelle thought. And he knew Quinn knew he was thinking that. "No, thank you, Your Honor."

Quinn turned to Jackson and excused him, then she looked at the clock. As Jackson walked by the prosecution table, Brunelle kept his attention focused on the judge.

"We're approaching the end of the court day, ladies and gentlemen," Judge Quinn explained. "I'm going to adjourn us for the day. We will reconvene tomorrow morning for more witnesses from the state's case."

She then dismissed the jurors to the jury room and the lawyers from the courtroom. Brunelle was glad to have survived the day. They'd have a break of sorts as they next called a series of forensics and patrol officers who didn't have anything controversial to say. Direct would be simple; cross would be limited. And then they'd hit their real test. Derrick Shanborn wasn't the only snitch in the story.

CHAPTER 38

"The state calls Amanda Ashford to the stand," Carlisle announced to the courtroom several days later.

In the spirit of partnership, Brunelle and Carlisle had split up the two 'cooperating codefendants,' *i.e.*, snitches. Carlisle would do Ashford while Brunelle did Rittenberger. It wasn't a girl-girl, boy-boy thing. It was that Rittenberger had more information and was more likely to go sideways, and Brunelle was still the lead attorney. The greater among equals. Or at least the one who would be blamed if things went wrong.

Brunelle fetched Ashford from the hallway as Carlisle set up her materials on the bar. She was a transcripts and binders kind of lawyer. Brunelle was more of the 'I'm pretty sure I read that somewhere in one of the reports' kind of lawyer. But he had presence, so that made up for a lot.

They'd told Ashford to dress conservatively. Apparently that meant a tiny white sweater over her skin-tight tank top and miniskirt. Welles was with her—he was getting paid, after all—and the two of them walked in together, but Welles took a seat in the front row of the gallery while Ashford stepped forward to be sworn in by the judge. When Brunelle looked back momentarily at Welles to make sure everything was okay, Welles gave him a far too obvious wink and nod. Brunelle ignored it, save a grimace the jury couldn't see with his back to them. He faced forward again and gave his full attention to the Carlisle and Ashford show.

"Could you state your name for the record?" The usual beginning.

"Amanda Ashford," came the reply. Her voice wasn't quite too high, or too whispered, but it was close.

"How old are you?" Standard second question.

"Twenty."

Brunelle nodded. Yeah, that seemed about right. He stifled the urge to glare at Hernandez.

"And how are you employed?" And a typical third question. Let the jury get to know the witness a little bit.

"Uh," Ashford hesitated. "I'm not, really. Not exactly. I mean..." she looked around a bit nervously. "I waitress sometimes, but I get paid under the table."

Brunelle nodded to himself. Always good to start off testimony with an admission of tax fraud. But in a strange way, it actually bolstered her credibility. They needed the jury to believe she was the type of person who would be in a drug dealer's house when a snitch got murdered. Sunday school teachers and hospice nurses need not apply.

"Okay," Carlisle responded. "And do you know any of the people in the courtroom today?"

Ashford nodded. "Yes."

Carlisle was going to have to pull teeth, apparently. "And who would that be?"

Ashford listed the names, but didn't look at any of them. "Lindsey and Nate," she started. "And Sammy."

"Anyone else?" Carlisle prodded.

Brunelle hoped she didn't say, 'My lawyer, Mr. Welles.'

"And Bur—uh, Elmer," Ashford finished. "Mr. Hernandez."

Understandable that she wouldn't want to call him by his street name. And she never called him 'Elmer,' but knowing where this was going, the 'Mr. Hernandez' gave it a definite pedophile vibe.

"All right," Carlisle interrupted before she did identify her lawyer, or Brunelle, or anyone else from the court system she'd encountered since the murder. That wasn't what the jury was interested in. At least, it wasn't what the prosecution was interested in. But there needed to be some additional identification beyond just first names and 'Mr. Hernandez.'

"What's Lindsey's last name?" Carlisle asked. "And how do you know her?"

Ashford again didn't look over at the defense tables. "Lindsey Fuller. I knew her and her boyfriend, Josh. We would hang out sometimes, I guess. At… Mr. Hernandez's."

Carlisle nodded. "And Nate? What's his last name and how do you know him?"

"I think it's Williams, or something like that."

Close, Brunelle thought with a slight frown.

"Or Wilson. I don't know. But he was a friend of Mr. Hernandez."

"Okay," Carlisle didn't try to fix the name. One, it would have been impermissible leading of the witness to ask, 'Wilkins, right?' And two, it didn't matter if she knew his exact name, just so long as the jury believed she was talking about the same Nate that was sitting in the courtroom. "What about Sammy? Do you know her full name?"

This is where it would start to get interesting. You might not know the name of the friend of the guy you're sleeping with, but you're gonna know the name of his long-time girlfriend.

"Yeah," Ashford sneered. She didn't even try to hide her disdain. "Sammy Keller. Samantha, I guess."

"And how do you know her?"

Brunelle eagerly awaited the response. How do you describe the girlfriend of the man you're fucking? That probably wasn't covered in the typical etiquette handbook.

"She was…" Ashford started. Then she cast a disparaging glance at Samantha Keller. "She *used to be* Mr. Hernandez's girlfriend. She lived with him, I guess."

'Used to be.' *Nice*, Brunelle thought. Maybe even accurate since they were now housed in different parts of the King County Jail. But probably more like wishful thinking on Ashford's part.

Carlisle hesitated, either as she processed the previous answer, or prepared for the next question. "And what about Mr. Hernandez? How did you know him?"

Ashford looked at Hernandez too, and smiled slightly. Brunelle didn't turn to look, but he supposed Hernandez probably didn't smile back. Ashford's grin faded quickly and she looked down. "I dated him."

"Dated?" Carlisle repeated. "Could you expand on that a little?"

'Date' was one of those words that could mean a lot of different things. Any more, people could regularly meet for sex but deny they were in a dating relationship. On the other hand, prostitutes and johns called their 20-minute encounters 'dates.' So, it was a good idea to clarify exactly what she meant by that.

"You want me to explain it?" Ashford asked. She narrowed her eyes at Hernandez, then at Keller. Then back to Carlisle. "He gave me drugs and I gave him sex."

How romantic, Brunelle thought. Maybe Amanda could be the next Disney Princess. Crack-whore-ella.

Carlisle let the response sink in for a moment, then made sure the jury got it. "So he would supply you with drugs and in exchange you would perform sex acts on him?"

Ashford frowned. "I don't know about 'sex acts.'" She made air quotes with her hands. "But we would do it. And then he'd make sure I got what I needed."

"And what did you need?" Carlisle followed up quickly.

"Heroin, mostly." Ashford shrugged. "Maybe some crack, if that's what he had. But I'm clean now," she added hastily. "Eighteen days clean."

Brunelle tried to be happy for her, but eighteen days was barely enough time to detox. Staying sober was going to be a monumental struggle. And it also meant she'd been using basically the entire time since she and Welles first met with him.

Carlisle nodded for a few moments. Enough with the defendants. There was one more person who wasn't there, but still was. "And did you know Derrick Shanborn?"

Ashford raised an eyebrow, somehow making that gesture express indifference. "Derrick? Yeah, I guess I knew him too."

The only way she could have looked less interested was if she'd been allowed to chew gum on the stand. Loudly.

"And how did you know Derrick?'

Ashford shrugged. "He was just another drug addict who would crash at Burn—Mr. Hernandez's house."

"So you had seen him at Mr. Hernandez and Ms. Keller's residence?"

That provoked a glare from Ashford. "Mr. Hernandez paid the bills. All the bills. Ms. Keller," she pronounced the name in a mocking sing-song, "didn't pay for shit."

Like you? Brunelle thought. Luckily, Carlisle was doing the examination.

"Okay," Carlisle soothed. Authenticity was all good and well, but she didn't want to get bogged down in a heroin-funded love triangle. "Let's talk a little more about Derrick. How long did you know him?"

Ashford shrugged. "I don't know. A while, I guess. It's kinda hard to say. He was just another guy, ya know?"

Carlisle nodded. "Of course." As if she'd spent a lot of time in junkie flop houses. "But you knew him before his death?"

Ashford nodded. "Yeah."

"And were you there the night he died?"

Another nod, but still no real emotion. "Yeah." Then, after a moment. "I mean, I didn't see it or anything. But yeah, I was in the house."

"Can you tell us what happened that night?"

But before Ashford could begin her story, Jacobsen stood up. "Objection, Your Honor. The question calls for a narrative response."

Brunelle frowned. Because Jacobsen was right. Lawyers could tell all the stories they wanted, but not witnesses. Witnesses— the ones who really knew what happened—were limited to answering the questions put to them. Specific questions, not 'tell us what happened' questions.

"Objection sustained," Judge Quinn said. She didn't wait for a response from Carlisle. Carlisle didn't bother trying to offer one. "Rephrase your question, counselor."

Carlisle nodded and tried again. "Where were you when Derrick was killed?"

"I was upstairs," Ashford answered. "Waiting for ... Mr. Hernandez."

Brunelle shook his head ever so slightly. Even 'Burner' would have been better than 'waiting for Mr. Hernandez.' In part, because everyone knew what she waiting for.

"Did Mr. Hernandez ever come upstairs?"

Ashford shook her head. "No. I went downstairs."

"Why?"

"I heard gunshots."

Brunelle smiled slightly. That's all they really needed from her. Well, that, and what she saw when she came downstairs.

"And what did you see when you came downstairs?"

Ashford nodded again, but more to herself, and she closed her eyes as she remembered the scene.

"Everybody was in the kitchen. Derrick was on the floor, kind of up against the wall. There was a bunch of blood on the wall behind him and on the floor and stuff. Nate was just kind of standing over him. And Sammy was freaking out, screaming something. I don't know what."

Carlisle waited for more, but after a moment had to follow up with, "And what about Mr. Hernandez? Was he there?"

Ashford frowned slightly. "Yeah," she admitted quietly.

"And where was he?"

The frown deepened. "In the kitchen."

Yep, pulling teeth, Brunelle thought. But Carlisle seemed the competent dentist.

"Where was he in relation to Derrick?"

Ashford shrugged. "Standing over him, I guess. Kind of next to Nate."

"Did you see a gun?"

Ashford nodded, but didn't reply audibly.

"You have to say it out loud," Carlisle instructed her. "Did you see a gun?"

"Yes," Ashford snapped. "Yes, I saw a gun, okay?"

"And who was holding the gun?"

Ashford didn't answer.

"Who was holding the gun, Amanda?"

Ashford looked at Hernandez, then at Keller. Brunelle wondered if she'd decide to verbally plant the gun on her romantic rival. There were ways to impeach a witness with her previous statements, but that wasn't a road they wanted to have to go down. Luckily, Ashford looked back at Hernandez, and then down again. "Mr. Hernandez."

Carlisle knew enough to sit down. Difficult witnesses rarely got better with additional questions. She thanked the judge and sat down again. It was time to see how Amanda would hold up under cross examination. Jacobsen, per usual, was first. He stood up and approached Ashford.

"So, you're a prostitute?" he started.

Nice, Brunelle thought. *Wow.*

"No!" Ashford shouted back. She knew she couldn't say, 'Fuck you,' but her face said it for her.

Jacobsen didn't bother arguing the point. "You're a prostitute, and a drug addict, and a liar."

Technically it wasn't a question. But all it really lacked was a final, 'right?' so there was little point in objecting.

"I'm not lying," Ashford crossed her arms in protest. Apparently, she wasn't going to challenge the prostitute allegation after all. Or the drug addict one.

"You lied to Ms. Keller, didn't you?" Jacobsen pointed to Keller. "About your relationship with Mr. Hernandez?"

But Ashford shook her head vigorously, her arms still crossed. "Nope. Burner—Mr. Hernandez—did that. She knew why I was there. And I wasn't the first one, or the only one." She shot a glance at Keller. "I mean, how do you think she started with him?"

Robyn stood up. "Objection, Your Honor!" It was a personal attack, which brought Robyn to her feet, but those weren't necessarily objectionable. She'd need to give a reason. "Lack of personal knowledge."

Brunelle's eyebrows shot up. *Lack of personal knowledge?* So basically, it was true, but Ashford wasn't around to know it firsthand. Weak. And surprising.

Judge Quinn frowned. But she sustained the objection. "Ask another question. Mr. Jacobsen."

"Gladly," Jacobsen replied with a grin. "So you traded yourself to Mr. Hernandez for drugs, correct?"

Back to the prostitute angle. Although, that didn't exactly make Hernandez look like a saint either.

Ashford hesitated, not wanting to answer yes to that particular question. But before she could, Jacobsen interjected anyway.

"Just like you sold yourself to Mr. Brunelle to get a plea bargain, isn't that correct?"

Oh, so she's a prostitute to me, Brunelle realized. But he resisted the urge to object to that personal attack. It wasn't like it didn't have some truth to it. Plus, he knew Welles was dying in the first row, unable to object because he wasn't the lawyer to any party, but desperately wanting to defend his client's honor. Or at least hear the sound of his own voice.

"I don't know," Ashford answered. "I told him what I knew and they never charged me with anything. So yeah, whatever."

Jacobsen turned around and pointed at Welles, conspicuous in his tailored suit and silk tie. "That's your lawyer, Mr. Welles, correct? And he worked out a deal with Mr. Brunelle to keep you from getting charged like everyone else in this room, didn't he?"

"That's my lawyer," Ashford admitted with a shrug. "But I don't know exactly what the deal was. I just know I told him what I just told you, and they didn't charge me. So yeah."

"So yeah," Jacobsen mimicked. Then, "No further questions."

He retook his seat and Edwards stood up. "Just to be clear," she said, "you got your drugs from Mr. Hernandez, not my client, Mr. Wilkins, correct?"

"Correct," Ashford agreed with a nod.

"And you were having sex with Mr. Hernandez, not Mr. Wilkins, right?"

Another nod. "Right."

"And when you came down the stairs and saw Derrick Shanborn lying on the floor bleeding, the gun was in Mr. Hernandez's hand, not Mr. Wilkins', right?"

A final nod. "Right."

"No further questions."

Brunelle was impressed. It was absolutely surgical. The best type of cross. He wondered if Robyn would follow suit.

Dunn approached Ashford. "Let's talk a little bit about your relationship with Mr. Hernandez."

Nope. Brunelle sighed. *Not surgical.*

"Okay," Ashford replied cautiously.

"You called him 'Burner,' right? That was his nickname?"

"Everybody called him Burner," Ashford answered. "Not just me."

"And my client, Sammy." Dunn pointed back at Keller. "Everyone called her 'Burner's old lady,' right?"

Ashford shrugged. "I guess. I mean, that's what she was. I don't know if people called her that. I called her Sammy."

"And being Burner's old lady is a pretty sweet gig, right?"

Dunn asked.

Ashford frowned. "I guess so. I don't know."

"Lots of perks, right?" Dunn pressed. "Free rent, free drugs, social importance. All that, right?"

"I don't know," Ashford said. "I guess I never really thought about it."

"Sure you did," Dunn countered. "Because you were doing the same thing, weren't you? Drugs, a place to crash, but it wasn't official. You weren't important, were you? You were just another girl he was using for sex, weren't you?"

"I'm important," Ashford insisted. "I didn't need to be his old lady to be important."

"Maybe not in your eyes," Dunn offered, "but everyone else saw you for what you were. That must have made you angry."

Ashford shook her head. "No. I don't care what other people think of me."

"Really?" Dunn replied. "Well, that would make you the first person in the history of the world. You wanted to be Burner's old lady, didn't you?"

"No," Ashford insisted. "It was just how things ended up. It wasn't serious."

"And you still want to be his old lady, don't you?" Dunn accused. "You want Sammy to go down for murder so you and Burner can be together, don't you?"

"I don't care what happens to Sammy," Ashford spat back. "She didn't even do anything to Derrick. She was just standing there, screaming 'What did you do?' at Burner."

"You want this jury to believe that you don't want Sammy Keller convicted of murder?" Dunn scoffed. "That she didn't have anything to do with the murder of Derrick Shanborn?"

"Yes!" Ashford answered. "I don't want to convict her of

murder. She didn't do anything!"

Dunn stopped. Then she smiled. "No further questions, Your Honor." And then she sat down.

Damn. Brunelle looked after her. Everyone did. Even the judge, who took a moment before she managed to say, "Mr. Lannigan. Any cross examination?"

Lannigan stood up. By then, everyone knew the drill. Lannigan stood a few feet in front of his table. "Ms. Ashford," he said, "did you see Lindsey Fuller shoot Derrick Shanborn?"

Ashford was still upset from her exchange with Dunn. Her cheeks were stained red and her breath was fast. But she managed to focus enough to answer, "No."

So ended the examination of Snitch #1;

But Snitch #2 was still to be done.

CHAPTER 39

"Joshua Rittenberger."

Rittenberger identified himself from the witness stand in response to Brunelle's first question. They'd had to make special arrangements for Rittenberger's testimony. Unlike Amanda Ashford, who'd avoided ever being charged at all, Rittenberger started out as another murder defendant, held pending bail in the King County Jail. And he was still charged with murder; he would only get his charges reduced after he testified. So he was still in the King County Jail.

But the case law was clear that jurors couldn't see a witness in jail garb. Criminal defendants were always dressed out for court in street clothes so the jurors wouldn't know that the judge thought they were guilty enough and dangerous enough to detain pending the outcome of the trial. That would prejudice the jury against the defendant. The same rationale applied to witnesses. And not only did Rittenberger have to be dressed in street clothes, the jurors couldn't see him being marched into the courtroom in handcuffs by two corrections officers. That would probably give it away too.

So Rittenberger had been brought into court—in handcuffs

and by two corrections officers, to be sure—but after a break in the proceedings and with all of the jurors safely behind the closed door of the jury room. When court was reconvened, the jurors stepped out to see a nice young man already on the witness stand, two extra corrections officers hanging out in the back of the courtroom, and a professionally dressed woman, Barbara Rainaldi, sitting in the first row of the gallery. The judge then swore Rittenberger in and Brunelle began his examination.

"Mr. Rittenberger, did you know Derrick Shanborn?"

When Ashford had identified her relationships, they had started with the defendants and ended with Shanborn. Mainly because they wanted to get her relationship with Hernandez—and Keller—out first. With Rittenberger, they reversed it because there was no awkward, sex-for-drugs love triangle going on. At least, not as far as Brunelle knew. Or cared to know.

It was also to mix things up for the jury a bit. It could get boring hearing the same questions put to witness after witness. And it was also to bring Shanborn back to the forefront. Murder victims could get forgotten in the midst of a trial about the conduct of the police and the future of the defendants.

Brunelle wanted the jurors to think about Shanborn when they listened to Rittenberger. Because Rittenberger was both the most important and the most troubling witness. He was the only eyewitness to the shooting, but his story was short on details and long on heroin.

And it wasn't as if they would be able to hide Rittenberger's heroin use from the jury. The ability of a witness to perceive and remember went to the heart of the witness's credibility. If Brunelle didn't bring it out on direct exam, the defense attorney sure as hell would on cross. So he had to 'draw the sting' and admit the weaknesses in his case. Then hope the jury would believe

Rittenberger anyway.

"Yes," Rittenberger answered. "I knew Derrick."

"How did you know Derrick?" Brunelle followed up.

Rittenberger hesitated, then admitted, "We used drugs together."

Brunelle himself didn't hesitate. He had written out every question and answer he planned to pull from Rittenberger. Shooting from the hip was possible with law enforcement witnesses, maybe even innocent bystanders, but not with druggie codefendants. When he was done checking all the boxes, he would sit down again. "What drugs?"

"Uh, well, heroin mostly," Rittenberger said. "Sometimes something else, if there wasn't enough heroin, or just to try something different. But yeah, mostly heroin."

"Are you using heroin now?"

Rittenberger made a confused face. Brunelle knew he'd been locked up since the murder. But wasn't he supposed to not say that?

"It's a yes-or-no question," Brunelle pointed out.

"No."

"Were you using heroin the night Derrick was murdered?"

Rittenberger's expression relaxed. "Yeah. Definitely."

He almost sounded relieved at the thought of it. No doubt he'd be back on the junk as soon as he got out again.

"Where were you that night?"

"At Burner's house."

So, no trouble using the nickname. Not like it mattered now. "Who's Burner?"

Rittenberger pointed at Hernandez. "That's Burner. His last name is Hernandez, but everybody calls him Burner. I think his first name is Alman or something."

Great. Real close friends. How did grown people end up sleeping in the homes of people whose names they didn't even know?

"Why were you at Mr. Hernandez's house?" Brunelle kept his thoughts to himself and his examination on track.

"Uh, well, I was still using back then," Rittenberger said, "and so I was just gonna crash out there after I, uh, after I took a dose."

"And did you take a dose?" Brunelle asked, using Rittenberger's own euphemism. As if it were medicine.

"Uh, yeah."

"Was Mr. Hernandez there when you took the heroin?"

Rittenberger nodded. "Well, yeah. I mean, I bought it from him."

Brunelle nodded. *Makes sense.*

Before returning to Shanborn, Brunelle moved through the cast of characters again. "So, you know Mr. Hernandez. Do you also know Samantha Keller?"

"Yeah, of course," was the answer.

"Who is she?"

"She's Burner's girlfriend. Like, his main, long-time, real girlfriend."

Which led to: "Do you know Amanda Ashford?"

"Uh, yeah," Rittenberger answered. "She was like a side, short-term, not-real girlfriend."

As tempting as it might have been to linger on that sordid detail again, Brunelle pressed on. "Do you know Nate Wilkins?"

Rittenberger nodded. "Yeah. He's like Burner's enforcer. If I didn't pay on time or something, Nate was the one who came to talk to me."

Brunelle raised an eyebrow. He knew everyone in the courtroom wanted to know if the enforcement ever went beyond talking. Brunelle sure did. Which meant the jurors did too. Edwards might object, but he couldn't not ask a question the jurors wanted to know the answer to. "Just talk?"

Edwards didn't say a word and Rittenberger answered the question. "Oh, yeah. Just talk. I always paid up. I mean, I usually had to pay up front anyway. But once or twice, they let me pay them a couple days later. But I always did."

Brunelle frowned. That little detour wasn't especially helpful. If anything, it made them seem charitable. On the other hand, Rittenberger said 'they' so that brought Wilkins tighter into Hernandez's operation. Back to the script.

"And do you know Lindsey Fuller?"

Rittenberger frowned and looked over at her. "Yeah."

"How do you know her?"

"She's my girlfriend." Rittenberger looked away again. "Or she was, anyway."

Brunelle definitely wasn't going off script again with that Pandora's box.

"Let's get back to the night Derrick Shanborn was shot," he said. "Was Derrick already at Mr. Hernandez's house when you arrived?"

Rittenberger's face twisted up in attempted memory. "I'm not really sure actually. He might have been. Or he might have come right after I got there. I don't really remember. Sorry."

Brunelle shrugged off the apology. "At some point, though, were you, Derrick, and Mr. Hernandez all in the house at the same time?"

"Yes." Rittenberger was sure of at least that much.

"And was it during that time that Derrick Shanborn was murdered?"

Rittenberger paused long enough to digest the question, then nodded and answered, "Yes."

"Did you see Derrick get shot?"

Brunelle had to ask it. Even though he knew what the answer would be, or roughly what it would be, he still had to ask it. Again, the jury wanted to know.

"I think so," Rittenberger tried. "I remember him being there, and remember him not being shot yet, and then I remember him being shot. So, yeah."

Brunelle frowned a bit at the answer, but it was about what he'd expected.

"Were you high at the time?" Again, it had to be asked. Better by him, than by Jacobsen. And Edwards. And Dunn and Lannigan. Well, not Lannigan. He only had one question he asked.

"Oh, yeah," Rittenberger practically laughed the answer.

"But you remember at least some of what happened when Derrick was shot?"

Rittenberger got serious again. "Yes. Definitely."

"What do you remember?"

Brunelle half-expected another 'calls for narrative' objection from Jacobsen, but it never came. Rittenberger's opiate-soaked memory probably made a true narrative impossible anyway.

"Well, okay," Rittenberger started, "I had just shot up and was laid out on one of the mattresses in the front room."

Great start, Brunelle thought to himself.

"And then I heard some kind of argument, or yelling, or something. So I looked over and saw Derrick and Burner in the kitchen."

"Could you tell what they were arguing about?" Brunelle interjected.

Rittenberger frowned. "No, not really. I was pretty high. I mean I'd just shot up—I think. Unless I blacked out and woke up because of the yelling." He frowned deeper, trying to remember. "I don't know. I mean, I was already kinda high when I got there. I was just trying to get higher."

Even better, Brunelle thought.

"But you're sure they were arguing?" he tried.

"Well, maybe it was more like yelling. Like, Burner was yelling at Derrick. I don't think Derrick was really yelling back, you know? He was more like apologizing and stepping back."

Okay, that was good.

"Did you ever hear the word 'snitch'?" Brunelle asked.

Rittenberger nodded. "Yeah, I think I did."

"Who said it?"

Rittenberger thought for a moment. "I think maybe both of them did. Or maybe Nate. I'm not sure. It was a dude, though, I remember that much."

"Could it have been Derrick?" Brunelle probed.

Rittenberger paused as he tried to remember. "Yeah. Maybe him too. Like, 'I would never snitch on you, Burner. I know what would happen.' Or something like that."

Brunelle stopped. There were times to go off script. "And what would happen to someone who snitched on Burner?"

"Exactly what did happen, man," Rittenberger answered with wide eyes. "Burner would kill them."

"Did you see Mr. Hernandez shoot Derrick Shanborn?" The million-dollar question.

"Uh, Well, I saw Derrick get shot," Rittenberger gave a two-bit answer, "but I can't say who shot him exactly. I was looking at him. And I was pretty high. I had tunnel vision, you know. So, uh, yeah. I saw him get shot, but I didn't see who pulled the trigger."

"Well, right before the shots," Brunelle tried to bolster the account a bit, "where was Mr. Hernandez?"

"He was standing over Derrick, yelling at him."

"For being a snitch?"

"Right."

"And where was Mr. Wilkins?" Brunelle continued. "Right before the shots."

"Standing next to Burner."

"Where was Ms. Keller?"

"She was in the house, I think," Rittenberger said. "But I didn't see her in the kitchen."

"And what about Ms. Fuller? Was she in the kitchen too?"

That was supposed to be the last question. Get all the defendants in the room, or at least the house, then stop asking the junkie questions. But the junkie had other plans.

"Uh, no," Rittenberger answered. "I don't think she was there. She wasn't there."

Brunelle stared at Rittenberger for several seconds. They had made sure to ask him that during his initial interview. And he had been clear—well, as clear as he could manage—that Fuller was present when Hernandez shot Shanborn. It was recorded. Brunelle could go back to counsel table and dig the transcript out from his briefcase. He could show Rittenberger the line where he'd previously told the cops that Fuller was present. Confront him with the inconsistency. Make him admit that either he didn't really remember after all, or he was lying.

But neither of those seemed like a good option. Fuller was the least culpable, after Rittenberger anyway. Should he really undercut the credibility of his one eyewitness to make sure Fuller was convicted? It wasn't like Lannigan was going to ask him any questions about it anyway. Even if he wanted to go beyond his one and only question, there was no reason to challenge a witness who said your client wasn't there.

Brunelle was actually surprised how well Rittenberger had

done. But he looked tired. The jury would likely understand why a man would omit his girlfriend. He could readdress it in closing, maybe. But he wasn't going to finish his direct exam doing a boring transcript-dance ('Please turn to page forty-seven and read lines sixteen through nineteen to yourself...') with an unpredictable witness and no promise of what might happen.

He looked up to Judge Quinn. "No further questions, Your Honor. Thank you."

When Brunelle returned to his seat, Carlisle tugged at his arm. "He said she was there when he talked to us before," she whispered.

"I know," Brunelle whispered back. Then, the worst thing a man can say to a woman, "Trust me."

Jacobsen stood and strode confidently to the bar.

"Hello, Mr. Rittenberger," he started.

Rittenberger hesitated. He really did look tired. And scared. Hard to blame him. "Hello," he offered weakly.

"You're a drug addict," Jacobsen started.

"I was," Rittenberger claimed, unconvincingly.

"You're a murder defendant," Jacobsen continued.

"I was," Rittenberger said again.

Jacobsen paused. "You still are, aren't you? You don't get your deal until after you testify, correct? Until then, you're still awaiting trial for the murder of Derrick Shanborn."

For the first time, Rittenberger looked past his inquisitor to the front row. Rainaldi gave a short nod. Then Rittenberger looked back up to Jacobsen. "Yes, I guess that's right."

"So, you're a drug addict," Jacobsen repeated. "And a murder defendant. And you're a liar."

Rittenberger shook his head. "No. I'm not a liar."

Jacobsen smiled and crossed his arms. Brunelle noticed he

hadn't brought any paper up with him. Unscripted, but clearly not unprepared.

"Didn't you tell the police," Jacobsen asked, "when they first talked to you, that you didn't remember anything?"

Rittenberger thought for a moment. "Uh, yeah. I think so."

"And then you were charged with murder anyway," Jacobsen said, "and you suddenly remembered everything. Is that right?"

"Not exactly," Rittenberger answered.

"You told the police you didn't remember anything, but you told the prosecutor you remembered everything," Jacobsen recapped. "So either you lied to the police or you lied to the prosecutor. Which is it?"

"It's not like that," Rittenberger said. "I was still really strung out when I first talked to the cops."

"And after you got charged," Jacobsen pressed, "you told Mr. Brunelle what he wanted to hear and you got a deal."

"I just told the truth, man," Rittenberger insisted.

"The truth?" Jacobsen asked.

"Yeah."

"You want to tell the truth?" Jacobsen followed up.

"Yeah," Rittenberger said.

"Okay, let's see if you can tell the truth." Jacobsen leaned forward. "Was Lindsey Fuller there when Derrick got shot?"

All eyes shot over to Fuller and Lannigan. But no objection from Lannigan. It probably wouldn't have been sustained, but still. Do *something*.

The eyes returned to Rittenberger. "I, uh, I..." he stammered.

"So you're a liar?" Jacobsen repeated.

"No!"

"Was Lindsey Fuller there?!" Jacobsen demanded.

Brunelle could only watch and wait. It almost didn't matter what the answer was. The damage was done. Well, most of it.

Finally, Rittenberger hung his head. "Yes."

"She was there?" Jacobsen confirmed.

"Yes, she was there."

"Which," Jacobsen raised both his voice and a finger to the ceiling, "proves you are in fact a liar. Not ten minutes ago you told this jury she wasn't there. That was a lie."

Rittenberger didn't look up. "I was just trying to protect her. She didn't have anything to do with this."

"In fact, it was more than a lie, wasn't it?" Jacobsen ignored Rittenberger's assertion as to Fuller's culpability. "You were under oath. So it was perjury. Your testimony is perjury."

Rittenberger shrugged. "I guess so."

"No further questions," Jacobsen declared, with a surprising amount of disgust for a person defending a murderer.

Edwards stood up next. She picked up the club Jacobsen had been beating Rittenberger with.

"You lied about Lindsey Fuller not being there, is that correct?"

Rittenberger nodded. "Yes."

"So how do we know you're not also lying about Nate Wilkins being there?"

"I'm not," he insisted

"Maybe," Edwards allowed. "But now that you've admitted to lying under oath, how can we know if you're telling the truth about anything?"

"I am."

"But how do we *know*?"

Rittenberger stared at the floor for several seconds. Then he admitted, "I guess you don't."

And Edwards was finished.

Dunn rose to take her place. "You didn't see Sammy in the kitchen that night when Derrick was shot, did you?"

Rittenberger was clearly still rattled, but he responded to the friendliness in Dunn's voice. "No," he agreed. "I mean, she usually was around, you know? She lived there, right? But I don't remember seeing her. She didn't like it when me, or Derrick, or anybody like that would come over and crash, so she would usually leave and go someplace else."

Dunn nodded. "No further questions."

And then Lannigan offered his single question for the witness: "Did you see Lindsey Fuller shoot Derrick Shanborn?"

Rittenberger shook his head and looked at his ex-girlfriend, who looked away. "No, man. She didn't shoot Derrick. She was there, but she didn't shoot nobody."

Lannigan sat down again and Judge Quinn looked to Brunelle. "Any redirect examination?"

As entertaining as it might have been to try to rehabilitate someone who'd just admitted to lying on the stand, he decided to pass. "No, Your Honor. Thank you."

Rittenberger was finished, but he couldn't get up and leave the courtroom because of that whole 'still being held on murder charges' thing. So the judge called a recess and the jurors filed back into the jury room. When they were done, the judge left the bench and court was adjourned for fifteen minutes so the guards could take Rittenberger back to his jail cell.

Rainaldi checked in with Rittenberger before the guards took him away through the secure side entrance. Then she checked in with Brunelle and Carlisle.

"He did good enough, right?" she asked. "That bit with

Lindsey wasn't great and I'll talk to him about it, but he gave you Hernandez. He said Hernandez shot Derrick."

Brunelle frowned, but it was Carlisle who responded. "He didn't quite say that. He said he didn't see but it was probably Hernandez. And he admitted to lying on the stand, so I don't know. The deal might be off."

Rainaldi was about to protest, but Brunelle spoke up first. "The deal was to testify truthfully. He didn't do that. At least at first. But I think the jury may forgive him trying to protect his girlfriend."

"Exactly," Rainaldi responded. She looked at Carlisle. "Exactly."

"Why don't we wait to see what the jury says?" Brunelle suggested. "If these defendants get convicted, even if your guy didn't really live up to his end of the bargain, we're probably not going to want to try the entire case a second time just to get him."

"Exactly," Rainaldi said a third time. "Okay, I'll talk to him. And if you need him in rebuttal or something, he'll be ready. I'll make sure of that. He'll be ready."

Rainaldi excused herself and left Brunelle and Carlisle to consider.

"That wasn't great," Carlisle started.

"Yeah, but it could have been worse," Brunelle opined. "Did you believe him when he admitted to lying to protect Lindsey?"

Carlisle thought for a moment. "Yeah, I guess so."

"So did I," Brunelle said. "And I bet the jury did too."

"You mean, you hope they did," Carlisle said.

Brunelle smiled weakly. "That too."

CHAPTER 40

Start strong. Finish strong.

Those were two of the (probably too many) rules of trial practice. But when the witnesses with the most information also have the least credibility, strong becomes more art than science. They didn't want to end on Rittenberger; they knew he might struggle, although admitting to perjury was worse than they'd expected. So Brunelle and Carlisle were both glad to wrap up their case with the medical examiner.

In truth, Dr. Albrecht's testimony was perfunctory. No one was contesting that Derrick Shanborn died from three gunshot wounds to the torso. But it never hurt to remind the jury how the victim died. A grisly description of blood filling a chest cavity to collapse a lung could help the jury feel the level of fear and indignation they would need to find someone guilty of murder. And it was better to finish with images of Shanborn's bullet-ridden corpse on the autopsy table than with Rittenberger's perjury-ridden testimony on the witness stand.

Brunelle glanced around the courtroom as Carlisle approached the end of her direct examination. The jurors seemed politely interested. Contested or not, the cause of someone's death was always interesting.

The attorneys were visibly less attentive. It had been a long trial already and keeping up appearances of interest became harder with each day. They also knew cause of death wasn't the issue in the case. They each had other issues to focus on, so they were all eyes-down, taking half-hearted notes. Except Lannigan. He was enthralled. Brunelle wondered if he'd ever heard a medical examiner testify before.

"And so," Carlisle wrapped up, "at the conclusion of your autopsy, were you able to determine a cause of death?"

"Yes," answered Dr. Albrecht. He sat erect in his chair, his deep set eyes fixed on his questioner.

"And what was the cause of death, doctor?"

"The cause of death," Albrecht turned to the jurors. "was homicide."

Carlisle nodded and grabbed up her binder. "Thank you, doctor. No further questions."

Quinn invited Jacobsen to cross examine. He paused before standing, then stepped forward. "The cause of death was homicide, correct?"

"Correct," Albrect confirmed.

"And you can tell that because someone else shot him, right? He didn't shoot himself three times in the chest, right?"

"Right," Albrecht answered. "A single gunshot to the head or chest might be suicide, but the number and trajectory of shots indicate another person caused the injuries which led to his death."

"But an autopsy can't show you *who* shot him, can it?"

Albrecht nodded. "Correct." Again he turned to the jurors. "I can tell you that he was shot, but I can't tell you by whom."

"Thank you, doctor," Jacobsen said and he returned to his

seat.

Edwards stood up. "You also can't say why he was shot, can you doctor?"

Albrecht smiled slightly at the question. "No, of course not."

"Thank you. No further questions."

When she sat down, Judge Quinn turned to Dunn. "Any questions, counsel."

But Dunn demurred. "No questions, Your Honor."

That left Lannigan. "Any questions?" Quinn asked.

"Yes, Your Honor," he replied.

Of course. The same question he'd posed to every single witness. The state's case would end with the assistant medical examiner confirming he also hadn't seen Lindsey Fuller shoot Derrick Shanborn.

"Doctor," Lannigan said from right up at the bar where the other attorneys always stood, "how can you do that job? Isn't it gross and depressing?"

Brunelle dropped his pen.

But Albrecht didn't miss a beat. "Oh no. I think it's absolutely fascinating."

Lannigan smiled. "Wow. Really? That's great. I mean, someone has to do it, right?" Then he looked up to Judge Quinn, who looked as shocked as Brunelle felt. "No further questions, Your Honor."

Quinn took a moment to watch Lannigan retake his seat. Then she remembered to ask, "Any redirect, Ms. Carlisle?"

"No, Your Honor," Carlisle responded. "The state rests."

Brunelle always felt a huge sense of relief when the state rested its case. Like wet snow falling off a tree branch. Quinn started to instruct the jurors about coming back tomorrow to start the defense case, and keeping an open mind because they haven't heard all the evidence yet, and to avoid discussing the case even among each other until all the evidence had been submitted, but Brunelle wasn't really listening. It wasn't directed at him and he'd heard it all before more times than he could count.

As the courtroom packed itself up for the day, Brunelle was thinking about going home, pouring himself a glass of whiskey, and lying awake all night worrying they'd forgotten to elicit that one piece of evidence the jury would need to hold the killers responsible. That is, his usual post 'the state rests' routine.

But Carlisle put a hand on his shoulder. "Good job, partner," she congratulated him. "Shall we grab a drink?"

CHAPTER 41

Carlisle took them to a new bar that had just opened up on Broadway. On Capitol Hill. Where Robyn lived. Again.

Apparently, Carlisle lived there too. Small world.

"My first apartment was just around the corner from here," she was saying as they sat at the bar waiting for their drinks. The after-work rush hadn't quite started, so they'd had their choice of seats at the bar. Soon enough, the place would be full with Seattleites washing away their workdays, but just then it was at that pleasant equilibrium between too empty and too full. "Of course, they're condos now. They completely renovated them. Wood floors, state of the art appliances, rooftop garden. No way I could afford it now on my government salary."

Brunelle nodded politely and offered an affirmative grunt. He was distracted by the thought that Robyn could walk in any moment. And even more distracted by his distraction. Why should it matter? He wasn't dating Robyn any more. And he wasn't dating Carlisle. Not yet anyway.

Their drinks arrived. Brunelle got a pour of whiskey. Carlisle got a classic daiquiri. She raised her glass. "To the successful completion of our case-in-chief. May the defense cases suck ass."

Brunelle almost spit out the whiskey he'd started sipping. "Wow. Glad you didn't talk like that during the trial."

Carlisle laughed. "Just wait. I'm giving closing, remember?"

Brunelle smiled. "I can hardly wait." He finished that sip. "But don't get ahead of yourself. We're not quite there yet. We should figure out who's going to cross which defendants if they choose to testify."

"Do you think any of them will?" Carlisle asked. "I kinda like civil cases where you can call the defendant and make him testify. How do you prepare to cross examine someone if you don't know until the last second whether they're even going to testify? They should have to tell us before the trial starts or something."

Brunelle shrugged. "That might undercut that whole presumed innocent, right to remain silent, thing."

"Why? It's just giving us sufficient notice to prepare," Carlisle argued.

"Well, yeah, you have a point," Brunelle agreed. "But they'd just say, 'I haven't decided whether my client will testify, Your Honor. We're going to wait until we see what evidence the state puts forward.' So, basically, 'We reserve.'"

"Like Lannigan did with opening," Carlisle nodded, then her eyes flew wide. "But oh my God! How hilarious is his whole 'Did you see my client shoot Derrick Shanborn?' to every single witness thing? That was crazy, right?"

Brunelle couldn't disagree. "I've never seen anything like that. Pretty brave."

"Or pretty stupid," Carlisle countered over her glass. "The jury's going to want to hear more than that. She could have shot him without any of those people seeing it. Lannigan better hope

Hernandez doesn't take the stand and say she was the shooter. What's he going to ask then, huh?"

She punctuated her question with a light laugh. Brunelle smiled at the sound.

"Do you think Hernandez will testify?" he asked.

Carlisle thought for a moment, her mouth twisted up in consideration. "No, probably not. I mean, court and strategy and lawyer stuff aside, he was the shooter. It's hard to take the stand and lie."

"You think he would murder somebody but he wouldn't lie on the stand?"

Carlisle shook her head. "No, of course he would. He's a piece of shit. No, I mean, lying is hard because you have to get all the details right. It's too easy to get tripped up. You didn't shoot him? Okay, then who did? Whose gun was it? Where, exactly, were you standing? All that stuff. He won't have thought of all of that, so he'll get shredded on cross. He knows that. And so does Jacobsen. No way Jacobsen lets that happen. He'll just get up in closing and say we didn't prove it. That's better than having his client prove it for us."

"Good analysis," Brunelle complimented her.

Carlisle demurred. "Like I said, I used to try civil cases. Why do you think we always called the other side to the stand? So we could expose them for the liars they were. Jacobsen does civil too. You can bet he's sat at counsel table, watching helplessly as his client torpedoed whatever bullshit claim he was bringing."

Brunelle raised his glass. "And to Matt Duncan for being wise enough to put you on this case with me."

Carlisle smiled at Brunelle, but didn't reply immediately. She took another sip of her drink. "Okay, so Hernandez probably doesn't testify. What about Wilkins?"

Brunelle narrowed his eyes as he considered. He didn't know Wilkins, of course. Not beyond what he'd learned through the case. But he knew Edwards. "I bet he testifies. Jessica knows juries want to hear defendants say they didn't do it. We tell them a thousand times that they can't hold it against a defendant if he doesn't testify, but we do that because we all know they're going to. Jess doesn't do civil. She does criminal. And she can put Wilkins on the stand to say he didn't shoot Shanborn without it being a lie. Probably," he added with his own light laugh.

"But what about that crazy 'Murder on the Orient Express' story he gave us?" Carlisle pointed out. "If he testifies differently, then the statement comes in as impeachment. And if he tells the same story—"

"—then no one believes him," Brunelle finished. "Yeah, good point. I bet Jess regrets letting him talk to us."

"Not half as much as Robyn Dunn does," Carlisle laughed. "God, did you see the way she was looking at you during the trial? It was like she wanted to murder you herself."

Brunelle couldn't stop the half-smile that crept onto his face. "She was looking at me during the trial?" he asked. "Huh, I didn't notice."

Carlisle let out a loud laugh. "Now who's lying? You're obviously still very hung up on her."

Brunelle raised an indignant eyebrow. "I most certainly am not," he protested. "And I don't see what business it is of yours," he probed.

Carlisle shook her head and laughed. "It's my business if my trial partner can't keep his head in the game because he's thinking of putting his head someplace else."

Brunelle's other eyebrow shot up. "Wow. Just... wow."

Another laugh from Carlisle. "I'm sorry, did I upset your

delicate sensibilities?" Brunelle noticed her drink was already gone. "Fine, let's stick to business. Do you think Samantha Keller will testify?"

Brunelle frowned. "I'm not sure. I mean, Robyn knows the same thing Jessica does. But she was really upset about how the interview with Jackson went. So I don't know…"

Carlisle motioned at the bartender for another daiquiri then turned to Brunelle. "She's cute, isn't she?"

"The bartender?" Brunelle asked. He looked over. He'd seen cuter. "Uh, sure. I guess." It was a little awkward, so he joked, "I mean, she's no Amanda Ashford."

Carlisle laughed. "Or Robyn Dunn."

Brunelle felt like he'd been punched in the chest. The wind was knocked out of him. Carlisle could see it.

"If Keller does testify," she said, "let me do the cross exam."

Brunelle cocked his head. "Why?"

"Because you'll go easy on her," Carlisle accused. "Because you feel bad about what happened with Jackson."

"No, I don't," Brunelle insisted.

"Again, look who's lying," Carlisle shot back. "I mean, at least be honest about it. Say, 'I do feel bad about it, but I won't let that affect my professional responsibilities.'"

Brunelle smiled. "Fine. I do feel bad about it, but I won't let it affect—"

"Yes, you will," Carlisle interrupted. "You can't help it. You're a nice guy."

Brunelle was about to protest with an 'I am not,' but stopped himself. He didn't know what to say.

"Trust me on this one, Dave," Carlisle put a hand on his. "If Keller testifies, I'll do the cross. The jury needs to hear what she told Jackson, and we both know we can't trust you to go after her as hard as you should. You might. But you might not. This way, you don't have the responsibility."

Brunelle was again about to protest but again stopped himself. He looked down at Carlisle's hand on his. Then he nodded. "Okay. I'm not admitting you're right. But you can do the cross of Keller, if she testifies."

"Good." Carlisle gave his hand a squeeze then returned hers to her drink glass. "And you can do Fuller. 'Did you see Mr. Lannigan shoot Derrick Shanborn?'" she mimicked in a goofy voice.

They both laughed.

"That," Brunelle pointed at her, drink in hand, "would be hilarious."

He finished his drink and only hesitated a moment before ordering another.

After a moment, Carlisle smiled at him. "She's lucky to have a nice guy like you hung up on her."

Brunelle was taken off guard. Yet again, he wasn't sure what to say. More feelings than he could name—or wanted to think about—flashed through his gut. Then he shrugged and answered honestly. "Thanks."

They continued to discuss the case and what they thought the various defense attorneys might do in their own cases-in-chief. But there was a big difference between two drinks and three, and when the second glasses were empty, Carlisle slipped the bartender her credit card and the evening was over.

"Need a ride home?" she asked. She'd driven them from downtown.

But Brunelle lived within walking distance. And he kind of wanted time to think. But driving home meant waiting at the bar with Gwen while the buzz wore off, then arriving at his apartment, probably still buzzed and still slightly reeling from the punch to the chest. He might well do something stupid like invite her up. He did stupid things like that. But at least he knew it. "No, thanks. I think I'll just walk. It's a nice enough night."

Carlisle nodded and stood up from the bar. "Understood," she said. "Maybe next time."

Brunelle smiled at that. He liked the idea of a next time with Gwen Carlisle.

Yeah, it was good he was walking home alone.

CHAPTER 42

When court next convened, it was time for the defense to put on their cases. Maybe. Most defendants didn't put on cases. Character witnesses were generally inadmissible unless a character trait was specifically at issue. Most people don't have friends who can testify as to whether they're 'murdery.' Alibi witnesses were rare in real life too. It was one thing for a friend to maybe lie to a cop and say the defendant crashed on his couch the night in question. It was another thing to come into court and testify to it under oath—especially when it was a murder case. That left just the defendants themselves to testify. And Brunelle and Carlisle had already laid odds on that.

"Mr. Jacobsen," Judge Quinn began. "Do you wish to put on a case?"

The judge had to ask it that way. First of all, she had to ask in front of the jury so they wouldn't wonder why one or more of the defendants hadn't put on any evidence. Secondly, she had to make it sound like it was truly an option, because each defendant was presumed innocent and any suggestion that they *should* put on a case would be a claim on appeal that their right to be presumed innocent was undermined by the judge asking, 'So after all of that evidence the state just put on, you're not going to just sit there and not deny it, are you?'

Unfortunately, the defense attorney never just said, 'No.' Instead, the jury also got to hear the explanation as to why the defendant wasn't putting on a case. And it was never the truth. It was never, 'No, Your Honor. My client is guilty of the crime charged and so I've advised him not to take the stand and admit as much.' The kind of crap Jacobsen was about to pull.

"Thank you, Your Honor." Jacobsen stood to address the court. "As the court knows, Mr. Hernandez is presumed innocent, and that presumption continues throughout the trial until and unless the state overcomes the presumption beyond any and all reasonable doubt. Now that the state has presented its evidence—that is, what little evidence it has—it is clear that they have failed to overcome the presumption of innocence, and certainly have failed to do so beyond a reasonable doubt. Accordingly, Mr. Hernandez will not be presenting any evidence in this trial, as is his absolute constitutional right."

Brunelle rolled his eyes. Judge Quinn kept a poker face, although Brunelle suspected her eyes were also rolling on the inside. The judge turned next to Edwards.

"Ms. Edwards," Judge Quinn asked, "Do you wish to put on any evidence?"

Brunelle realized if this ended with four 'no's', they'd be giving closing arguments by the afternoon. He hoped Carlisle was ready.

Edwards stood up. "We'd like to reserve that decision for the time being, Your Honor."

Brunelle looked up. That was a new one. Quinn looked perplexed as well.

"Can she do that?" Carlisle whispered to Brunelle.

"I, I'm not sure," he admitted.

Judge Quinn clearly wasn't sure either. "Reserve?" she inquired. Everyone knew she needed to be careful in front of the jury. They probably should have discussed this possibility before the jury was brought out, but again, a defendant doesn't have to tip his hand before he, or she, plays it.

"Yes, Your Honor," Edwards replied calmly. "The court established an order of defendants for presenting argument and conducting cross-examination, but I don't believe the court can require any one defendant to decide whether to put on evidence before any other defendant." Edwards turned to Jacobsen. "I respect Mr. Jacobsen's independent decision not to put on a case. However, my decision may be impacted by evidence that might be put on by the other defendants. Therefore, I'm asking to reserve. I do not wish to put on any evidence at this moment, but that may change depending on what evidence, if any, is put on by Ms. Dunn or Mr. Lannigan."

"Kinda makes sense," Brunelle admitted to Carlisle in another whisper. She nodded in reply.

Quinn nodded as well. "Thank you, Ms. Edwards. You may reserve." She continued down the line. "Ms. Dunn, do you wish to put on any evidence... at this time?"

Edwards sat down and Dunn stood up. Brunelle's heart began racing despite himself. He wouldn't relish watching Carlisle destroy Robyn's client on the stand. He'd allow it, but he wouldn't enjoy it.

Don't put her on the stand, don't put her on the stand, he repeated in his mind.

"Your Honor," Dunn began. "Thank you. As you know, the decision whether to put an accused client on the stand is the most difficult decision a criminal defense attorney has to make. Mr. Jacobsen is correct that each and every defendant is presumed innocent. He's also correct that the state has to prove every element of every crime beyond a reasonable doubt. Every defendant must decide for herself or himself whether to take the stand to tell their side of the story, knowing that, if they do so, the prosecutor will have the opportunity to cross-examine them. And this cross-examination will be done by an advocate for the state, while the defendant sits alone on the witness stand, with no opportunity to discuss her answers with her attorney.

"An unsophisticated defendant, one like Ms. Keller who, the evidence has shown, has never been investigated for anything before, could very well come across as dishonest or dissembling. It is a difficult decision in any case. But in this case, the situation has become impossible due to the misdeeds of the state prior to the commencement of this trial…"

Brunelle jumped to his feet. "I'm going to object at this point, Your Honor. The question was whether Ms. Dunn was going to put on evidence. It was not an invitation to give a Shakespearean soliloquy on the moral failings of her adversary."

Quinn raised an eyebrow and regarded both Brunelle and Dunn. She'd heard the rumors like everyone else in the courthouse. But she wasn't about to let the attorneys' personal lives ruin a murder trial.

"Mr. Brunelle," she started. "You can sit down."

Then, "Ms. Dunn, do you wish to make a record as to the reasons why you may or may not be putting on a case? That's a yes-or-no question."

Dunn nodded respectfully. "Yes, Your Honor."

Judge Quinn turned to the jury. "Ladies and gentlemen, I'm going to send you to the jury room while I discuss this matter with the attorneys. I will be calling you all back into the courtroom within just a few minutes."

The jurors displayed a collection of nods and shrugs as they stood up and followed the bailiff back into the jury room. When the bailiff stepped out again and closed the door behind him, Quinn turned to Dunn.

"Make your record, Ms. Dunn. I'll let you know what, if any, of it you can say in front of the jury."

"Thank you, Your Honor," Dunn answered. "My client gave a proffer to the state prior to the trial. She didn't want to, and refused repeated invitations to do so. Eventually, Mr. Brunelle came to me with an offer to have just Detective Jackson and me in the room, to allay Ms. Keller's concerns about speaking about the case. I reluctantly agreed, a decision which I now regret, because Detective Jackson subsequently lied in his police report about what my client said in that interview."

Quinn's eyes widened. She looked over at Brunelle and Carlisle, but didn't say anything. She looked back to Dunn. "Go on."

"So now, Your Honor, I am put in the position of having to decide whether to put my client on the stand knowing that even if she tells the truth and says the exact same thing she said in that interview, the state will cross-examine her using Detective Jackson's report and accuse her of lying on the stand. Presumed innocent or not, we all know the jury is going to believe a seasoned detective over someone accused of murder. As a result, I can't risk putting her on the stand, although under any other circumstances, I would. And so rather than simply answer, 'We won't be putting on any witnesses,' I want the jury to understand why my client won't be testifying."

Judge Quinn thought for a moment, then sighed. She turned

to the prosecution table. "Any response, Mr. Brunelle?"

"She's my witness," Carlisle whispered to him. "Let me respond."

But Brunelle shook his head. Keller was her witness, but what happened between Robyn and Detective Jackson was his problem. His fault.

"Your Honor," he began, trying to sound as reasonable and understanding as he could. "I appreciate Ms. Dunn's frustration. And I appreciate why she would want to explain to the jury why she's deciding not to put her client on the stand. But Your Honor, none of what Ms. Dunn is saying is evidence. Evidence comes from the witnesses, not the lawyers. In every trial, the jurors are instructed," he recited the pattern jury instruction from memory, "'the attorneys' remarks, statements, and arguments are intended to help you understand the evidence, but they are not evidence. You are to disregard any remark, statement or argument that is not supported by the evidence.' To allow Ms. Dunn to tell the jury her reasons for not calling Ms. Keller to the stand are certain facts which were never admitted into evidence would create a situation where the jury might base their decision on Ms. Dunn's assertions even though there is no evidence in the record to support them.

"If she wants the jury to know her theory about what happened between Detective Jackson and her client, then she puts her client on the stand, or maybe even recalls Detective Jackson. But she doesn't get to just tell the jury some story and then sit down without any of her assertions being subject to cross-examination."

Brunelle avoided looking over at Robyn. Partly because it was unprofessional to mean-mug your opponent. Mostly because he didn't want to see what expression she was throwing at him.

"She's made her record for the appeal," Brunelle wrapped up. "Now, let's bring the jury back in and she can say yes or no to the question of whether she's putting on a case. If it's no, then Your Honor can proceed to Mr. Lannigan and we can keep this trial moving. Thank you."

Brunelle gave in and stole a glimpse of Robyn as he sat down. He expected her to look angry, or frustrated, or sad. But she just looked like any other lawyer. Like a stranger to him. That hurt even more.

"Any response, Ms. Dunn," Judge Quinn asked, "before I make my ruling?"

"Just that Mr. Brunelle makes my point for me," Dunn replied. "There's a story the jury needs to hear, but thanks to the malfeasance of the government, I can't put my client on the stand to tell it. And I'm certainly not recalling Detective Jackson. If I put him on the stand, I'd be suborning perjury."

Cheap shot, Brunelle thought. But he didn't object. There was no jury and Quinn was going to do what she was going to do. And all the sympathy in the world wouldn't change the simple fact that a lawyer isn't allowed to testify.

"I'm sorry, Ms. Dunn," Judge Quinn said, "but Mr. Brunelle is right. My question was whether you intended to put on a case, not why or why not. You've made your record. I'm going to bring the jury back in now and then I'll ask you again whether you intend to call any witnesses. I want a yes or no answer. Understood?"

Dunn set her jaw, but acquiesced. "Yes, Your Honor."

Quinn nodded to the bailiff and a few moments later the jury was escorted back into the jury box. The judge apologized for the delay, then looked down at Dunn. "Ms. Dunn, do you wish to present any evidence?"

Dunn presented as pleasant a face as the circumstances allowed. "No, Your Honor. Thank you."

Quinn nodded and turned to the last defense attorney. *They were almost there*, Brunelle thought. *No way Lannigan has anything to put on.*

"Mr. Lannigan," Quinn asked, almost perfunctorily, "do you wish to present any evidence?"

Lannigan stood up and smiled. "Yes, Your Honor."

All heads turned to the lawyer at the end of the row.

Lannigan ignored the gazes and kept his smile. "I call Lindsey Fuller to the stand."

Fuller stood up and moved forward to be sworn in by the judge.

"I forget," Carlisle whispered, "who did we decide was going to cross Fuller?"

"We didn't decide," Brunelle whispered back. "And I'm doing it."

When Fuller was all sworn in and seated on the witness stand, Lannigan stepped up to the bar from which the other attorneys had questioned the witnesses. It looked like he might be ready to actually at least try to keep up with everyone else.

"Ms. Fuller," he started, "did you shoot Derrick Shanborn?"

Fuller shook her head vigorously. "No, I did not."

Lannigan smiled again then looked up to Judge Quinn. "No further questions, Your Honor."

Brunelle and Carlisle looked at each other as Lannigan returned to his seat.

"Any cross examination?" Quinn asked, as if it were normal to call a murder defendant and only ask one question. Well, Brunelle could play that game too.

"Yes, Your Honor," he said as he stood up. He didn't bother coming out from behind his table.

He looked Lindsey Fuller square in the eye across the courtroom. "Who did?"

But Fuller gave the safest answer possible. "I don't know."

Brunelle considered for a moment. He could ask her where she was, what she'd been doing, what, if anything, she'd seen. But he knew she would just deny everything. She wasn't accused of shooting Shanborn herself; she was accused of being an accomplice to whoever did shoot him. Lannigan had been clever with his one-question-wonder routine, but he hadn't taken the time to have Fuller deny what she really needed to deny: that she was there, that she knew what was going to happen, and that she helped. If Lannigan hadn't given her the chance to deny that role, why should Brunelle do it for him?

"No further questions," he said and sat down.

"That's it?" Carlisle demanded in a whisper.

"That's enough," Brunelle replied. He hoped he was right.

Lannigan didn't have any redirect, of course, and a minute later Fuller was back in her seat next to her lawyer. They were almost done with the defense cases. Edwards had said she might put Wilkins on the stand, depending on what evidence the other defense attorneys put on. Fuller denying she did it, or knew who did, didn't seem like the type of thing that required a response from Wilkins. Brunelle looked at the clock. If they worked through lunch, Carlisle would have almost three hours to get ready for her closing argument.

"Ms. Edwards," the judge returned her attention to the last remaining defendant to answer the question, "do you now wish to put on any evidence?"

Edwards stood up. She wasn't the drama type. Not like Jacobsen, or Welles. She was hyper-competent and no-nonsense. But that didn't mean she wasn't a trial lawyer. And trial lawyers can't help but enjoy the showmanship of the job at least sometimes. Everyone thought they had finally, after weeks of testimony, reached the end of the trial. So there was the slightest smile tucked into the corner of Edwards's mouth as she announced, "Yes, Your Honor. We call Nathan Wilkins to the stand."

CHAPTER 43

Wilkins made his way to the witness stand to be sworn in by the judge. When he was seated and ready, Edwards began. Pretty much where Lannigan left off.

"Mr. Wilkins, did you shoot Derrick Shanborn?"

Wilkins kept his eyes glued on Edwards. Professional witnesses turned and delivered their answers to the jury. Brunelle used to think it seemed artificial or ingratiating, but he'd heard enough jurors comment, post-verdict, how much they appreciated that kind of response that he didn't question it any more. Hopefully, all the reasons they liked it when the cops talked directly to them would lead them to not like it when Wilkins didn't.

He shook his head. "No, ma'am."

Having asked Lannigan's question, Edwards next asked Brunelle's. "Do you know who did?"

But the response was different. "Yes, ma'am."

Brunelle decided it didn't matter which way Wilkins was facing; everyone was hanging on his next response.

"Who shot Derrick Shanborn?" Edwards asked.

Wilkins looked past his lawyer and pointed. "Elmer

Hernandez."

Brunelle tried not to look excited. He couldn't force Wilkins on the stand, but he could sure as hell take his testimony and use it to hang Hernandez.

"Why did Elmer Hernandez shoot Derrick Shanborn?" Edwards continued.

"Because Derrick was working as a snitch for Detective Jackson," Wilkins answered. "And Mr. Hernandez found out."

"How did he find out?"

Wilkins didn't hesitate. "I told him."

Brunelle's eyebrows lowered slightly. Wilkins had just told the jury he was an accomplice. Brunelle didn't know where this was going. He didn't like not knowing where a witness's testimony was going.

Edwards paused. For effect, Brunelle knew. She wasn't taking the time to form her next question. She had all her questions memorized. The pause was to give the jury a moment to digest the answer before she shifted to a new topic. Brunelle wondered—and feared—what that topic might be.

"Mr. Wilkins," Edwards continued, "do you recall giving a statement to the prosecution prior to the start of this trial?"

Murder on the Orient Express, Brunelle thought. He'd need to actually read that eventually.

Wilkins nodded. "Yes, ma'am."

"Did you tell the truth in that statement?"

Wilkins shook his head. "No, ma'am."

Brunelle's brows dropped deeper. Where was this going?

"Why not?" Edwards asked.

"Because," Wilkins finally turned to the jurors—which just added that much more emphasis to his answer, "Detective Jackson was there."

What did he just say? Brunelle thought to himself.

Carlisle whispered it out loud. "What did he just say?"

Oh, shit, Brunelle thought. *Here it comes.* He still didn't know what exactly, but he knew it was going to be bad.

"Why did it matter that Detective Jackson was there?" Edwards asked the question everyone in the courtroom wanted answered.

"Because," again Wilkins delivered his answer directly to the jurors, "Detective Jackson was the one who told me Derrick was a snitch."

That had the expected effect. Everyone turned to whoever was next to them as if to say, 'Did you hear that?!'

Edwards paused again, longer this time, to really let it sink in. Then she posed the next question everyone wanted answered "Why would he do that?"

"Because he was never quite able to get Mr. Hernandez for the drug dealing," Wilkins explained. "He'd been going after us for years, but we were too good. You can cover up a drug operation if you're smart and you're disciplined. And if the people who know about it are too loyal, or too scared, to snitch on you. But you can't cover up a murder like that. Dead bodies don't just go away. And when someone goes missing, people eventually start asking questions. Even if the person who's missing is a loser drug addict like Derrick Shanborn."

Edwards nodded. "So why did he tell you?"

"Because he knew I'd tell Mr. Hernandez. I had to. If he found out I knew about a snitch and didn't tell him, I'd be the one who ended up in a ditch. Detective Jackson knew exactly what would happen. He knew I worked for Mr. Hernandez. He couldn't prove anything, but he knew it. He knew I'd tell Mr. Hernandez. And he knew Mr. Hernandez would kill him."

Wilkins had answered Edwards' question. But he kept talking. Brunelle let him.

"That's why I made up some crazy story when I talked to the cops. Jackson was right there. I didn't know what he might do. I wasn't looking to be the next inmate who ends up dead in his jail cell, no questions asked. And that's why he made up that stuff about Sammy too. I read the report he wrote. There's no way Sammy would say she saw Burner shoot Derrick, 'cause she wasn't there. But he wanted her to shut up too."

Brunelle looked over to Robyn. She actually looked back at him. There was a touch of 'told ya so' in her gaze, but it was mostly 'holy shit.'

"So yeah, Mr. Hernandez killed Derrick," Wilkins concluded, "but it was Detective Jackson who set it all in motion."

Edwards knew to stop on that. "No further questions."

Carlisle started to stand for cross-examination, but Brunelle pulled her back into her chair and stood up himself.

"No questions," he said before Quinn could even ask. "And we move to adjourn for the day."

Quinn nodded. "Of course, Mr. Brunelle." She banged her gavel. "Court is adjourned."

Brunelle was halfway out the door before the echo died away.

CHAPTER 44

"Where is he?!"

Brunelle stormed into Chen's office. Chen looked up from his work, but didn't immediately reply. Strong, silent types don't respond to being yelled at unexpectedly.

"Jackson," Brunelle clarified. "He's not in his office. Where is he?"

Chen took another moment. "I don't know," he answered with deliberate calmness.

"I need to find him," Brunelle insisted. "Help me find him."

Chen thought another moment, then stood up. "Okay. Let's find him."

They started by backtracking Brunelle's steps to Jackson's office. He still wasn't there, of course.

"Do you want to tell me what this is about?" Chen finally asked.

"He blew Shanborn's cover," Brunelle replied. "Jackson. Jackson told Wilkins that Shanborn was a snitch so Hernandez would kill him."

Chen stood there for several seconds, staring at Brunelle,

assessing him. Then he turned around.

"Martinez!" he called out to one of the patrol officers seated in a nearby cubicle. "Have you seen Jackson anywhere?"

The young, heavy set officer spun in his chair. "Sorry, Detective. I haven't seen him today."

Brunelle clenched his fists, but then a uniformed officer yelled to them from the end of the hall. "I just saw him heading toward the elevator," she said. "I think he said he was going to the gym."

Brunelle clapped Chen on the arm. "Let's go."

After a quick elevator ride and a long walk through several subterranean corridors, they arrived at the door to the fitness center. Chen flashed his badge over the scanner and the door unlocked with a beep and a clunk. Jackson was inside, dressed in workout clothes and sitting on a weight bench, facing the door. He was tying his shoes and didn't look up when the door opened.

"Jackson!" Brunelle yelled, rather unnecessarily in the small room.

The detective raised his head. "Oh, hey, Dave. Hey, Larry," he said pleasantly enough. "What's going on?"

"That's what I want to know," Brunelle responded. He stepped over to Jackson. He tried not to feel ridiculous wearing a suit and tie in a workout room. "Wilkins just testified that you're the one who told him Derrick Shanborn was a snitch. That you couldn't catch Hernandez dealing drugs, so you set him up with a murder he couldn't refuse."

Jackson didn't immediately reply. But he stood up. "What else did he say?"

"He said," Brunelle added, "that he figures you lied about Samantha Keller's proffer so she wouldn't take the stand. Which worked, by the way."

Jackson tightened his jaw and nodded slightly. "And you believed him?"

"It doesn't matter what I believe," Brunelle snapped. He was trying to control his temper. "But the jury is going to believe him unless I put you on the stand in rebuttal to say it isn't true."

Again Jackson took a moment to reply. "Look, Hernandez was a menace. Kids were dying up there, O.D.'ing every day with needles still stuck in their arms. Now he's off the street and looking at spending the rest of his life in prison. I don't care how we got there, I'm just glad we did. I'd call that a win."

It was a non-answer. Trial lawyers don't accept non-answers. "Did you tell Wilkins that Shanborn was working for you?"

Jackson grinned and looked toward the ceiling. "You know, Mr. D.A., I have so many conversations with so many of the lowlifes you don't have to deal with until I put my ass on the line to catch them, it's hard to remember everything."

"That's why you write reports," Brunelle countered.

"That's why I *don't* write reports," Jackson answered. "If I put the name of one of my informants in a report, they're as good as dead. I said that on the stand."

"Yeah," Brunelle said, "but you didn't say the same thing happens if you blow their cover yourself."

Jackson clenched his fists, flexing his thick arms. "I do my job. I don't need bean-counters and pencil-pushers like you going over every line in my reports looking for a mistake. If there's no report, then there are no witness statements. If there are no witnesses, it's like it never happened."

"Or if the only witnesses are a charged murder defendant and her lawyer," Brunelle realized, "then you can write whatever you want in the report."

Jackson grinned again. "Now, you're getting it." He stepped in close to Brunelle. "Maybe if you wore a badge and a gun instead of a suit and a tie, maybe then you'd understand what it's really like to try to protect people from scumbags like Elmer Hernandez. Maybe if you worked against the other side instead of sleeping with them, I could have some respect for what you do. But the bottom line is, I didn't shoot anyone. I didn't tell anyone to shoot anyone. Wilkins chose to tell Hernandez and Hernandez chose to kill Derrick. And if Sammy Keller gets washed away with the tide too, so be it. I'm not going to lose any sleep over it."

Brunelle took a moment to root himself to the ground and slow his breathing. He wanted to be calm for this.

"So," he confirmed, "if there are no witnesses, it's like it never happened?"

Jackson spread out his arms and smiled broadly. "Now you get it."

"No. You do." And Brunelle punched him square in the nose.

Jackson tripped backward over the weight bench, landing ass-first and cracking his head on the thin mat covering the floor.

Brunelle turned to Chen even as he shook the sting out of his fist. "No witnesses, right?"

Chen looked at Jackson, still prone and grabbing the back of his head. "I didn't see anything."

EPILOGUE

Brunelle dismissed the cases against Samantha Keller and Lindsey Fuller. If he couldn't charge Jackson—and he couldn't, there were too many intervening actors making independent decisions—he could hardly send those two off to prison. As for Hernandez and Wilkins, the jury took less than an hour to convict them both.

As for Jackson, he wasn't charged with murder, but he was suspended pending an internal affairs investigation. Apparently, outing your snitch to a murderous drug dealer is conduct unbecoming a police officer. Maybe. The union was contesting the suspension. And it was with pay anyway. Brunelle figured it was 50-50 he'd keep his job.

That left the small issue with Gwen. He liked her well enough, but the thought of dating someone inside the office was just too much. It was stressful enough having exes in the medical examiner's office and the local defense bar. He didn't need to worry about running into Gwen at the office after they broke up. Because, of course, eventually, they would break up.

Besides, he hadn't completely screwed up his relationship with the cops yet. There was probably some female detective at

Seattle P.D. or the King County Sheriff who'd be willing to date him for a few months before a drama-filled breakup

On the other hand, she'd have a gun...

So it was Brunelle who had invited Carlisle out to dinner. He took her to The Pond, the Vietnamese restaurant Robyn had introduced him to. Ostensibly, it was to celebrate their victory. But it was also to let her down easy.

It turned out to be even easier than he'd hoped.

"You thought I wanted to date you?" She asked once she'd stopped laughing. "Dave, you idiot. I'm a lesbian."

Brunelle's jaw dropped. "Gay?" Could he really have been so wrong? Did he really misread all those signals? "But, but you're divorced."

As if he could prove she was wrong or something.

"Yes, Dave," Gwen replied with another bemused laugh. "Gay people can get married now. That means we can get divorced too. Why? Do you have a problem with that?"

"What? Oh my God, no," he was quick to defend, hands raised. "No, no problem at all. I think it's great."

"You think it's great I got divorced?" Gwen teased.

Brunelle didn't get it, not at first. "What? No, I just... I mean..." He trailed off. After a moment, he asked, "So, Chris?"

"Short for Christine," Gwen explained. "We were dating when gay marriage was made legal. We sort of got caught up in the moment and just decided to get married too. It was a mistake. We were trying to save something beyond saving. It didn't take us long to figure it out. The divorce was amicable. I mean, it sucked, but that's life sometimes, right?"

"Yeah," he agreed. "That's life sometimes."

He thought for several more seconds. "So that's why you said Robyn was gorgeous," he tried.

"I said it because it's true," Carlisle replied. Then she laughed. "And yeah, I'd totally hit that."

Brunelle's embarrassment at being so dense was joined uncomfortably by jealousy at Carlisle being revealed as a potential rival rather than confidante. He didn't fully understand. So he decided to just shut up about it. "Well, I'm glad we had this little talk."

Gwen laughed too. "Me too."

They finished dinner and Gwen picked up the check. To pay him back for mentoring me through my first murder trial, she'd said.

When it was time to go, Brunelle decided to linger and have one more drink. Even Vietnamese restaurants have whiskey in the back. Gwen thanked him again for the opportunity, and wished him a good night. The waitress brought his drink, and he took a sip as he glanced around the restaurant.

He'd picked the place because Robyn had taken him there. Not because he remembered the decor was classy and the food was excellent, although both of those were still true. He'd picked it because he hoped if Robyn used to come there a lot, she might still come there. And he would run into her.

She would walk up to his table when he wasn't looking and say something like, 'Hiya, Mr. B.'

He'd look up at her and smile, then say something like, "Well, hello there, Miss D.'

She'd sit down and they'd talk about the case they'd just finished. She'd thank him for dismissing the case. He'd shrug and say it was the right thing to do.

Eventually there'd be a pause and then she'd say, 'I miss you, Dave.'

He'd say, 'I miss you too.'

She'd say, 'I know it'll be hard to make it work, what with you being a prosecutor and me being a defense attorney, but it's not impossible. As long as we don't have any cases against each other, we can make it work. Let's give it another try.'

And he'd say, 'I'd like that.'

But she wasn't there.

And she wasn't coming.

He was there, sipping his whiskey, and ending his day the way he always ended his day.

The way Burner Hernandez should have murdered Derrick Shanborn.

Alone.

END

ABOUT THE AUTHOR

Stephen Penner is an attorney, author, and artist from Seattle. He writes a variety of fiction, including thrillers, mysteries, and children's books.

His other novels include the Maggie Devereaux paranormal mystery series, beginning with *Scottish Rite*. He also wrote and illustrated the children's books *Katie Carpenter, Fourth Grade Genius* and *Professor Barrister's Dinosaur Mysteries*.

For more information, please visit *www.stephenpenner.com.*

Made in the USA
Coppell, TX
23 November 2020